FIRE FORCE

Hardin crouched up on one knee, the toe of his boot dug hard into the earth. He was trying to count numbers, but it was difficult; the men he could see kept shifting around in the gloom. Then he muttered "This is it!" as fire from the trees lashed the chopper's nose. It went on for five seconds, and then the bushes sprouted human beings. Hardin sprang out of cover like a sprinter off the block, hearing Garrett's Armalite rattling off its staccato deathsong, joined an instant later by a searing blast of rounds from Olsen's direction.

As he ran Hardin pumped bullets in a tight arc to his left and saw EnVee grunts go down like pins in an alley. Those behind were running and yelling, but the yells turned to screams when two grenades sailed out of the trees and exploded in front of them, hurling them back with a roaring detonation and a red-cored eruption of fire.

THE SURVIVALIST SERIES
by Jerry Ahern

#1: TOTAL WAR   (960, $2.50)
The first in the shocking series that follows the unrelenting search for
ex-CIA covert operations officer John Thomas Rourke to locate his
missing family—after the button is pressed, the missiles launched and
the multimegaton bombs unleashed . . .

#2: THE NIGHTMARE BEGINS   (810, $2.50)
After WW III, the United States is just a memory. But ex-CIA covert
operations officer Rourke hasn't forgotten his family. While hiding
from the Soviet occupation forces, he adheres to his search!

#3: THE QUEST   (851, $2.50)
Not even a deadly game of intrigue within the Soviet High Command,
the formation of the American "resistance" and a highly placed
traitor in the new U.S. government can deter Rourke from continuing
his desperate search for his family.

#4: THE DOOMSAYER   (893, $2.50)
The most massive earthquake in history is only hours away, and
Communist-Cuban troops, Soviet-Cuban rivalry, and a traitor in the
inner circle of U.S. II block Rourke's path. But he must go on—he is
THE SURVIVALIST.

#5: THE WEB   (1145, $2.50)
Blizzards rage around Rourke as he picks up the trail of his family and
is forced to take shelter in a strangely quiet Tennessee valley town.
Things seem too normal here, as if no one has heard of the War; but
the quiet isn't going to last for long!

FIRE FORCE
GUNSHIPS

BY JACK HAMILTON TEED

ZEBRA BOOKS
KENSINGTON PUBLISHING CORP.

To Jonathan Mirsky (journalist), and Jerry Way (ex-grant), both of whom were there.

ZEBRA BOOKS

are published by

KENSINGTON PUBLISHING CORP.
475 Park Avenue South
New York, N.Y. 10016

THIRD PRINTING JANUARY 1984

Printed in the United States of America

Prologue

Stratton never knew who killed him; never even heard his killer come up behind him.

He was lying in thick undergrowth atop a hillock overlooking the trail. Overhead, high above the tangled network of branches and vines and jungle topgrowth, the noonday sun beat down with remorseless, punishing force. Even down here, 120 feet below the tips of the tallest trees, the steamy heat was almost solid; almost something you could touch.

Stratton felt he was stifling. Breathing was like taking in chunks of hot cotton wool down his throat and into his lungs. Under his heavy jungle fatigues his body was slick with sweat; it seemed like he didn't even have to move for it to pour out of him. He was running a Goddamn river, and the only plus side to this lousy patrol deep into the heart of Laos was that by the time they got back into Nam he was going to be pounds lighter.

On the other hand, he'd soon put what he was losing back on again. He was a sucker for pastries and pies, and junk food that tasted good but played hell with your body metabolism.

He eased the M-16 he was holding forward and sighted along the trail, snapping off an imaginary shot. The weapon was slippery in his sweat-soaked hands, but not too much; in any case, he'd rubbed up the underside of the stock with a heavy-duty file, leaving it rough and coarse, easier to grip. He eased the Armalite in a half-circle and snapped off another phantom round down the trail.

His eyes took in the trail from left to right. At this point, immediately below him, it was wide and quite straight, though starting to curve round to the right about 30 yards to his left before disappearing completely into the riot of green undergrowth and tangled creepers. A much-used trail, by the Pathet Lao as well as the North Vietnamese Army. It was one of the link-roads that cut through the jungle and finally, after 30 or 40 miles, joined the Ho Chi Minh Trail. If the Ho Chi Minh was a main artery—and Command often described it in such terms—this trail was a tributary blood-line that fed it: fed it arms and ammunition and troops and anything else the NVA could dump on to the South Vietnamese and American forces to make their lives miserable.

Though nothing, thought Stratton, could be more miserable than lying in the grass sweating a river and slowly broiling in heavy canvas fatigues. He thought longingly of the river.

These jungle suits were supposed to provide warmth by night and let your skin breathe by day. That was the theory. Stratton didn't believe it. Not for a moment. Someone had been lying to him.

Or maybe he was wearing sabotaged fatigues? Maybe some gook hit-team had made it across to Okinawa and neutralised the quartermasters' stores, so that all the jungle fatigues kept you cold by night and shit-hot during the day? And maybe he ought to keep his mind on the job and not fuck around fantasising when he was supposed to be on look-out. Just in case a battalion or so of EnVees should decide to drop by for a Coke.

Not that there were any North Vietnamese in the immediate vicinity. No very large contingents, anyhow. Maybe a few isolated patrols or scouts. No sweat (Stratton's mind back-pedalled. No sweat. That was a joke. If only it were true).

In any case, the EnVees often gave themselves away with their Goddamn monkey-talk. You could hear the little fuckers chattering and jabbering for miles. In general, they weren't the hot jungle-fighters they were cracked up to be, and the VC—the black-pajamaed irregulars who worked solely in South Vietnam—were even worse. Stratton recalled a patrol into bandit country just below the DeMilitarized Zone when it had seemed like a herd of rogue buffalo was stampeding through the jungle. Turned out to be a small party of VC on an intelligence-gathering mission. Jesus! Sure had been open season that day.

But you still had to keep your eyes open, just in case. Not all the VC were like that, and certainly not all the EnVees. The EnVees were very fierce on discipline; quite often they kept their mouths shut and their movements quiet, and you always had to be on the alert in case you tripped over a bunch of real pros.

His eyes flicked to the right as he caught a sudden movement up the trail, but it was only a scarlet-hued bird swooping through the upper foliage, letting out a weird, whooping shriek as it vanished from sight.

Although his throat was parched and dry, Stratton

was aching for a cigarette. Taking in smoke deep into his lungs would be worse than hot cotton wool, but out in the jungle you sometimes got totally irrational desires like that. This was his third patrol in Special Forces, and he was due for an extended R-and-R, outside of Nam. Probably Japan. He'd never been there—on R-and-R anyhow—but he figured a month out there would stop the irrational desires for a good Goddamn while. You'd be too busy indulging in all the rational desires you could think of, for a little jungle craziness to bother you.

He thought about the river again, and began to feel irritable. Those fuckers back in the clearing were in it now, washing the shit off their bodies and out of their systems. He glanced at his watch. Schwaab should be relieving him any time now and it couldn't happen soon enough. He thought about stripping off all his clothes and jumping into the fast-moving coolness of the river, diving right down to the bottom and rolling a couple of times then arrowing up to the surface and coming out in a surge of spray. The thought made him sweat some more, it was so good.

Then a cigarette, and then some food. Then check that the cache was well hidden for the last time and head back into the jungle again and up north.

Stratton thought about the cache and chuckled to himself. A smart move on Command's part, to order a cache to be dumped not a hundred yards from an EnVee feed-trail. The EnVees'd never figure that one out, not in a hundred years. Right under their noses. Right under their slanty little eyes, Goddamnit. They'd be walking right past an Aladdin's Cave, figuratively speaking—rucksacks of dried food, dobie bags stuffed with ammunition and grenades, sets of clean fatigues, socks and underwear, medical supplies in tight greased wraps—and not even be aware of it.

Stratton didn't know who they'd left it for. You never did when you were dumping a cache. Some other Special Forces group who'd got a long trek ahead of them, or maybe a long trek behind them. Whoever it was, and for whatever purpose it was needed, those who'd find it would be well content. There was nothing in the world like finding a full cache after a hard month's, or even week's, haul through the jungle. It was Thanksgiving, Christmas and your Birthday all rolled into one.

Fat City!

He chuckled again, then grunted with shock—as he heard an answering chuckle behind him and his head was suddenly yanked back hard, fingers gripping his curly hair and tugging viciously.

Schwaab. It had to be Schwaab. Just like Schwaab to sneak up behind him. The beanpole fuckhead fancied himself a joker.

"Get the fuck off, Schwaab," Stratton hissed—then felt the kiss of a blade on his throat, for a microsecond, was almost a ticklish sensation against his taut skin. Then blood fountained into the air above his eyes. His own blood.

Stratton didn't scream. He couldn't.

Suddenly, he had no vocal chords.

Suddenly, he was dead.

Dettweiler said, "You better relieve Stratton."

Schwaab, a tall, skinny blond from Minnesota, nodded and climbed into his pants. A cigarette was

9

glued to his lower lip and smoke curled up from its tip, lazily. The rest of his clothes were in a neat pile beside him, and his M-16 was leaning against his backpack, well within reach.

Dettweiler pulled his own shirt over his head and threw it down. His heap of clothes was untidy, strewn across the grass, but his Armalite, like Schwaab's, was close at hand, primed and ready to fire. At the first sign of trouble, all Dettweiler had to do was grab it and pull the trigger. He knew that there was no heavy concentration of NVA troops within 10 miles, but you still didn't take stupid risks in bandit country.

"Strat should be getting very pissed off, right about now," he said. "He'll be right pleased to see you, Schwaab."

"Affirm on that, Sarge."

"Strat's probably shooting his boots for a cigarette, too."

"Yeah."

Dettweiler yawned and stretched, letting the hot sun beat down on his chest. Down here by the river it was cooler, and the small clearing seemed to have a better circulation of air. Around the clearing the jungle was like a solid wall; you only spotted the gaps and openings in the thick foliage when you were right up against it. A gentle slope led down to the river, and a natural hollow in the bank dropped to the fast-moving waters, which surged and sprayed over rocks and gurgled round smooth, eroded gaps in the overhang. Across the river the jungle crowded the bank, a dense mass of tangled vegetation that stretched out of sight both sides. Macey, sitting cross-legged a couple of yards away, with his rifle across his knees, was watching that.

Two birds suddenly whirred overhead, heading for the opposite bank, and Dettweiler snatched up his M-16, gazing back at the surrounding jungle wall in nervous expectation. His tense naked body, with the Armalite held out in front of him as straight and unyielding as a steel tie, pointing at the foliage, was like an idealised representation from the 1930s, or a part of a modern heroic relief that you might find in Russia, say or Czechoslovakia, with a title like "War!" or "To Arms!" or, better, "Defending His Motherland!"

That was what Macey thought, anyhow, as he watched Dettweiler from up the bank.

Macey read a lot, and drew a lot. On his right knee was balanced a small notebook with impressions of the jungle on almost every page, drawn with a soft 2B pencil, of which he had four or five stubs hidden in various pockets of his fatigues. Before he'd joined the army he'd submitted work to a number of agents, but none had expressed much interest. Good but not brilliant. Macey had a gift for faces, swiftly sketched, but that was all. He had the depressing feeling that some-day, when he'd maybe finished with the army, he'd probably gravitate towards advertising, or drawing comicbooks, or something equally soul-destroying.

Dettweiler relaxed, let the tension seep slowly out of him.

"Just birds, Sarge," said Schwaab.

"Yeah. Just birds."

Dettweiler was 25 and a couple of months. He was five foot seven and stocky, but not bulky or fat. He kept himself in excellent shape. This was his seventh mission out into the jungle, and the first one over which he had sole command. He just hoped it wasn't to be his last.

For some reason he couldn't define or analyse he had bad feelings about this one. Dumping a cache in enemy territory wasn't the reason; that was no big deal. It was part of the job. But some psychic alarm bell had started ringing as soon as he'd been briefed back at the Special Forces HQ in Nha Trang, down in the south-east of South Vietnam, and it just hadn't stopped ringing since. If anything it had gotten louder in the past couple of days, as they'd threaded their way through southern Laos, and he'd had the strong feeling they were being followed. But he'd tried every trick Special Forces had taught him and come up with a big fat zero. No one was tracking them.

Shit! he suddenly thought. Maybe whoever it is was *pacing* us? Maybe they were deep in the jungle on each side of the trail, keeping the same Goddamn *pace?*

That explanation hadn't occurred to him at the time, but it could have been so. And suddenly the sur-rounding jungle was full of hidden eyes—hostile eyes—watching every move they made.

Dettweiler shook his head irritably. Go on like that and he'd end up *dinky dau*—off his head completely. Sure, you had to be on the alert the whole time in this game—had to have eyes in the back of your head, damn near—but once you started to get too paranoid, you'd blow a circuit. End up on the funny farm.

Butler hauled himself over the lip of an overhang and bounded up on to the grass, his black body glis-tening. Grinning, he shook himself like a dog, and droplets of water sprayed Schwaab and Schwaaab's neatly piled clothes. Schwaab erupted.

"Goddman black motherfucker!"

"Fuckin' honky sackashit!"

"Jesus, Butler, you're like a fucking two-year-old."

"Cool it, man," said Butler. "Gimme a cigarette."

Muttering, Schwaab reached for his packet and threw it across to the black. Butler lit up and took smoke in deep, then let it out in a long relaxed plume.

"Damn, that's good." He nodded to Dettweiler. "Like I always say, Sarge, ain't nothin' better'n a cigarette after splash-down in a cool mountain stream." He took another long drag. "Well, on'y one thing, anyways."

Up the bank Macey shifted his position and half turned his head. He knew the routine.

"One thing, Butler?"

"For sure, man."

"Tell me, Butler, d'you smoke after *intercourse?*"

"No, man, I *incandesce.*"

He let out a loud guffaw, and Schwaab snorted, grinning.

"Crazy Goddamn nigger," he said.

Butler jabbed the cigarette in his direction.

"You jus' wash yo' mouth out, whitey," he said, mock-sternly. "I am a crazy Goddamn *black.*"

Dettweiler dragged his backpack to the edge of the bank, and placed his M-16 against it.

"So get your craziness together," he said, "and take over from Schwaab when he goes to relieve Stratton."

Butler made an O of his thumb and forefinger, and began to dry himself. Schwaab unfolded his shirt and put it over his head. As he did so, a man stepped out

13

from the jungle.

Dettweiler had the Armalite in his hands and pointing at the man almost before he'd fully emerged from the trees. Then he relaxed, dropping the rifle clumsily, so that it bounced off the side of his pack and fell to the ground, its butt sticking out over the lip of the river-bank.

The man was an American soldier.

"For Christ's sake," said Dettweiler angrily.

The man grinned.

"Don't panic," he said.

He was tall, rangy, dressed in jungle fatigues and floppy camouflage hat. His skin was burned a dark brown, and there looked to be about a month's growth of beard on his face. His teeth gleamed whitely as he smiled.

He was carrying a Russian Kalashnikov AK-47 assault rifle, but that didn't mean a thing, except the guy knew a good deal when he saw one. When the chips were down the AK-47 had it over the American standard issue M-16 all ways and every way, and even the meanest draftee grunt coveted the weapon. Sure, the M-16 was lighter, had a faster fire-rate, and a greater effective range, It was a sophisticated and sensitive piece of hardware. But that was its main drawback: a hell of a lot of things could go wrong with it, and usually did.

It was all very well having it drummed into you at boot camp that your rifle was your mistress, your lover—that you had to look after it, pamper it, keep it sweet. But when you staggered out of a heavy combat situation you were usually shocked, exhausted and as hungry as all hell—and the last thing you wanted to

14

think about was stripping down and cleaning the God-damn thing.

The AK-47, on the other hand, could be treated like a wife—the kind of wife stone-age man clubbed unconscious and dragged around by the hair, like in the funnies. You could haul it through the mud, piss on it, kick it around some, and then, more often than not, nail a low-flying gunship with it, if the mood took you that way. The AK was a hell of a killing-machine that could take a lot of shit and still come up blasting. The Armalite, for all its good points, could not.

Dettweiler gazed sourly at the AK in the man's hands. It looked to be in healthy shape. He wished he had one. Then his mind grasshoppered to the thing that had been worrying him earlier. At least he knew now that he'd been right about that—they *had* been followed, or at least, paced.

"What the fuck is going on?" he snapped. "Why the shadow-play?"

The man laughed.

"You noticed. That was right smart. We figured . . ."

But what they—whoever they were—figured, Dettweiler never discovered, because Butler suddenly cut in. He was pointing at the guy, frowning in puzzlement, as though racking his brain for an elusive memory.

"Shit man, I know you. You're . . ."

"You got a good memory, nigger," the man cut in. "Too bad."

The AK swung up and the man sent a single shot into Butler's chest, punching him backwards. The hole was not too large, but most of the black's back, from his shoulderblades down to his kidneys, exploded outwards in a scarlet shower of minced bone, blood and tissue. The thought flashed through Dettweiler's mind, in the brief instant before he jumped backwards, that the guy was loaded up with soft-nosed rounds. Then he was rolling over the edge of the bank and crashing into the river.

He came up almost instantly and scrambled up the slope, lunging for the M-16. It was pure luck that the butt was so near. If he hadn't dropped it so clumsily, it would have been way out of reach.

On the slope the man from the jungle, laughing harshly, had switched to automatic, and the clearing was filled with the AK-47's distinctive high-pitched chatter. He sent a burst into Schwaab's body, stitching an irregular pattern of bloody blotches across his chest. Schwaab was still struggling to pull his shirt down over his head. He jack-knifed as the bullets tore into him, and was bundled over, screaming, by the force of their impact, arms still high in the air, his face still covered by the shirt.

Macey had swung round and was firing, but his cross-legged position hampered his movements. The man jumped to one side and let him have it in the head. Macey's head burst apart like an over-ripe peach.

Dettweiler slid over the top of the bank, resting the Armalite on the ground. He was half-hidden from the killer by his backpack. He triggered a long hammering spray of rounds in a short arc across the clearing, catching the man in the stomach. The American was flung backwards, arms waving and legs kicking in the air, as though he'd been electrocuted.

16

Then the M-16 was smashed out of Dettweiler's hands and it was as though he'd been pounded across the left shoulder by a jack-hammer. Blood sprayed across his line of vision, and he was lifted into the air and sent cart-wheeling over into the water below.

His last coherent thought before he lost consciousness was, Should've raked the jungle before I wasted the sonuvabitch.

Then he blacked out.

The current took him by the legs and jerked his naked body round in a half-circle. He caromed off a rock, then crashed head-first into another. The current tugged greedily at him again, dragging him under for four or five yards before smashing him into a half-submerged boulder and throwing him bodily out of the water. Firing from the bank broke out and bullets flayed the boiling froth around him, then the current flipped him over on to his stomach and whirled him away into the middle of the river. A scarlet stream fanned out from his body, staining the clear rushing water.

The big man was very drunk, hovering on the verge of being murderously so.

"Ah hear you s'pose t'be one of them shit hot Special Forces bimbos," he said slowly, staring down through narrowed, red-rimmed eyes.

Hardin Zippoed the cigarette that dangled from his lips and replaced the lighter in his shirt pocket. His eyes flicked round, taking in the rest of the bar that was not hidden from view by the big man's bulk.

No one seemed to be taking much notice. Not even those at the table from which the big man had staggered were looking his way. It was a typical Saigon bar, near the Thieves' Market, full of hustlers, hookers, pimps, grunts and R-and-R, a journalist or two seeking local colour. There was no reason why anyone should take any notice. The scene that had to be played out now probably took place two or three times a day, somewhere in Saigon.

Hardin finished his drink and breathed out irritably. The big man was a Marine Sergeant, but he didn't look as though he'd seen much action recently. Certainly not in the last year or so, and probably you could multiply that figure by fifteen.

His stomach sagged over his belt and his thighs quivered against the slack material of his pants every time he moved. His jowls shivered like a turkey's wattles and his face was red and blotchy. Only his hands and arms looked dangerous. The arms were like hairy hamhocks, but corded and knotted with muscles that had not yet gone slack; his fingers were long and thick.

"Y'hear me, bimbo?" said the big man.

Hardin felt anger rising up from the pit of his stomach like bile. It occurred to him that if he wasn't very careful he was suddenly going to explode and kill the man. Which would not be a very smart move. He stared at his empty glass and thought about the situation.

He could get up and walk away, but then the big man would almost certainly go for him and there'd be a tangle of broken tables and chairs and smashed glasses at the end of approximately 30 seconds. And noise and fuss and gabbling waiters and shrieking bargirls, and the manager would holler for the MPs or the

Arvins, and there might even be some shooting.

Or he could quietly and reasonably point out that he was a Colonel and the big guy was a Sergeant and Sergeants don't go shooting their mouths off at, or throwing their weight around in front of, Colonels even in a Saigon bar near the Thieves' Market, and why not just cool it, huh? But then the big man would probably not even listen to this, he was so juiced up. And even if he heard the words, their meaning would not penetrate that thick skull into the tiny dinosaur's brain beyond, and the end-result would be the same as for option one.

Or he could just hit the man now in the right place and have him fold up quietly on the floor, and probably no one would even bat an eyelid.

"You got Colonel's tabs on," said the big man, as though he'd just figured out the secret of the universe.

"You git it, soldier," said Hardin wearily. "Now why don't you just back off, and we'll forget all about this."

The big man leaned over the table, the folds of flesh on his face creasing up into a loose-lipped leer.

"Y'know something, *Colonel?* Ah don' b'lieve you a *Colonel* at all." The word "all" came out as two syllables: ah-wull.

"Get the fuck out of here, Sergeant," said Hardin tightly.

"You Special Forces bimbos ain't worth a good jackshit, *Colonel*. You ain't worth diddley-spit. Ain't nothin' spay-shull 'bout *you*." The big man belched. "Pardon me, *Colonel*. Pardon me for burpin' in your spay-shull face. In fact," he reached into his pants pocket, "pardon me for nailin' your spay-shull *ass*."

His hand came out holding a switchblade. He gazed at it reverently, as though it was a precious object, a family heirloom handed down for generations. He thumbed the trigger and the blade sprang out with a metallic hiss. He leaned over and stabbed it towards Hardin's face.

Hardin's head jerked to the right, and the blade just twitched at his left ear-lobe before travelling past.

"Fugger," slurred the big man peevishly.

Hardin's balled left fist shot out and sank deep into the man's stomach. It was like punching a bean-bag without the rattle, and Hardin felt no satisfaction whatsoever. The big man jack-knifed over the table. His mouth gaped open and his small red eyes bulged, tears springing out round their rims. Whisky-breath soured the air between the two men.

The big man dropped the knife and his left hand drove forward like a piston, clutching at Hardin's throat and shoving his head back against the wall. Hardin spat out his cigarette, gagged, then couldn't breathe any more as the fingers squeezed in. The big man's speed had startled him, but even as the emotional shock-wave was travelling through his mind he was thinking he'd been right about the man's hands and arms being the most dangerous part of him.

He couldn't kick the table away because the big man's weight was holding it down to the floor, his right hand on the table-top to steady himself. Hardin, red stars popping in front of his eyes, groped for the knife on the table, gripped it, brought it up and smacked it down through the big man's splayed right hand, deep into the flesh and beyond, skewering it effectively to the wood.

The big man gave a thin, intense scream and reeled away, and the pressure on Hardin's throat was gone. Hardin jerked his left foot forward under the table and hooked at one of the big man's legs, and the big guy toppled over sideways slowly, like a falling tree, taking the table and two chairs with him, his hand fixed firmly to the wooden top.

He lay sprawled on the tiles, the table half on top of him, his left arm waving slowly in the air, the fingers feebly clutching and unclutching a few inches from the switchblade handle. Blood welled from his right hand, round the embedded blade, seeping down the table-top and dripping on to his face. He'd stopped screaming now, and was merely making incomprehensible gargling noises in his throat.

Hardin stood up and brushed himself down. A couple of pimps had vanished, but no one was yelling or creating a fuss or calling for the MPs. A waiter was hovering nearby, his face impassive. From the look of him, it didn't seem likely he was suddenly going to jump at Hardin.

Hardin said, "You better see to him."

He walked swiftly across the bar-room to the table where the rest of the Marines were sitting, playing cards. There were four of them, all NCOs of one rank or another. Same mould as the big man, but not yet his size. They stared up at him. Hardin felt adrenalin shooting into his blood-stream.

"Any problems?" he said tightly.

One of them, a corporal, shook his head. A nerve ticked under his right eye.

"Hay-ull, no, Colonel." He tried a friendly chuckle, which ended up as a series of short coughs. "Ole

Gunny was a-beggin' for it. He gets a skinful inside of him, he gets t'be as mean as a goaded bull." He turned to his companions. "Ain't that so?"

The others laughed nervously, and Hardin turned on his heel and headed for the door. Outside bright sunlight beckoned him. He tossed a handful of paper money at the manager behind the formica-topped bar and went out into the sun-splashed street.

Chapter One

Major Tollmarsh sang out "*Ho-ohhh!*"—his voice going up on the first syllable, and down on the second. At the same time he whipped off his white cavalry Stetson and flourished it in the air—then snapped "*Shit!*" when it caught on a piece of metal hanging from the cabin roof, pulled it down to see if the cloth had torn, glared up at the offending piece of metal (a loose strut) and said "*Fucker!*" in a voice that had enough acid in it to sear the fingerprints off a man's hand. Then a big beaming smile broke out on his reddish, freckled face, and he let off an ear-splitting Rebel yell.

Captain Frank Marco, sitting at the controls of the Bell UH-1D Huey helicopter gunship, winced and glanced across at his co-pilot, Hanks, who shrugged wearily. Hanks had been through all this before, many times.

"Well, come on, Cap'n Marco," bawled Tollmarsh, "why the fuck don't we-all get the shit up outta here and a-*waaaay!*"

"You mean, like Superman, Major?" enquired Marco, half-turning in his seat.

Tollmarsh threw him a stony look.

"Don't give me any crap, Captain. Just lift us off,

right? We got a date with some gooners, and I don't intend for us to be late."

He scrambled backwards into the main cabin area and plumped himself down in what he always referred to as the "hot seat," a steel swivel-chair fixed aft of the port boarding door, which, like most doors on the choppers under his command—indeed, like most doors on most Hueys in the whole of South Vietnam—had been taken off, leaving a wide gap through which the port M-60 gunner had a clear field of fire.

Why Tollmarsh called his chair the "hot" seat was something of a mystery. It was in fact anything but hot—in the dangerous sense of the word—since it was placed well back from the actual door-opening, and thus out of any lines of fire from below, which, if they hit anything at all, would hit the door-gunner, a bulky man who went some way to filling the entire gap. It had been remarked on more than one occasion that the door-gunner on Tollmarsh's Command chopper was invariably a man of some bodily substance.

One of them, conspicuously more intelligent (perhaps with more of a sense of humour) than the rest, had once pointed this out and tried to claim extra-hazardous-duty pay on top of the normal hazardous-duty and mission-over-hostile-territory pay he regularly drew. Within hours he'd found himself not only back on the ground, but way out in the front line in the Mekong Delta, the shittiest place in Nam. Major Tollmarsh had a short way with "disrupters."

He had a short way with pansies, too, and peaceniks and pinkos and anyone else who deviated from the course he'd set himself ever since, as a teenager back in the early 1950s, the appalling and insidious threat

24

to world peace and the American way of life represented by international Communism had been brought starkly home to him by such hard-hitting documentary style films as *The Red Menace* and *I Married A Communist*.

Door-gunners were not there to argue about how much pay they drew, they were there to shoot gooks. And gooks being Communists, that made this war something of a Holy Crusade. And you didn't argue about money on a Holy Crusade. And if you did, there had to be something wrong with you.

Major Tollmarsh didn't at all begrudge the time and effort it took to root out and neutralise people with something wrong with them. In fact, he revelled in it, especially if they were of a similar, or, better, higher rank than he was. He'd been known to spend days—weeks, even—plotting some devious entrapment of a fellow major, or a colonel, who'd earned his displeasure for one reason or another (usually for not taking what Tollmarsh considered to be a strong line against the VC, and since he privately believed that most of the population of South Vietnam were VC, this meant he had his work cut out keeping ahead), and then tying them up in so much bureaucratic red tape that the guy's career was usually strangled there and then.

Tollmarsh was also a great admirer of the late Senator for Wisconsin, Joseph McCarthy. True, he didn't wave a list of card-carrying members of the Communist party around wherever he went, but then he didn't need to. A word—a hint, an insinuation—dropped in the right ear at the right moment played far more havoc than any amount of hard documentary evidence (Tollmarsh actually believed that the Senator for Wisconsin's famous shit list was hard documentary evidence). In any case, why bother collecting boxfilesful of proof when you could pull the trick just as — or, rather, far more — effectively with a throwaway line to a general of similar persuasion standing in front of the pisser in a men's room in Nha Trang.

Major Tollmarsh shifted his position irritably in his hot seat, and thought about Captain Frank Marco. He had a strong suspicion that Marco was a trouble-maker. As far as Tollmarsh was concerned, the guy had two strikes against him already: one, he'd been in some kind of trouble before (losing a couple of gunships, and then getting himself involved in some dubious situation or other about which Tollmarsh was none too clear), and, two, he was a Goddamn black.

That last was a major strike in Tollmarsh's book, blacks being almost as vicious a threat to the American way of life as Reds.

And now he had a third strike against him: he was a smart-ass. That crack about Superman had stuck in the major's craw. It rankled. It had not been at all funny. Okay, so Superman was comicbook crap, but you could look at it another way. Superman was getting to be Americana — maybe had got there already. Hell, he'd been going for over 30 years, hadn't he?

And there was nothing wrong with the values he represented, either. Fearless, pure-hearted, morally upright — Goddamnit, he was a positive force for good. An example to follow. White, too.

Well, brooded Tollmarsh, it was not too late to do something about Marco. Not too late to fix him good, the way Tollmarsh liked to see troublemakers fixed. Not too Goddamn late at all.

Up front Marco adjusted his dark glasses and said, "That dude for real?"

Hanks grinned.

"Nah. Figment of our imaginations, Captain."

"Man, he's gung-ho. All that Stetson-waving shit. Tell you, Hanks, I am wondering what I have gotten myself into now."

There was a subtle inflexion on the word "now" that Hanks caught. He knew that Marco had been transferred to Tollmarsh's troop after a longish, and unexplained, lay-off from active duties. The scuttlebutt drifting around Base had hinted at spook activities that had somehow fouled up, plus some kind of a connection with a major shake-out in the higher echelons of Special Forces Command in Saigon and a sudden eruption in South Vietnamese government circles. But further than that no one, least of all Marco himself, would go.

Hanks had heard that Marco was a five-star chopper pilot, and he had ribbons to prove it, but this was the first time he'd flown with him. He knew that prior to whatever upheaval Marco had been involved in he'd spent most of his time ferrying Special Forces small units into and out of bandit country. Solo jobs, for the most part: shadow patrols, clandestine hit-teams. Hanks wondered how Marco would take to this kind of work—large, organised hunter-killer swoops on EnVee sanctuaries across the borders of Laos and Cambodia. He figured he'd soon find out.

Marco stared through the plexiglas windscreen. Dawn was coming up fast, pushing back the darkness to the east, fingering the tree-lined horizon with an almost sinister light. Gunships, warming up, ready for the crank, were, he knew, stretched away behind him in an inverted V. All he had to do was lift off, and suddenly the air would be full of these roaring, racketing death-birds, heading west for yet another confrontation with Charlie. Marco wondered if this confrontation would turn out to be at all decisive, one way or the other, and then thought probably not.

You rocket-blasted villes, bombed the jungle, napalmed rice paddies, killed lots of gooks. But whatever you did, and however violently or savagely you did it, it never seemed to make much difference. The war dragged on; resolution seemed as far away as ever.

Sure, Nixon was dragging men out of Nam and back to the World by the scruffs of their necks, thousands at a time; de-escalation was the buzz-word of the moment. And that meant they were winning, didn't it?

Didn't it?

No way, he thought sourly. No way were they fucking winning. They were simply clearing out before the rising tide of shit swamped them utterly.

Marco was only 24, but he felt worn out and tired and old. Like, about a thousand years old.

"You think we'd better move it, Captain?" said Hanks.

"Like, set the wagons a-rollin', man?"

"Something like that, sir."

Marco nodded briefly.

"Jus' tryin' to work up a little enthusiasm for the war," he said. "You is right, though. We better move it on down, or ole Custer's like to bust a gut back there."

He set the throttle and thumbed the starter. The turbine rose from a whine to a shriek, emitted a throaty cough, then took hold with an ear-shattering bellow. Above, seen through the overhead greenhouse panels, the whirling rotors became suddenly invisible. Marco felt that old familiar feeling of weightlessness for a second, as the rotors clawed at the air, then the Huey tilted forward on its skids and almost drifted upwards.

Still low, he tilted the cyclic over, touched the pedal, and began to swing round from old habit in a long gentle curve to the left, glancing at the terrain below quickly and professionally. All-seeingly. Taking in every detail.

Then he pulled on the collective lever at the side of his seat, and the chopper began to climb higher. He glanced at the altimeter—450 . . . 500 . . . 550 . . . 600. Smoothly and easily. He touched the right pedal, then the left, and the gunship waggled slightly. Then he swung the cyclic back and forth, getting the feel of the machine as it rolled.

The sun could now be seen, an incandescent curve on the rim of the eastern horizon. Marco climbed higher, then turned in a half circle and hurtled towards the dying darkness in the west.

The target was about twenty-five miles across the border into eastern Cambodia. Here the terrain rolled gently upwards through tracts of dense forest towards the foothills of the *Plateaux Montagnards* that stretched its brooding bulk across from South Vietnam.

Marco watched as the ville suddenly sprang into view beyond the uneven carpet of green that looked solid enough to walk on, way ahead. Medium-sized, no overspill at the rear, long-houses placed neatly around three sides of a central plaza, rice paddies like a patchwork quilt falling away to the left, an old temple to the right.

By now the inhabitants would know they were coming. In fact they would have been warned of the gunship pack's approach some minutes before by a kind of subdued growling sound, sometimes faint, sometimes more distinguishable, carried by the wind. The sound would grow, and so would their alarm, if Marco knew anything about it. It was a weird sound—a sound imbued with a terrifying menace—the far-off but fast-approaching racket of many rotors.

This vile had been tagged as an EnVee sanctuary and arms-dump, so any moment now all kinds of shit would be zeroing in on the pack. They'd have pulled out rockets, MGs, AKs, maybe a heat-seeking missile or three by now. They would fight. Rarely, in Marco's experience, did Charlie take it on the lam into the jungle. Rarely did they do a fast fade. The bellicose little fuckers would just stand there and take it, and throw back all they had. Defiant as a bastard.

Marco's eyes narrowed behind his shades, then flicked to left and right as the ville hurtled towards him. No incoming yet. They were leaving it until the last possible moment for some reason. Unusual. He frowned suddenly, pushed down on the collective. The chopper swooped towards the forest, and skimmed along at tree-top level.

"We stay out back!" yelled Hanks. "Behind! Let the

30

rest go in!"

Marco gave him the finger, and increased speed. Below him the endless acres of green abruptly ended—disappeared as though magicked away by a wizard's spell. Various shades of dusty brown replaced them. Marco swept over the central plaza, low, and noted that it was totally empty. Not even an old mama-san scurrying for cover. Not even a fucking dog.

"I got a bad feeling," he shouted at Hanks. "This ville sucks!"

He was suddenly aware of something hammering down on his right shoulder and glanced around. It was Major Tollmarsh's left hand. Tollmarsh was jabbing the forefinger of his right hand downwards.

"Go in! Go in!"

"Bad ville!" yelled Marco. "Bad vibes!"

Tollmarsh's pinky-red face turned a dull scarlet.

"*Go in!*"

Marco shrugged.

"Why no incoming?" he bawled at Hanks. "You tell me that. Ain't natural."

As if on cue yellow flashes suddenly starred the greenery way to the left, flicking on and off like an ineptly operated light-show. And then, just as suddenly, ceased. Marco shook his head.

Tollmarsh was shouting into a mike, and ahead a chopper peeled away from the rest of the pack. It swooped down over the jungle then veered off to one side in a sharp bank, two barrel-shaped objects bucketing away from its belly. Nothing happened for three or four seconds, then orange fire bloomed upwards and outwards, roaring through the trees like dragon's breath. Black smoke belched into the air. Another chopper made a pass, this time across the path of the first machine. More fire express-trained along under the forest canopy, searing the rich green ugly black.

Marco circled away to the rear and hovered, sinking down in his seat to watch the show.

Gunships lanced down at the ville from left and right and raced away, and huts fountained into the air, exploding like angry orange flowers. Red streams of tracer soared over the central square and down, lashing the entire plaza, sending chunks of stone, brickwork, hard-caked mud dancing in all directions. Giant palm fronds fluttered through the dust-haze like dying birds, and smoke rolled across the scene, half-shrouding it before a tremendous eruption of mud, roof tiles, lumps of concrete, burning hootch-thatch and bits of trees cleared it away again. Then, scant seconds later, the smoke of that explosion boiled up, almost hiding the ville completely.

"Weapons bunker!" bawled Hanks.

Marco said nothing.

He felt like some grass, or a pipe of opium, or a couple of tabs, or something—anything—to shift the tight feeling out of his stomach. It was as though an invisible hand had reached inside of him and was clutching at him, squeezing hard.

He had no doubt at all that Tollmarsh, for all his combat experience, had fucked up on this one. It was a plant. The ville was a dead one. Below, he could now see the small temple more clearly, with vines and creepers trailing out of its empty windows, with clumps of grass on its wide, cracked approach-steps. A hut, a few yards beyond, caught his eye. There was a hole in its roof-thatch; an old hole, black round the edges. Another hootch beyond that, half of one wall rotting and exposed, sagging outwards. No one had lived here in a long, long while.

Tollmarsh was bellowing more orders in the mike, and choppers were dropping down into the ville and on to the flatland outside. Loose grass, dust and bits of debris were whirled into the air, and the thick black smoke tore apart, thinned and dispersed, shredding into nothing.

Marco took hold of the cyclic again and pulled the chopper out of hover, sending it into a long, wide turn away from the shattered ville.

Tollmarsh was suddenly close behind him again, screaming over his shoulder.

"*Down* Goddamnit! We go *down!*"

Marco didn't bother replying. He wanted to place himself well behind the rest of the pack. As he began his spiralling approach, his eyes were taking in the ground below and he had a strong feeling that he ought to be seeing figures in green camouflage suits and pith helmets flitting from cover to cover, closing in on the ville, ready for the pounce. But he saw nothing like that at all. That worried him even more.

The ground was not quite even and covered with short tough grass, dotted with occasional stunted bushes. Marco put the gunship down with only the slightest bump behind the rest of the choppers and slightly to their left. Paddy fields stretched away on a gentle slope; he was a long way from the nearest tree-line. That suited him.

Ahead men were clambering from their choppers

and heading into the ville, fanning out in well-drilled skirmish line, M-16s at the ready. Two MG teams sprinted across his nose and split up, one, with a black gunner and back-up, setting up a few yards away, the other disappearing behind the nearest hootch.

"Burned their damn balls off them," crowed Tollmarsh, hitching the mike. "You see that bunker blow? Fuckin' Commie dinks. That'll take the starch out of their attack capability, yes sir."

Marco turned in his seat.

"Got to say I don't think this smells so sweet, Major."

Tollmarsh's face underwent a rapid shift from good-time joviality to thin-lipped outrage.

"And what in Hell is that supposed to mean, Captain?"

"Christ, Major, this a prepared ville. I mean, man, it's like a ghost-town out there, all set up." He pointed at the temple. "Ain't no one gone down on bended knee in there in a hog's age. Huts ain't been lived in since Christ was a teenager. It's a fuckin' *trap*, man!"

Tollmarsh's expression was sour now, as though he was about to burp bile. Then a tight death's-head smile broke out across his features.

"God preserve me from the wise-ass element in this man's army, Captain."

"Sir," said Marco through his teeth, "this an unsafe ville."

"Crap," said Tollmarsh.

He ducked down and turned away. Marco watched him double-timing it past the black MG team and on into the smoking ville.

"You won't take this to heart, Captain," said

Hanks, "but I have to say I doubt you're gonna be with us long."

"That your considered opinion, babe?"

Hanks, who'd never been called babe by his wife, let alone an officer, coughed.

"Yessir."

"Damn right," said Marco, as though he was thinking about something else entirely. "Ain't it the truth. Got a feeling—*Holy Christ!*"

Hanks stared at him. Marco was gazing upwards through the windscreen.

"That pissant little turdbird gone pulled *all* the Goddamn choppers down! We ain't got us no fuckin' air-cover!"

He leaned right across Hanks to peer up through the opposite side-window—and stiffened, as though electricity had lanced through him. Outside, on the ground below, a man was coming up from the crouch, an AK-47 assault rifle in his hands. Marco could not have recognised every member of Tollmarsh's troop, but whoever this guy was he did not belong to it. No way.

In his two-second appraisal—all he allowed himself—Marco saw that the man was white, but dressed in soiled jungle fatigues with bandoliers of spare rounds hanging crosswise over his chest. His face was dirty, his hair unkempt. Shock flickered across his face, and something else. Another emotion. Baffled rage. Marco's hand snatched at the door's release-handle and slammed it down, ramming the door open and into the man's face.

The man went over backwards with hardly a sound—apart from the meaty crack of steel on bone—and hit the dirt, blood pouring from his shattered nose.

Marco, adrenalin burning through him, snarled "*Kill him!*" and threw himself backwards into his own seat, his left hand scrabbling for an open hold-all beside it. He yanked out a heavy .45 automatic and fired left-handed past the shrinking figure of Hanks, through the open door. The man outside had rolled on impact with the ground, and was now rising fast, his Kalashnikov swinging up for a burst. Marco's bullet took him full in the throat and punched him solidly backwards. Hanks saw the back of the man's neck and head burst outwards in a wash of blood and brains, and knew that Marco's rounds had to be soft-nosed and crossed.

Marco, breathing fast, was punching buttons on the instrument panel. The rotors howled.

"Fucker! Knew it! Shee-it, I *knew* it!" He jabbed the gun at Hanks, and Hanks gulped in air and shrank back in his seat, totally bemused. "Shut the fuckin' door. We gettin' outta here fast!"

Corley, the fat door-gunner, had jumped across the cabin and was now leaning half across Hanks, peering wide-eyed at the sprawled body outside.

"What the fuck is doin', Captain?"

"Christ knows. Get to your gun. We under attack."

Corley didn't get a chance even to move. Suddenly he screamed and pitched forward over Hanks, blood welling out of a hole in his back. Hanks yelled, tried to shove the feebly squirming body off him. Corley was moaning and kicking his legs in the air.

Ahead, Marco could see men running towards the chopper, dodging and weaving as they neared him.

None of them was from Tollmarsh's troop, and all had assault rifles. The black MG team lay like broken dolls around their weapon; Marco had not even seen them killed. He opened up with his forward cannon as he lifted the gunship off the ground, and grinned savagely as the close-range fire bowled his attackers over like pins in an alley, bursting at least two of them apart completely and spraying what was left over a wide area.

Then he was in the air, lifting straight up, soaring high above the smoke and confusion below.

He threw a glance to his right. Corley appeared to be dead now; at least, he wasn't making any sound or kicking his legs in the air as Hanks struggled to heave him away.

"Can't get him off," Hanks was babbling, his voice pitched high. "Snagged somewhere. Fucker's died on me. Can't shift him off me."

Corley was in a kind of a sideways foetal position wrapped round Hanks, his bulk trapping most of Hanks's upper body and right hand against the cabin door. Blood was gouting out of the hole in Corley's back and Hanks's face and free hand were liberally splashed with it. Hanks looked panicky.

"Cool it down, Hanks," rapped Marco. He dropped his .45 back in the hold-all. "Jus' ease the mother off. Do it slow. We outta the shit-pan, man."

As he said this the distinctive foresight and curved gas piston on the pockmarked barrel of a Kalashnikov slid past his nose.

Marco had once read the expression "his heart lurched" in a book and had instantly dismissed it as unrealistic bullshit, the sort of crap only a fifth-rater would use to fill out space. Now he realised that the line might be a cliché but, like all clichés, it had a solid foundation of hardcore truth in it. He felt his own heart jump as though it had been socked by a fist. It truly was an almost physical sensation.

He kept his hands on the cyclic and slowly turned in his seat. The Kalashnikov was held by a tall man in dirty fatigues wearing a helmet with a skull-and-cross-bones decal on the front. He was grinning nastily. He was black. Behind him, just glimpsed, was another man, white, also gripping an AK. This one was big-boned, with a heavy, drooping Zapata moustache almost hiding his mouth. Special Forces, both. Marco could smell Special Forces in a Force 9 gale blowing in the opposite direction.

"Outta the shit-pan into the firing-line," said the black, deep-voiced. "Take us back, brother."

"Shove it," said Marco tightly.

"Sho' nuff," said the black playfully. "Where you want it shoved, brother? Up your ass? Or straight 'tween yo' baby-blues?"

After the initial shock, Marco's brain was shifting into top. The black had the drop on him; he couldn't reach for his own gun. Since he was in front of the other guy, it followed that he was the one who'd iced Corley. But it also followed that his AK was on single-shot, and he'd probably not switched to full auto-matic. Could be, thought Marco, some salvation there. Start blasting on automatic in an enclosed chopper cabin high off the ground and you might not get down in one piece. Or maybe these guys didn't care? Marco couldn't believe that.

He drifted some way away from the ville and all he

could see of it, out of the corner of his eye, was a thick curtain of oily smoke rising above the sea of green. But he had a strong feeling that Tollmarsh and his troops were now non-existent. Then his mind jumped back to choppers, and the thought hit him that that was what these mothers were after. That was what they wanted.

The choppers.

Ergo, figured Marco, the guys back here wanted a smooth ride down and the chopper intact.

Marco was not inclined to give it to them. Hell, if he did, this'd be the third Huey he'd had taken off him, one way or another, in less than six months! He'd be getting a rep for being an easy touch, Goddamnit. Every asshole in Nam and out of it would be after him. Frank Marco, the numbnuts who was so stupid they were gonna have to open up a whole new category of stupidity for him. It was not, thought Marco, to be borne.

"C'mon, c'mon," said the black. "Back to the ville, brother. We got business to conclude."

Marco said, "Look, man, what the fuck is this? You supposed to be killin' Charlie, not us. You Special Forces."

The big man behind the black guffawed.

"He wins a Kewpie doll."

"This a take-over," said the black. "This what this is. Principles are getting fucked up in this shooting war. Time someone took a stand."

The big man said, "Shut it!" loudly.

"Take it easy," said the black. "It's cool. He a brother." He suddenly leaned over Marco, put an arm round his shoulder. "Listen, all we want's the materiél. Dig? You put us down real smooth, an' disappear. Or maybe join us. There are choices, man. Choices all over."

Marco didn't believe this for a moment. These cats were heavy. He knew the type. They were natural-born killers, and Marco had an idea that whatever he did he'd end up with a hole in his head.

He made to rise from his seat, noting Hanks's pop-eyed expression—now set fast in a mask of blood—as he did so.

"You wanna go down—take her the fuck down yourself," he said. "Brother."

The tall black stopped being playful. He slammed the barrel of the assault rifle against the side of Marco's head.

Marco grunted and lurched back into his seat. Pain like white fire roared behind his eyes. He hunched over the cyclic, nodding dully.

"Okay, okay."

The black stepped back.

Marco sucked in his breath then suddenly shoved the collective all the way to the bottom and kicked the chopper over on its left side with full left pedal, cyclic hard over. The black staggered and yelled, then screamed as he spun round and collapsed back against the M-60 mounting, face-first. Corley's body jerked off Hanks and fell across Marco but the black pilot had been ready for this. He let go of the controls for three seconds at most, grabbed the dead gunner and heaved him bodily back over the seat, then lunged for the cyclic again.

Corley's body tumbled over the black and across the narrow space of the rear cabin. It struck the big man with the moustache, and both went sailing out of the port door. The big man didn't even have time to yell.

The altimeter was down to 150 when Marco pulled right and aft on the cyclic, gritting his teeth. The engine bellowed lustily. Below left, all he could see was the colour green, different shades of it jazzing around and melding crazily as he spiralled. His head was hurting and he was desperately trying to keep from vomiting all over his console.

Then he came on with the power, and eased the cyclic forward for airspeed, levelling off about five feet from treetop level. He was drenched with sweat.

The chopper raced along for some seconds before Marco took her straight up again, vertical, shooting high like an express elevator. He knew he hadn't gotten rid of the black, and he knew he had to keep jinking to stop the guy from using his gun, and he knew he couldn't throw this bird into another fast spiral because the mother'd be ready for it this time.

Hanks! Hanks could nail the fucker.

He glanced right, and cursed. Hanks was slumped in his seat, held in by his belt, his head sagging sideways, the skin at his temple broken and his own blood mingling with Corley's. The kid had been cold-cocked somehow when the chopper had keeled over.

The altimeter showed a thousand and Marco levelled off again as fast as he dared, then risked a look over his shoulder. The black, hate and rage writ large across his face, was clinging to Tollmarsh's hot seat, still gripping his AK. He was yelling, but Marco couldn't hear a word. Probably, he thought, starting to regain his cool, just as well.

For a second he considered simply taking him back

to Base, but rejected the idea almost as soon as he thought it. The guy could still cause problems. Maybe he wouldn't dare shoot up the ship, but you couldn't count on it. He looked mad enough for anything. He looked mad enough to suddenly flip his wig. Go bananas utterly. Forget any danger to himself and simply cut loose with the AK on full automatic.

The thought made Marco sweat some more. The fuck with you, he thought.

You for the high jump, brother.

There wasn't a hell of a lot you could do with a Huey aerobatically when all was said and done, but Marco had by no means shot his bolt. One way or another that son of a bitch was going to take a dive into nothing, and by the time they scraped him up off the ground there really wasn't going to be enough of him left to make up a half a can of C-rat jam.

He checked his seat-belt. Firm. He hoped Hanks's was likewise, otherwise Bye-bye Hanks. Then he pushed the cyclic forward and down until the Huey was racing nose-first for the jungle.

He eased back and the rotors tore at the air, the gunship coming up out of the swoop and climbing. He'd lost the jungle now and all he could see was sky. This was going to be hairy. He'd done it before, and knew exactly what he was doing and what he was going to do. But he'd never done it with a trigger-happy madman out back and that was what pitched the manoeuvre right out of the barnstorming league and smack into hold-tight-keep-praying-and-hope-to-save-your-ass tactics.

Whole different ball-game.

He was almost vertical. Any second now and it was

42

going to be stalling time. Already the engine-noise sounded as unhealthy as a guy with a knife stuck in his windpipe. He checked out his console and eased the cyclic over to the right.

The gunship peeled away at the top of its climb and turned right over, on its side, its rotors hammering, the entire machine vibrating and juddering at maximum stress. Like some strange futuristic torpedo, it continued rolling as it hurtled onwards, loose fittings spraying out of the open doorways, showering the jungle below. Upside down, the tall black with the skull-and-crossbones decal on his helmet tumbled out on the port side, bounced off the 20mm cannon mount, and shot away at an angle straight at the churning rotors.

In his seat, Marco felt the entire Huey kick savagely at the bottom of its roll and thought, Sweet-Jesus-I-is-done-for-something's-hit-the-fucking-blades.

At the same time as he thought this a large round ball rocketed past the windscreen, leaving a spatter of crimson across the plexiglas in its wake, and he realised that (a) the black was out, and (b) the rotors had sheared the son of a bitch's head off.

All this took little more than an instant of time, and then he was rolling right way up, on even keel, and he was centreing the cyclic and pushing it firmly forward.

He wanted speed. He wanted speed more than he'd ever wanted anything before in his entire life.

He got speed.

He maintained it.

Still gripping the cyclic as though it was a talisman, Marco hunched back in his seat and breathed out gustily. Executing a wing-over in a helicopter gunship was not the smartest move one could think of. Sure, it was a perfectly feasible manoeuvre, aerodynamically—but that wasn't the point. It was just not the cleverest stroke to pull when you were menaced by a crazed, gun-toting killer, with your co-pilot out for the count, and you'd just jumped out of a heavy ambush situation and your skull was throbbing after a side-swipe from a rifle-barrel and your guts were about ready to heave themselves up out of your mouth.

Marco gazed around him, taking the chopper in a slow easy turn to the left. Far away on the horizon the sky was smeared with grey: the smoke of the bombed ville. He debated whether to head back there and recon the area, and decided no way was it worth it. He had no doubt that the choppers were taken and the men either dead or prisoners. If he went to see what was doing down in the ville, chances were they'd chase him, shoot him down. There must be some pilots amongst the attack-force, else why in hell would they want the choppers?

Whoever they were.

Marco couldn't figure that out, or, indeed, any other detail of the ambush. The guys who'd jumped his ship were Special Forces, without the shadow of a doubt, but that only made the whole crapping business crazier. Specials killing Specials? It didn't make sense.

And killing it was, for sure. They'd nailed that black MG team like they meant it—without a thought, fast and smooth, no argument.

So who in Christ's name were they?

Marco had heard of deserters banding up in the jungle, preying on small isolated villes, living like wild dogs off the land. But this was different—way different.

These guys weren't simply punk deserters. They were heavy dudes, and they knew exactly what they were doing. This was an organised effort. Team-work. What had the black said? Principles are getting fucked up . . . time someone took a stand?

There was a Goddamn brain behind this.

They'd set up the ville and then let the intelligence filter through somehow to Command across the border that it was a juicy target. A hunter-killer strike is ordered. The gunship pack moves in, gets fired on from the jungle just in case anyone gets worried about the lack of heavy stuff from the ville itself (and you could bet your last pack of Luckies that tracer from the trees had been triggered by some guy who'd jumped the hell out fast before the napalm came down—or, more likely, had been some kind of jury-rigged MG set to shoot from a long way away), and Bam-bam-bam! The gunships expend on the ville, blow its shit away, and drop down—all ready to be grabbed by the guys who've been waiting in nice deep bunkers underneath, shooting craps or playing poker or just yawning their ass off while the shit is flying upstairs.

That, thought Marco, would be the way of it.

If only that peckerhead Tollmarsh had listened to him, none of this would have happened.

That would not be left out of his report.

He thought about radioing for an assist, played around with the idea for a while, then rejected it. This was Cambodia; it might be un-cool. The dust had not entirely settled from the US incursion of a couple of months back, and to bounce a major air-strike into the country while the crap was still flying back in the World might not be the smartest of moves.

Tollmarsh's own strike had been different, of course. Strictly officially-unofficial. It would not have logged. As a matter of fact, there were almost as many missions into Cambodia now, air and ground, as there had been before the official invasion, but they were kept well under wraps. In any case, Marco figured that if he pulled in a large strike to nail the chopper-bandits and things went wrong (always a possibility) he might well find himself in very deep shit in double time. Scapegoats were badly needed these days.

He looked at Hanks. Still dead to the world. Marco dived for the jungle and levelled out, then streaked east for the border.

Chapter Two

"How much you had to drink?" said Steeger.

Hardin shrugged.

"A shot of bourbon. Nothing to speak of."

"When?"

"Hour or so ago. More. Why?"

Steeger grinned like a vampire.

"Got some good stuff in the Diplomatic Bag this morning." Still grinning he put his hands up in the air and waggled them about, like Al Jolson doing his "Mammy" act. "Wanna try some?"

Steeger was a highly regarded freelance who had a foot in many camps. Under his own name he religiously attended the Five O'Clock Follies at the Joint U.S. Public Affairs Office (progaganda, 98 proof), solemnly accepted all the official handouts from the MACV Information Office, and wired back long and enthusiastic reports to various journals like *Newsweek* and *Esquire* and *New York Magazine* in the States about how the Marines were winning the war and the Arvins were winning the peace. Under the pseudonyms Guy La Douche (swiped from a favourite novel called *The Man Who Wrote Dirty Books*) and Rolk La Rue (because he used to read *Lash Larue* comicbooks, *inter alia*, when he was a kid) he sent scurrilous pieces back to radical papers like *Rolling Stone* and *Village Voice* about how everything was so fucked up over here, and Command didn't know its ass from Wednesday, and it was quite clear that the ruling Thieu regime was doomed, doomed, doomed because it was riddled with corruption and venality. And under the even more absurd name Fred Katzenzammer he wrote occasional stories for drug-oriented Underground sheets about the grunts who used to come off the Medevac choppers with their arms and legs blown away but feeling no pain because their minds were blown away too on all kinds of tabs and pills, and how up in the Highlands the Montagnards would trade you a pound of legendary grass for a carton of Salems.

The joke was, Steeger also contributed occasional very gung-ho articles to the CIA-controlled *Saigon Post* (a notorious rag), and was very well in with the spooks who operated out of the Embassy on Thong Nhut Street. That was where he got most of the information and scuttlebutt he blew to the radicals. Naturally, the spooks were unaware of this.

Just as they were unaware that Steeger was really a freak of the first water who was running a contact on the diplomatic staff who brought in all kinds of high class dope from all over via the Diplomatic Bag.

Naturally, if they had known any of this they would have been somewhat pissed off about it—and even more pissed that the secret, such as it was, was shared by a much-decorated colonel in Special Forces who, contrary to what much-decorated officers in Special Forces were expected to do in off-duty periods, had a habit of getting stoned out of his skull on the proceeds of Steeger's forays into the drug culture.

Steeger said, "You had an ear-bleed, or something?"

"Someone took a lunge at me with a switchblade in a bar near the Thieves' Market couple of days ago."

"Wow!" Steeger's thick eyebrows lifted. "You Special Forces bravos really live dangerously. You stomp on him?"

Hardin got up from the lounger he'd been sitting on and strolled towards the open French window. The mingled smells of poincianas, frangipani and bougain-villea drifted in from the villa's large garden beyond, where Eileen Satkis was throwing bread crumbs on to the lawn and making vaguely birdlike twittering noises. No birds seemed interested in these offerings. Eileen Satkis turned and shrugged, wide-handed, at Hardin.

He lit a cigarette; said over his shoulder, "I skewered his hand to a table, but not before he half-throttled me."

"You're losing your touch," said Steeger. "Time was, old Special Forces buddy, when you'd've creamed the guy with both legs tied behind your back."

"Getting out of practice," said Hardin.

"Must've been a big guy, to half-throttle you."

"Big, and drunk as a bastard."

"But you let him half-throttle you."

Hardin said, "Cut it out, Will. I have enough problems without any smart-ass shirt from you."

Steeger dumped himself down in the swivel-chair behind the big, old-fashioned roll-top desk he used for working and heaved himself round a couple of times. The chair creaked and cracked in protest.

"They're still keeping you on a leash?"

"They're still keeping me on a leash."

"Sounds to me they don't know what the fuck to do with you, Hardin."

"I get the same impression, Steeger."

Steeger pondered this. He knew Hardin well; had known him on and off for fourteen, fifteen years. He knew Hardin to be a tough nut with a soft centre — or maybe softish was the better word. It was difficult to analyse the guy, and it had always been like that, even right back when he'd first bumped into him in San Francisco. Then, Steeger had been studying at UCLA, editing one of the student newspapers, and Hardin had been — what? A kind of a bum, hanging around on the waterfront, mixing with the Beats. Steeger had met him while browsing round the now legendary City Lights bookstore; Hardin had been one of the kids behind the counters — although not so much of a kid at that.

Steeger used to spend weekends in San Francisco, on a phantom quest for phantom copy ("Our Frisco Correspondent"), and he and Hardin would meet up at one of the jazz cellars down by the harbour and drink Millers and smoke dope and nod their heads and tap their feet to the sounds. Even then Hardin had been restless. At times, he'd simply take off, Steeger never knew where. And Hardin rarely told him. Sometimes he'd get postcards from weird places: Acapulco, maybe, or La Paz. Once from some port in Morocco. Steeger recalled the occasion when he'd been staying the weekend in Frisco at a loft rented by Hardin's current old lady — Kate? Jeannie? Fran? — and had woken up on the Sunday to find a note pinned to his door: "See you in a couple of weeks, maybe." In fact he didn't see Hardin for five months, and the first indication of his whereabouts was a cryptic card franked in some hick town in Venezuela, that wasn't even marked on a large-scale atlas. Hardin's current old lady—Jo? Stella? Marge?—hadn't seemed too bothered. "He often does that," she'd said.

There was no doubt that, sometime during the late '50s/early 60s, Hardin had gotten himself into some strange and exotic situations. Steeger had often wondered whether Hardin was in the CIA during those years, but hadn't taken the thought too seriously. It hadn't seemed to him to be quite Hardin's style, somehow. Too clinical. Too Ivy League. Too seersucker suit. All the CIA guys he knew, from his newspaper experience, had very short haircuts and no sense of humour. Hardly the Hardin image (well, apart from right now, anyhow; but then Hardin didn't have too much to laugh about at the moment).

On the other hand he was doing something weird for some weird outfit or other. That had to be admitted. Often he'd show up when you least expected it, and then disappear again, and it was only later that you suddenly realised that he'd shown up—and this was almost an invariable—only days after some hot-spot had exploded the other side of the globe. A revolution, a seizure of power, an assassination.

And then there was the time Steeger had been on assignment for the *Los Angeles Times* in Cairo, about 1962, and had spotted Hardin across a street in deep conversation with one of the military attachés at the U.S. Embassy. There'd been too much traffic or he'd have crossed over, and seconds later both Hardin and his companion had disappeared down a side-street. But Steeger knew the attache, and later had button-holed him. The conversation had not been at all satisfactory. The attache had denied that the meeting had occurred; claimed he'd been in the Embassy all morning.

Three days later a strongly pro-Russian French wheeler-dealer had been gunned down outside his apartment block in one of the classier Cairo suburbs, and, as far as Steeger knew, they never did nail the killer. Steeger had done some digging, but no American by the name of Hardin—John or otherwise—was living in Cairo at that time, or had been living there, or had even been staying there briefly.

Well, you could add two and two together and you'd have to be a dimbo to deny they made four. Steeger was by no means a dimbo. He'd bumped into Hardin in New York about six months later, and casually mentioned he'd been doing a spell in Cairo. Hardin had expressed vague interest; it was, he'd said, one of the places he'd never been to, but he'd heard it was nice. Steeger hadn't pressed him.

Now he lit a cigarette and spun himself round in his swivel-chair a couple more times and watched Hardin gazing out of the French windows at Eileen Satkis, still trying unsuccessfully to seduce the local bird population.

He said, "Don't let it fuck up your mind."

Hardin turned away from the window angrily.

"Jesus, Will, I think it's fucked up already! Listen, I've been on ice now for two months, damn near, hanging around Saigon. They won't let me move an inch over the city boundaries. 'Take it easy,' they say, 'hang loose.' *Hang loose!*" Hardin's face twisted up with sudden intense rage. "The way things are, you'd think I'd been caught with my fingers in the till, not that son of a bitch Dempsey!"

Steeger knew all about the Dempsey affair—or, at least, as much as he guessed Hardin had figured it was necessary to tell him. Dempsey, a Special Forces general, had been secretely trading with the EnVees and because Hardin had refused to play ball had sent him out over Laos with a bomb in his chopper. To cover himself, Dempsey had then sent out a "rescue party," which just happened to consist of the dregs from the dirtiest brigs in Nam, none of whom were supposed to make it back alive. Somehow they had, with Hardin. Dempsey's career had then ended very messily on a Saigon street.*

As a story it was dynamite—political, military, any and every kind of dynamite you could think of—but it was one that Steeger had not blown to any of the radical sheets he secretly worked for. After Dempsey's downfall, a lot of worms had come wriggling out of the Saigon woodwork—Dempsey had had his fingers in some very strange pies—and the already shaky Thieu regime had come close to toppling altogether. Steeger had already had at least a half dozen frantic enquiries from papers and magazines in the States, straight as well as Underground, for the inside dirt on the upheavals shaking the South Vietnamese government, but he'd kept both his mouth and his typewriter-lid closed tight on that one.

Pity, really. It was the hell of a story.

*See *GUNSHIPS: The Killing Zone* by Jack Hamilton Teed

Corruption in high places, including the top echelons of the U.S. Command. Hell of a story. But Hardin had said, "Look, Will, why not leave it for your memoirs, okay?"

Well, you won some, lost some.

Hardin stubbed his cigarette out in an ashtray viciously, grinding it around until it shredded and fell apart.

"That damn Dempsey. You know what he did? Had a cousin of mine iced back in the World. Christ, I hadn't seen him in eight years — hadn't spoken to him for five — and that fat bastard put out a contract on him, just in case. Covering all Goddamn eventualities! Dropped the word to his crappy CIA contacts. Out on the spook network. The poor fucker probably opened his door one day and that was it — Thank you and good night. That fat son of a bitch. Well I nailed *his* hide for him."

There was a wealth of venom in that last pronouncement that surprised Steeger. It was unlike the Hardin he knew. Then again, maybe he didn't know Hardin at all, even after all these years. Steeger shivered slightly. That thought was actually quite scary.

"How would the spooks have dug out your cousin's location?"

"Easy. They had a file on him, you bet. He was always a radical son of a bitch."

Steeger pondered this for a couple of seconds. Mention of this twilight world of files and taps and bugs and general clandestine surveillance by those in authority never failed to trigger off a slight gut-churning reaction in him. Often, Steeger's news- and rumour-gathering activities caused him to tread a very narrow tightrope indeed, over what was cool and what was un-cool, and there had been occasions in the past when he'd had to use all of his considerable skill to save himself from falling off the wire completely.

"You think they have files on Guy La Douche and Rolf La Rue?" he said.

Hardin's face suddenly puckered up. His laugh started off as a snigger then exploded into a roundhouse gaffaw.

"Yeah, you bet. You bet they have files on those scurrilous fuckers. Fat files, too. Why, I figure the spooks have files on those vile, treacherous bastards a foot thick. At least."

"No shit? Hell, John, makes me queasy just to think about it. For all I know, the spooks could be planning a hit on those two very close friends of mine right now."

"They could indeed, Will. They could very well be doing just that very damn thing. Right now, in one of those nice air-conditioned conference rooms out in the complex at Langley, they could be beating their brains apart trying to figure out the perfect hit on one or other—and probably both—of those leaky scoundrels." Hardin's eyes narrowed; he jabbed a forefinger sternly at Steeger. "It's freaks like Guy La Douche and Rolf La Rue who're losing this man's war, Will, I can tell you. I am able to inform you of that fact. With their rotten freaky habits and their sneaky way of infiltrating Command and digging up the dirt on all the fuck-ups, and then, Goddamnit, spreading it around in their good-for-nothing nihilistic rags, they're doing more damn harm than old Charlie Cong himself."

"Sapping the nation's morale, the treacherous low-lives."

"Damn right."

"It's heinous, John."

"Heinous is the word, Will."

"La Douche and La Rue really ought to be deep-sixed."

"Yeah."

Steeger wriggled slightly in his chair and shot a veiled look at Hardin. All of a sudden he seemed to have loosened up, relaxed, as though all the tension and anger in him had drained away.

Steeger, said, "Christ, John, you don't like this war any more than any other intelligent guy does. You don't agree with US policy. You don't even think we ought to be here at all. And yet you're a colonel in Special Forces. Why in God's name d'you stick it out?"

Hardin sucked smoke into his lungs and let it out again through his nostrils, two plumes of light grey that drifted to nothing almost as soon as they were out. He shrugged.

"Can't explain it, Will. Not down to the last knot and bow. Maybe I like the adrenalin-burn in a bad situation. Maybe I just like the jungle. Maybe I like what Special Forces has to offer over the army, navy, air force."

"And that is?"

"Easy. You're your own man, to a hell of an extent. Listen, if you're in the army, you do what they tell you. You have to take a hill, you take it, and you take it exactly the way the guy on top of you tells you how to take it. That guy could be a military genius, and he could be a sack of shit. If he's a genius, likely as not you'll achieve your objective without too much hassle. If he's a sack of shit, you're in big trouble. You probably don't survive. All the time it's a crap game, and the dice are loaded against you. There aren't too many military geniuses over here right now, Will."

Steeger laughed shortly.

"Yeah, some of us noticed. You only have to go out on patrol with the grunts and see the fuck-ups from the top that turn a firefight piss-sour, and then come back and attend the Five O'Clocks next day and discover you were actually at the scene of a major victory, to realise that." He laughed again—the sour old newshound—and lit himself a cigarette. "They really do say," he said, shaking a sour old newshound forefinger at Hardin, "that it's us who're losing this war—the whole Goddamn press corps, you know?—but, truly, they don't need any help from us. Jesus, Command can lose this war their own sweet way." He took a drag on his cigarette. "So? Special Forces?"

"What it is," said Hardin, "is freedom. You have a mission. You get briefed up. You get ferried in. From there on out, it's yours. You take it the way you have to, the way it seems right." He waved a hand. "It's raw out there, Will. You don't just have to contend with Charlie, but the jungle too. The indifferent immensity of the natural world. A lot of guys feel they have to fight it, but that's not the way I've ever seen it. The way I figure it is you go with the tide. Dive right in. You can't beat the jungle, it's too damn big. So you join it. Easy. That way you win. And if you can beat the jungle, you can sure as hell beat Charlie." He shook his head, his eyes far, far away. "Jesus. So many crazy things. Listen, my last mission but two. I was heading a three-man team, and we got jumped. Fire-fight beneath the old banana tree. The other guys got wasted, but I managed to dodge out. The bastards were tracking me. Tight as leeches. I was living off the forest for a week. Then I managed to double-back on 'em; sneaked back through their lines. About noon one day I wanted to take a look around, get my bearings. Squirreled up this tree. Half way up I froze—my left foot resting on this real slender branch, about," he held up his little finger, "that thick, my right leg in a half-way-up position as I climbed with the knee about on a level with the top of my gut, my left hand holding a strand of loose creeper, and my right hand reaching up for the next branch but not touching a damn thing but air—and I *froze*." He shook his head, half in amusement, half in sheer incredulity. "Way below, a slope appeared out of the bushes. Just," he snapped his fingers, "like that. Stood there, rolled a cigarete, smoked it, stamped it out. Then, Goddamnit, he shoved his pants down, took a leak, then squatted down and had himself a crap. Then he smoked another cigarette. By this time, others had arrived. Eight of the fuckers. They had AKs, bandoliers of ammo, grenades, one guy even had a fucking rocket-launcher. And they were all down there, using my tree as a Goddamn crapper, while me, I'm in exactly—and, Will, I mean *exactly*—the same position as I was when the first guy turned up. My right hand is *still* not touching a Goddamn thing. Daren't! All it needed was one slight move, and something—a piece of bark, a twig, a lousy little leaf—might have broken off, drifted down to the ground. That was all it needed, and all one of those guys needed to have done was spot it and glance up, and I'd've been taking so much incoming they could've used me as a pepper-pot afterwards. Jesus!" He stroked his chin and laughed out loud, a sound of pure-grained triumph. "They were down there four hours, and when they left I gave them another 30 minutes—*and counted it out*—before I so much as shifted my position. And that was fatal, because my left leg, which'd been taking the whole fucking load, the whole weight of my body, was totally paralysed. Just seized up. I just fell down that tree, Will, straight down through the branches, must've sounded like a string of grenades going off, and landed slap-bang in EnVee shit. *Literally!*" He let out a wild howl of laughter and flung himself into Steeger's leather saddle-bag chair.

"How many times can you survive?" said Steeger dubiously.

"Jesus, Will, who knows? But that's what I meant by freedom. Survival is solely up to you. No one else can fuck things up. Whatever the nature of the mission—I mean, forget about that for the moment; it could be the dirtiest, most treacherous mission you can think of, but that's beside the point—you're free to do it how you like. You're free to make your own decisions—and your own mistakes. But the thing is, you don't make too many mistakes out there; you can't afford to. And you don't have a genius or a sack of shit telling you what to do, either. All you have is *you*." He shrugged. "Freedom."

Steeger eased himself out of the creaking swivel-chair and padded purposefully across the wide, book-lined room. Near an open doorway which led into a cool, spacious hall was a tall cabinet, which he opened out, gazing thoughtfully at an array of bottles inside. He stared at the bottles for some moments, his gaze shifting from label to label, then he closed the doors again with a sigh that was almost regretful. But not quite. He turned back towards his chair. Half way across the room he stopped.

"See, what I'm getting at, John, is what you've just mentioned. Mentioned in passing, damn it, like it wasn't there at all. Not worth bothering about. But, Christ, it's the most ambiguous piece of the tapestry." He bent over the centre table and stubbed his cigarette out in the ashtray. "I mean, look at that Operation Phoenix. Hell, word gets out, especially to guys with noses as big as their face, like me. Knocking off all those harmless jokers like they were shit. Where's the glory in that, for Christ's sake? Where's the fucking freedom? I mean, this undercover war—the stuff that never makes it to the front pages of the *New York Times*—it's . . . it's . . ." for a moment his hands quivered in the air like manic moths, "well, it's despicable, man. And I mean *rotten*-despicable, not funny-despicable."

"Orders, Steeger," said Hardin, his voice squeezed tight.

"Don't give me that shit, Hardin."

There was a long silence in the room. Sunlight filtered through the blinds at the windows and was a hot bright solid shaft through the open door into the garden. A butterfly, predominantly orange and blue fluttered into the room, circled it twice, then vanished outside again. Steeger thought you could almost hear the beat of its wings.

"If it makes any difference," said Hardin, "I've never knowingly killed, maimed or tortured a good guy."

He said this in a voice that was pitched very low and drained of all expression.

"Shit," said Steeger, aware that all of this was getting slightly out of hand but not at all sure how to slide things back to normal again (and what in fuck was "normal," anyhow?), "what am I supposed to say to that? How d'you spot the good guys? They don't go around with badges on their coats. I figure the EnVees are good guys, according to their lights." He paused. "You know, I once had you tagged for a spook, before you jumped into the army. Then I figured, no, he just isn't the CIA type. But I'm not so sure I wasn't right first time round."

Hardin said, "This is really depressing. This is worse than being crapped on by Command."

Steeger was aware that what Hardin was actually saying was, Let's for Christ's sake leave this alone; no good can come of this.

He had a feeling Hardin was right. Friendship was a strange game that had no fixed laws. Once you started creating ground rules, defining territory, that was the finish. Steeger thought about another close friend, an artist called Windsor. The guy was right of centre, disliked blacks, was intolerant, moody, arrogant, had a dangerous temper, and couldn't draw horses. Type all that out on a card and hang it round the guy's neck, and people would avoid him like he had the Black Death. Steeger certainly would. But there were, of course, compensations for all of these uncivilised attributes (none of which had appeared on the surface

61

in the early stages of comradeship), and the good—the kind, the funny, the thoughtful, the entertaining, the intelligent—vastly outweighed the bad. Steeger could not have done without Windsor, all things closely considered, and nor could he have done without Hardin, who was certainly a killer, an assassin, a man of blood. But, like Windsor, he was other things, too. In the last analysis, it was the other things that mattered.

"That asshole in the bar," said Hardin suddenly, "was really the final straw."

Steeger sat down in his swivel-chair again and reached out a hand for a small ivory box sitting on a low-lying bookshelf. He shook it; it rattled. He opened it, took something out and closed it again. He tossed the box at Hardin.

"Catch."

Hardin lazily stretched out an arm and caught it one-handed.

"Wrap your troubles in dreams," advised Steeger, grinning.

"Oh Jesus, Steeger, now what in hell are you getting me into now?"

"Take one. All you need. Expand your consciousness—or, as we say down on the funny farm, blow your fucking mind out."

Hardin opened the box. Inside were a dozen or so button-sized tabs, light pink in colour. He took one and sniffed it, passing it back and forth under his nostrils as though testing a choice cigar.

"You is shitting me," chuckled Steeger.

"Affirm on that. Okay, what is it?"

"Well I'm, not entirely certain."

"Jesus Christ, you trying to total me, Will?"

"No, no. This time I is shitting you. Half-shitting. Far as I know, it's a mescaline derivative, but further than that I do not care to go, not having the full facts at my disposal."

Hardin raised his eyes to the ceiling.

"Where in hell d'you get this stuff, Steeger? Jesus, I ought to blow the whistle on you, you rascal. You're a no-good, demon dope-pusher." He popped the pill. "My momma done warn me against evil guys like you."

"Yeah, see where it got you," said Steeger dryly. "Anyhow, you won't vomit up your breakfast with this junk—less you've been chuggalugging, in which case you'll truly, you know flip out. This baby's one of the miracles of modern chemical science. I once had peyote straight, and it was a case of first the Goddamn hangover, then the blast. Jesus, I don't believe I ever tasted anything so fucking malevolent in my life."

"Yeah, vile-oh," agreed Hardin. "I once got gathered in on a peyote hunt. Bumped into a tribe of Huichol Indians on a pilgrimage. They had these sacred grounds, couple hundred miles from the Sierras. I was heading for the Sequoias, wanted to see old General Sherman, but I kind of got side-tracked. Jesus, these guys had been using these rearing grounds for Goddamn centuries. They had clusters there I swear were eight feet across."

"Careful cutting," nodded Steeger.

"Da-da-da-uhmmm-rhye-ooom-hisss-isss . . ."

As Hardin said this, he was aware that he was not in fact saying "Da-da-da-uhmmm-rhye-ooom-hisss-isss" at all, but "damn right, you've hit it." It just sounded like that. In fact, it sounded to his ears as though he

63

was saying both versions together, in tandem, but with only one voice. There were different levels, clearly, although both came out with the same clarity and definition, and at precisely the same time.

This was something of a pisser, as he'd wanted to tell Steeger about his extraordinary experiences with the Huichol Indians—the prayers and hunting ceremonies engaged in when the peyote was first sighted, the cutting and storing of the cacti, the trek to the tribe, the ritual drying of the plant, the subsequent celebrations, which had extended into a high of truly epic proportions.

It had not been easily achieved. At first he'd been heaving up his guts with awful regularity—peyote being, as his Huichol friends had warned him, a "hard road to travel"—although this, oddly, seemed to sharpen his physical awareness, clarify the incredible effects. But after a while the appalling taste of the peyote buttons became less noticeable, and in any case he found that food was of minor importance in the general scheme of things.

He wanted to tell Steeger all this—but how in hell could he do it if he was talking gibberish?

Nevertheless, he persevered, and the strange thing was, Steeger appeared to be taking it all in as though nothing untoward was happening. There were still problems, of course; the major one being that Steeger, for one reason or another, had suddenly decided to turn himself transparent. As Hardin talked he saw Steeger's flesh turn a milky-white, then fade out altogether. Only the formal outline was left, and Hardin noted with mild interest the complex cross-hatching of interior veins and arteries through which blood raced at what he slowly began to realise was a quite incredible speed. In fact Steeger's blood was circulating at such a headlong pace that there had to be something seriously wrong with the guy; it was beyond reason for the flow to act this way.

And now, damn it, it was beginning to look like a 4th of July firework display. Crimson arrows fizzed and sizzled through his system like rockets, streaking this way and that, sometimes colliding in midstream and setting off miniature sparks, then hurtling off again in all directions. These tiny scarlet eruptions became more and more noticeable until the whole picture began to take on the appearance of an unheeded telephone switchboard or an out-of-control computer-wall. Red lights blipped on and off in a rapid though totally random and almost kaleidoscopic pattern—or non-pattern—until each fierce scarlet flowering began to hurt his eyes, and he de-focused quickly so that all that remained of Steeger was a scarlet blur. But even that did not remain constant for long. He became aware that something was happening within that red fog; some piece of internal machinery had—it seemed likely—broken loose from its casing, come adrift. Could be the heart, because what he was seeing now, through the blur, was something solid that pulsed with a regular pumping beat, but, at the same time, shifted from left to right and then back again. His eyes followed this fluid crosswise movement, and began to hurt again.

"No fair," he thought, lifting a hand to signal to Steeger to stop this visual onslaught. As he did so he noticed that his fingertips were extending. They pulsed redly like the landing lights of a plane, then dissolved into a spray of stars that soared across the room. Still speaking, he closed his eyes.

At once he was transported into what was clearly another dimension, possibly the fabled ninth.

Vast pyramid-shaped forms flowed smoothly past his point of view, on both sides, slowly and majestically, as though for his sole benefit. Or maybe it was he that was moving—perhaps on some sophisticated walkway system unknown to man? That was too complicated to consider for any length of time; he concentrated on the monoliths. They were thickly encrusted with huge precious stones glowing with every conceivable—and inconceivable—colour. And all of these colours were brighter and more intense than anything he'd ever seen before. These were no mere reds and blues and greens, but rich crimsons, deep ceruleans, vivid jades. And brilliant emeralds, livid carmines, radiant tangerines, glittering saffrons, shimmering magentas, luminescent heliotropes. It was an extravagant and gorgeous array, yet it occurred to Hardin that it had a kind of demented quality about it that might possibly drive someone—some firefight-blasted guy, for instance, wobbling on the hinge of paranoia—across the divide. Over the edge. Off the roof. That must mean something, because he could absorb it all with calm detachment.

The scene changed abruptly. The flow of events became swifter. It was like he was travelling through Alpha Centauri or maybe the Crab Nebula. Shooting stars hissed alongside him, then plunged on past; planets exploded, suns crashed, galaxies collided, spraying blast-furnace-like showers of incandescent stars across the sabled velvet of deep space.

And he was travelling faster and faster.

"Slow down," he thought. And an iridescent web, glistening with dew-drops, descended across his path of vision, a shimmering, dancing curtain of exquisite manufacture. He sailed straight into it and discovered that although he could actually feel nothing tangible, he *was* slowing down. Or *it* was slowing down (depending on whether it was in fact moving or not). Or *something* was slowing down.

He opened his eyes again, to discover that he was still talking. And quite rationally, too. He watched himself, sprawled in the saddle-bag chair gesturing at Steeger, and explaining the intricate drumming rituals of the Huichol Indians, and the stuff about the "shovel man" who went around tending those guys who were throwing up, and the complex . . .

Very weird, that. He'd never noticed it before. Steeger's suit. A white one. Well, sure it was white, but he'd been under the impression that, like just about everything in this damn climate, it was rumpled and grubby and sweat-stained. Not a bit of it. It was the colour of the eternal snows of the Himalayas, on a piercingly bright sunny day. Goddamn, it was positively *dazzling!* An albescent glare that could, laser-beam-like, destroy the eyeballs if you gazed upon it long enough. Better to shift to something else.

But the books behind Steeger were just as fierce. A polychromatic parade that leapt out at him, full-blaze. His eyes skipped along the rows of brilliant spines. Odd how he'd always thought of most of them as being dull and worn; well-used; dowdy. An absurd error. All glowed richly, those with jackets positively glittering at him. Better to shift to something else again.

The garden. A *riot* of gorgeous colour! Through the French windows each separate bloom that he could see almost sprang . . .

But the doorway was suddenly blocked. Eileen Satkis had given the birds best.

Hardin stopped talking to Steeger about the peyote rites of the Huichol Indians.

"Hey," he said, articulating slowly, "it's Ei-leen God-damn Sat-kis!"

Hardin woke in the pre-dawn twilight and stretched himself luxuriously under the fine linen sheet. The room was cool, but not cold. He felt relaxed, at ease, good inside. He thought, Fuck Command. The hell with them. Bunch of total assholes.

He rolled on to his back and stretched again, and his left hand came into contact with Eileen Satkis's satiny flesh. His fingers trailed down, twined themselves into the bush of fine black hair at the base of her stomach. He closed his eyes again and his fingers dove downwards, gently pushing themselves between her legs until they rested on the folds of warm skin there. Eileen Satkis shifted slightly and mumbled sleepily; her legs opened out.

Hardin let the tips of his fingers flutter lightly across the creases of her flesh, lazily enjoying the tactile sensation. He was still only half-awake, which made what he was doing and what he was feeling and what he was thinking acutely pleasurable.

He brushed his fingers over her skin, gently massaging her inner thighs, reaching right down and under until he could feel the puckered circle of her anus. Then he lightly dragged his middle finger back up so that it slid between her lips and opened them out, drowsily expecting her to be dry. She wasn't. The narrow cleft was slick and wet.

Hardin groaned in the back of his throat, the head of his penis tingling with exquisite sensations. It was like a spark jumping from his fingertips right down deep into the core of him. He turned his head on the pillow and he could just see Eileen Satkis's face in the half-light seeping through the blinds, her eyes wide and frank and knowing. He turned full over on to his left side, and the movement caused him to pull his hand away from her.

She said, "Don't stop that. Don't stop at all. Feels good."

"You're a cool lady, Eileen Satkis."

"You're not so hot yourself, Hardin."

She reached out for him, enclosing his length in her fingers and dragging the funnel of her hand upwards to the tip then pushing back down again. Possibly it was some after-effect of the drug, but Hardin felt he was on fire. He lowered his head over her right breast, lounging slightly off-centre, took the nipple between his teeth and ground it harshly, his free hand reaching down between her legs, his middle finger sinking into her almost to the knuckle.

Eileen Satkis said, "Oh Christ" in an agonised voice. She said, "Christ, do it. Get on me." She caught at him again, her fingernails pressing at the stem, where the scrotum was now firm and tight and furrowed. She said, "Jesus, John. Yes. Don't stop it."

He shifted over her and rubbed his face hard into the tightening flesh of her stomach, his tongue tracing a delicate circle round her navel then burrowing hard into its centre. She made a high fluting sound through her nose, a kind of "*Eeenngh*," then her whole body shuddered convulsively as he drifted on down, burying his nose in her hair. Her knees drew back and he could feel against his flesh the hard tenseness of the muscles in her calves which circled his shoulders. She smelt warm and musky and exquisitely delicious, and he wanted to do everything he possibly could to her, and it was going to be very hard to take it as slow as he would have liked. He ran his tongue round the outer lips and then started over, using his lips, flicking at her with his tongue, and nibbling all the way round, faster and faster, until in a kind of frenzy, hardly aware of her fingernails digging deep into the flesh of his shoulders, he nuzzled right into her, as deeply as he could, as lascivously as he wanted and she wanted.

Then, in one smooth, fluid movement, he slid up her and into her, and it was the easiest thing in the world, as easy as the way she interlocked with him, gripping him with her legs pulled high.

Hardin said, "Damn, this is good, Satkis."

Eileen Satkis said "Don't talk. No, talk. Yes. Talk. Do it. I don't care."

"Don't close your eyes."

"Fucker. You want them open."

"Right. All open. Your fucking *pores* open."

"Christ. I can feel it."

"Fucking boiling up, Satkis?"

"Christ. Fucking. Boiling. Up. Hardin."

Eileen Satkis then said "*Oh Gahhhd*" in a very loud squeezed voice, from deep down in her throat, her face slick with sweat, her eyes abyssal pools of exquisite torment. The sound went on for a long time.

Hardin bared his teeth. He leant on his elbows, drummed his toes against the sheet. From his stomach on down he was a twisted knot of tension. Slowly, very slowly, he relaxed. He nuzzled at the damp hair framing the long oval of her face.

"Just caught it."

"Christ, Jon," her voice was soft, the tone lazy and tender, "you on a strict regime, or something?"

He shook his head, easing his hand under her shoulders. He glanced at the shuttered windows.

"Not so's you'd notice. But we have a good couple hours before we need to face the world." He grinned. "Don't want to shoot my damn bolt yet a while. Unlike the studs in the fuck-books Superdick I ain't."

"Well. About that," said Eileen Satkis, "we will have to do something."

Hardin said, "Spoken like a true *summa cum laude* in English."

He bent his head and bit hard into her lower lip.

Hardin stared at himself in the long mirror as he ran a comb through his dark hair. His hair was short, but not close-cropped Army style; the gung-ho guys who went around with not much frizz on a lot of skull never failed to amuse him. The stockade-cut, as it was called, was cultivated by medium-echelon officers who wished to impress their superiors, but Hardin could think of few men in the high reaches of Command he even wanted to salute, let alone impress.

From somewhere in the apartment he could hear clattering sounds as Eileen Satkis made coffee. He had no idea how he'd ended up here; Steeger's rented villa on plush Pasteur (for which, Hardin suspected,

Steeger paid absolutely no rent whatsoever) was at least three miles away. In fact, he had no clear recollection of anything at all after about five o'clock of the previous day. It appeared that he and Eileen Satkis had made love for an hour or so before going to bed, but he only had fast flashes of that, and already they were beginning to merge with the past two or three hours.

He looked around the room. With the blinds up it was light and airy; there was a view of downtown Saigon scrapers disappearing into the distance. A helicopter chattered by, and Hardin wondered idly about its destination. But not for very long; it really wasn't worth wondering about. Sound of traffic rose from the street below; behind him a telephone shrilled.

On the dressing-table there lay, jumbled and disordered, the usual woman's detritus—tubes of cream, small bottles of perfume, make up boxes, pills, potions, powders. In the dressing-table mirror, as he turned away, he caught sight of a slight bulge in his shirt pocket. Frowning, he patted the pocket and unflapped it. There was a small linen bag nestling inside with a half dozen small pink tabs in it. Scrawled on a self-adhesive label on the bag, in Steeger's curiously clumsy handwriting, was the legend "*Not* to be taken 3 times a day!"

Not for the first time Hardin wondered where exactly the fuck Steeger got his junk from. The guy was like an octopus, his tentacles wrapped around the world. If Steeger had been half-way crooked he could have been a millionaire by now, but in many ways he was bizarrely straight.

Eileen Satkis came into the room and said, "It's for

you. Ben Weinraub. My reputation must be shot to shit if they traced you here."

"You're a journalist," said Hardin. "You have no reputation." Then he frowned. "Ben? What in the hell does he want?"

Weinraub was a friendly contact who lived and had his being on the upper plains of Special Forces.

Eileen Satkis regarded him with eyes that were cool and slightly sardonic.

"Looks like your troubles are over," she said. "They want you to come in."

Chapter Three

"It's not," said Lieutenant General Swales, "that you're in the craphouse. Get that notion out of your head, Colonel, right damn now. Doesn't do you any good. Doesn't do anyone any good."

He was a stocky man with sandy hair and the kind of florid complexion that did not take the sun too well. He was in shirtsleeves and his shirt, stiffly starched, creaked and rustled as he paced restlessly up and down the room, every so often punching his right fist idly into his cupped left hand with a soft smacking sound. So far he had not once looked at Hardin directly on an eyeball-to-eyeball level. If he did want to make some kind of point to Hardin, he stared at Hardin's left ear, or his right shoulder, or his chin, or his hairline. Hardin found this very slightly disconcerting.

But then that was only one aspect of this confrontation that worried him. There was a mission in the air, that was for sure, but from the way Swales was cat-walking round the subject, it had to be a very, very heavy one.

It had taken Hardin two days of chopper-hopping to get here, to this small air-base almost within spitting distance of the northern tip of the Cambodian border. The place had once been a flourishing and prosperous tea plantation, but Special Forces had soon put an end to that nonsense. Its position vis-à-vis all kinds of important locations—southern Laos and northern Cambodia to name but two—had made it an eminently desirable spot on which to extemporise a bustling and well-fortified Special Forces jumping-off point. It had never once been so much as touched by the VC, even during the heady days of the Tet Offensive—the Big One in 1968, when it seemed like Charlie had finally gotten his shit together, and had even on one memorable occasion gone so far as to subject the hallowed precincts of the U.S. Embassy in Saigon to the crump of mortar shells.

Up here in Da Thong Linh, amidst the rolling forested foothills of the Central Highlands, the only violent sound to be heard that horrendous day had been the snap and hiss of Coke cans being opened.

The room in which Hardin's briefing was taking place—if the word "briefing" could be applied to a situation where a lieutenant general had so far said nothing of consequence in a very long half hour—had clearly once been the tea planter's living-room. Swales had turned the room into his den. There were framed photographs on the wall—Swales talking to General William Childs Westermoreland; Swales nodding seriously at General Creighton Williams Abrams; Swales being clapped on the shoulder by Vice President Nguyen Cao Ky; a somewhat younger and slimmer Swales saluting the then (circa 1957) U.S. Vice President Richard Milhous Nixon; Swales laughing heartily at something National Security Affairs Assistant Dr. Henry Alfred Kissinger was saying—as well as various artefacts of destruction (hunting rifles, knives, bayonets, revolvers), many of them antique. The books that filled, and overflowed from, the bookshelves were mostly Big Game fare, with the odd hunting and fieldcraft manual thrown in for good measure.

A ceiling fan, which had probably been put in sometime during the 1930s, rotated lazily, doing nothing to dispel or even lightly freshen the afternoon heat. Bars of sunlight slanted through the loose-fitting blinds of the two main windows. Hardin, sitting in a cane chair near one of them could, if he glanced to his right, see the helmet of a guard through the gaps in the slats, and, beyond, a longish grassy slope leading down to an asphalt path. The other side of the path two more guards could be seen, standing against trees and bushes in full bloom. An incongruous sight.

Across from Hardin a tall man in casual fatigues slumped in an armchair. His face was deep-tanned and creased, leathery; his hair was short and snow white. He wore horn-rimmed glasses, and a pipe drooped from his mouth, the bowl resting on his chest. The pipe seemed to be dead. Hardin, from where he was, could see that most of the interior of the bowl was charred black. This was General Lewis J. Halderling.

In the centre of the room was a large round table, covered with a clutter of documents and maps. Papers lay in some confusion on the floor. On the other side of the table sat a thin man with a narrow bony face and a mouth that looked as mean as a rat-trap. He wore dark glasses. Hardin didn't know his name, but his trade was obvious.

Swales did an about-turn and began to walk back towards Hardin again.

"Y'see what I mean, Colonel?" he said, staring at the top button of Hardin's shirt. "Just makes things difficult. Difficult all round. You gotta think positive. Forget about the past. No one gives a crap about the past, anyhow. Jesus, if everyone was living in the past all the time, we'd still be weeping over Tet. Not," he suddenly held up a finger, warningly, and his eyebrows rose a quarter inch, "that we have anything to weep over. Tet. No way. There was a lot of journalistic hoo-hah with regard to that, and frankly . . ."

"Jesus Christ, George," said General Halderling. He said it wearily, as though he hadn't slept in a month or more.

Swales stopped pacing, and swivelled on Hardin. This time he managed to catch Hardin's right eyebrow.

"Okay. Colonel Hardin, have you at any time during the past year been asked by anyone—anyone at all—to desert the armed service of the United States of America?"

Hardin said, "*What?*"

Swales jabbed a finger at him.

"That is not an answer, Colonel. That is a God-damn question. You don't ask me questions, Colonel. I ask you questions. And you better answer my questions right damn now."

Hardin stood up quickly. He turned to Halderling.

"Now look, General—what in hell is all this about?"

Halderling breathed out hard and flapped a leathery hand at him. He uncoiled himself from the armchair and lounged to his feet, wincing as his right knee cracked. He was a tall, spare figure, almost scarecrow-like in build, who looked older than his 61 years, and tended to make much of his cracking knee-cap. He also tended to complain of other aches and discomforts when in company, as though they were trophies of advancing age. In fact, as Hardin well knew, Halderling had been badly shot up by a Nationalist MG-gunner while fighting with the International Brigade in Spain in 1938.

"Goddamn knee-cap," said Halderling to no one in particular. He leaned back against a bookcase, tugged a worn leather pouch from his shirt pocket, and began to fill his pipe.

"We gotta problem, John, Bad one. War's at a low ebb. We're taking a deal of shit, media and otherwise, about Cambodia. Cops are killing kids on campuses back home. Demonstraters are mobbing the White House. A lot of people want out." He set fire to the contents of his pipe-bowl with a book-match. "A lot of people are *getting* out. And they're not walking out by the front door either."

Hardin said, "Yeah, but it's been like that from the beginning."

Halderling nodded.

"Affirm. But as the conflict has escalated so has the desertion rate."

"Figures."

"You have any idea of the scale of the problem?"

Hardin shook his head.

"You were to give me a figure, General—an official figure, the kind of figure that surfaces at MACV or USPAO press corps briefings—I'd have to multiply by six, and I guess I still wouldn't be too close. It was

78

different a couple of years back, but now the grunts want to get the hell out, even the non-draftees. They resent Nam, and all about it."

"Jesus Christ!" erupted Swales. "See here, Colonel, I'm seeing hard-core loyalty wherever I go . . ."

"George," said General Halderling patiently, "let's quit playing piss-in-the-ring, shall we, George." He puffed smoke into the air. "You're in a kind of privileged position up here. Special Forces get a kick out of what they do, or they wouldn't be Special Forces. The grunts are different, George, and there's no denying the fact. You know and I know they're a dying breed. The long-term objective is what the think-tank strategists back in the World call the automated battlefield. The push-button war. And it's closer than we think. A situation, George, where the infantryman's eyes will be replaced by remote-control sensors, and his aim'll be substituted for by computer-operated target acquisition devices, and his Goddamn trigger-finger'll be turned over to extreme-range artillery batteries." Halderling chuckled, as though in disbelief, though the flintyness of his cornflower blue eyes belied this. "That's what they say. This is surely what they say. And maybe it'll happen exactly the way they say it. We'll still have Intelligence, Firepower and Mobility, but they'll all be combined in one wimpy little guy in a white coat playing buttons on a lousy console. But right now," he jabbed the pipe at Swales, who stared at it as though it was the barrel of a gun, "right here and now, George, we still need the grunt. Trouble is, the automated battlefield is half-way here, so the kind of grunt we need these days doesn't have to be as smart as the kind of grunt we needed twenty years ago, or thirty years ago. Getting right down to the nitty-gritty, George, he can be the dumbest son of a bitch you ever saw, and we'd whoop and holler and clap our crapping hands, because dumb sons of bitches are *exactly* what we need." He paused, sucked noisily at his pipe, then nodded slowly. "Cannon-fodder, George. Cannon-fodder is all."

Out of the corner of his eye, Hardin watched Swales.

Swale's face was getting redder and redder, and Hardin knew the man was very angry, about ready to explode with fury and only holding back because of Halderling's rank. Swale's face was getting redder and redder, and Hardin's laconic dismissal of ideas and institutions he felt to be almost sacred furred him up.

"Trouble is again," Halderling went on, "these kids may not be so damn smart education-wise, but they sure as hell are smarter than we take 'em for. Sure they know they're fodder. And like John says, they resent it. They know they're fodder, and they don't give a crap about isms or ologies or winning hearts and minds or why we're in Nam or what-all. They resent the whole kit-and-kaboodle, and so they're deserting. Shit in a bucket, George, they're deserting in droves." He sniffed hard and folded his arms across his chest, hunching down slightly against the book-case. "You get to feeling sometimes—in the long watches of the night—they may have the right idea," he said sourly.

"That's . . . an interesting viewpoint, General," said Swales tightly.

"But you don't think I ought to push it out?"

"Wouldn't like to give an opinion either way on that

one, General," said Swales, who looked as though he'd just swallowed a leech.

"I don't give a good jack-shit what I say, George," Halderling said. "Never have, never will. I've said the same to Creighton Abrams, and I'd say the same to Nixon, to his Goddamn face. Ain't no one gonna do a damn thing about it." He shot an icy smile at the man with the rat-trap mouth, and the man with the rat-trap mouth held the look for a micro-second then shifted his gaze, fidgetted with some papers.

"No one," said General Halderling softly.

He turned to Hardin.

"Thing is, John, that's not quite the problem. Not quite the problem at all."

He pushed himself suddenly off the book-case and strode to the table, riffling through the mess of maps and documents until he came to a green card file. He flipped it open.

"You ever come across a guy called Andrews— Samuel Philip Andrews?"

Hardin frowned.

"It's a common name, Andrews."

"Master-Sergeant, Special Forces."

"Narrows it down, but . . ."

Halderling held out a small notebook. It was creased and soiled, crusted with dried mud; the pages were beginning to flake at the edges. It was open, and on the left hand page was a detailed pencil drawing of a flower which Hardin didn't recognise. On the right hand page was a sketch of a man's face, quarter-profile, which, after a second or so, he did.

It was rough, clearly done at high speed. But the artist had managed to imbue the features with strong and recognisable characteristics. Even with a darker shading on the man's chin, Hardin knew him.

"Clever piece of work," he said.

"You know him?"

"Sure, Dump Andrews."

"Dump?" said Swales.

"Yeah, they call him Dump because he likes to dump on Charlie."

Swales frowned.

"Doesn't everybody?"

"Yeah, but with Andrews it's different. More hard-line, you know? As a matter of fact, Andrews doesn't like the Vietnamese whether they're VC or not. His plan for completely sanitising the situation would be to clear all the good gooks out of the country. Put 'em on cattle-boats, send 'em out into the South China seas. Okay, so now you can kill off all the rest, all those who remain. Clean country. But, just to make sure . . ."

Hardin glanced at General Halderling, who nodded sourly and said, "Yeah, yeah. I already heard it, John. You bomb the cattle-boats."

Swales sniggered explosively. He muttered, "Damn right."

Hardin said, "So what about Andrews?"

"Last thing we know about him," said Halderling, "is that another Special Forces Sergeant—by name Dettweiler—blew his shit away with an M-16."

"Kind of drastic, wouldn't you say, General?" said Hardin cautiously.

"Under normal circumstances, John, I'd have to agree with you. Fact is, however, prior to this, Andrews had blown Dettweiler's patrol shit away with an AK-47."

"Jungle crazy?"

"Unconfirmed, but we think no."

"He just didn't dig the rest of the guys on the mission?"

"Ah," said General Halderling, "now that is the strange thing. That is the very strange thing. Andrews wasn't on Dettweiler's patrol. Fact is, Andrews has been posted as a deserter for the past three months."

Halderling put down the green card file and puffed at his pipe, pushing his bony elbows back behind him and poking his chest outwards in a smooth, relaxed movement.

"Dettweiler was on a recon patrol in northern Laos, but on his way up-country he had instructions to drop a cache in a hide we've used before, beside one of the tributaries of the Kong river. Big cache, packed with goodies. Dettweiler reached the spot and offloaded, and he and his men were just grabbing some rest-time when Andrews stepped out of the greenery and blew 'em away. Dettweiler managed to nail him before he got hit from the jungle. Landed in the stream and floated off. Current's kind of fierce there, it seems, and Dettweiler got carried away before anyone could finish him off. He got dragged out by some Laotian friendlys a day later in a bad way, but he managed to recover and made it back to base. This all happened about a month ago."

"The sketch?" said Hardin, frowning at the notebook and realising that what he'd previously taken to be dried mud on the soiled pages was in fact blood.

"One of Dettweiler's men. Corporal Macey. Had a habit of taking a notebook out and sketching the jungle. Seems he did a lightning sketch of Andrews before Andrews cut loose with his AK. Dettweiler says he didn't know Andrews personally, but another of his men clearly recognised him. That was when Andrews started shooting. Naturally," Halderling picked up the notebook and gazed at it thoughtfully, "we sent a heavy patrol out to check the score. The rest of Dettweiler's men were still lying where they'd dropped, but Andrews's body had gone." Halderling shrugged. "Whoever was with Andrews must've dragged him away and buried him. Dettweiler says the guy couldn't've survived the burst he put into him. Dettweiler's men had been stripped of arms and spare rounds, medical straps, anything useful. The notebook was underneath Macey; they must've figured it wasn't important. They sure as hell didn't look at it too closely, which was lucky for us, because that sketch was the only way we could identify who in hell the guy was. Like I said, Dettweiler didn't know him."

"Didn't this Dettweiler character throw out a lookout, for Christ's sake?" said Hardin.

"Sure. Guy called Stratton. We found him with his throat cut in the trees."

"And the cache?"

Halderling laughed dryly.

"Nowhere to be found. Not unnaturally." He paused for several seconds, underlining, Hardin knew, the bad news—whatever the bad news was going to be. "That's the ninth cache to disappear in less than two months." He paused again. "And the fifth patrol to get chopped up."

"Jesus," said Hardin, "you think some of our guys've gone over to Charlie?"

"Worse than that, Colonel."

It was the man with the rat-trap mouth. He had a voice to match, thin and hard, with a sharp cutting edge. He sounded as though he didn't much like opening his mouth.

"We are strongly of the opinion that certain members of Special Forces have, to put it simply, gone rogue."

Chapter Four

The asphalt on the paths near to the bungalow was loose. Hardin's boots crunched through the top layers as he strode beside the lean, almost gangling figure of General Halderling. Halderling was bent forward with his head thrust out and his hands clutched behind his back, as though he was fighting a Force 9 gale. His pipe was clenched between his teeth, sticking straight out from his mouth.

"See, the thing is, John," he said, "the fact of the matter is, you *are* in the craphouse. And that's it. It's taken me all my damn time to push you into this one. Taken a lotta effort, too. Getting too old for this crap, John. Fighting all this Mickey Mouse shit. I can do without it."

"I appreciate it, General," said Hardin warily.

"Damn right. So you should."

Halderling was, and always had been, a man of action. Blocked by a mountain of Mickey Mouse bullshit, his immediate reaction was to reach for the biggest shovel he could find and start digging; confronted by festoons of red tape, he invariably lunged for his knife, preferably of the Bowie variety, with a big fat blade honed down to a razor-edge.

In the past these tactics had paid off. Halderling

went for results and got them, and had a reputation for being virtually unstoppable. Certainly, the hammering he'd taken in the Spanish Civil War hadn't stopped him, Hardin reflected as he glanced at the gaunt, commanding figure striding out beside him. He'd joined the army, been speedily commissioned, and, shortly before Pearl Harbor, had been sent to the Philippines where he'd served as an advisor to a Filipino infantry battalion in Luzon. But it was after Corregidor fell and the Japanese over-ran Luzon that Halderling began to show what he was really made of.

He'd refused orders to surrender, evaded capture and disappeared into the jungle. There, he'd spent most of the rest of the war organising the Filipinos into guerilla bands, and had eventually shaped up and taken command of a regimental unit of headhunters, creating appalling mayhem behind the Japanese lines — especially after the U.S. forces landed in Luzon in 1945 — and achieving a quite extraordinary kill-ratio of 25 Japanese for every American soldier lost.

Halderling emerged from the war a much-decorated man, but with the reputation of a rebel whose exploits often made his superiors wince. On the other hand, the exploits of his superiors often made Halderling despair. He delighted in recounting the story of the capture of a key Japanese airstrip towards the finale of the Philippines' reconquest.

He'd taken a small force of guerillas across the Cagayan River at night, and by dawn, after a major battle — during which he'd lost only five men, to something approaching 85 of the Japanese — he'd secured not only the airstrip but an important road junction nearby. Radioing this news to his superiors, he'd been told that a battalion combat team from the 11th Airborne Division would be capturing the objective later that day. When Halderling pointed out that he'd already taken it, he was told that this was going to be a major PR exercise, with the Press corps in attendance, and that frankly he'd better get his ass back to the strip fast, remove all signs of battle, clean up generally (particularly any pools of blood that might be lying around), and move his men beyond the perimeters and into tight concealment—in case more Japs came along and the paras needed support while they were posing for the photos.

The fake attack was a shambles. From start to finish. Most of the gliders either crash-landed or collided one with another in the air or on the ground. Over 50 of the paratroopers were seriously injured. Halderling and his headhunters had to emerge from their hiding-places to render emergency first aid, and a dozen of them were killed by uninjured paras who, in the confusion, thought they were Japs. A correspondent of the *New York Times* had his left ear shot away by a stray bullet.

Hardin knew the story and a lot of others like it about Halderling. He'd worked for the general for a long time; officially since 1964, unofficially since as far back as 1960. He'd ranged over not only the length of breadth of South East Asia for Halderling, on various exotic and dangerous and, at times, spectacular missions, but also across most of the rest of the world.

Now he said, "So where were you when I needed you most, General?"

What he meant was, Where were you when that fat bastard Dempsey dumped me neck-down deep in buffalo-shit—and the question was largely rhetorical because he knew precisely where Halderling had been: on a three-month briefing tour at the Pentagon.

"Soon as I leave town," grumbled Halderling, "you have to get your fool self involved in some Goddamn situation or other. Damn it, John, you could've kept clear of that son of a bitch Dempsey."

"I did," Hardin pointed out. "The mad fucker pursued me."

"In the last analysis, John, laying it right down there on the line, that ain't the point."

A guard by the side of the path snapped to attention as they passed him. Halderling acknowledged this with a vague gesture of his right hand, not even glancing at the man.

"Fact is," said Hardin, "Command are treating me like *I'm* the villain of the piece—you know, like *I* was the guy about to blow all this sensitive stuff to the En vees. For Christ's sake, Dempsey was waging a private war. I was on the fucking receiving end!"

Halderling shook his head slowly.

"You iced Dempsey," he said flatly.

"Dempsey got nailed by an Arvin patrol in a Saigon street."

Halderling crunched to a halt and swung round on Hardin, jabbing his pipe at him. His pale blue eyes were like chips of ice behind his glasses.

"Cut it out, Colonel. You know and I know that you nailed General Dempsey just as surely as though you'd pulled the trigger on the fat fucker yourself." He turned abruptly and continued along the path. "Let's just not piss around, okay? It was a classic exercise. We ran a similar operation when we took out that politico in Manila in '61, you and me both. You had some guy let off some *plastique* in a crowded street and you panicked Dempsey to start running. The Arvins did the rest. Just like you knew they would. Those triggerhappy dimbos'd shoot the President of the United fucking States if they saw him so much as twitch after a bomb-blast in a Saigon street."

Hardin was beginning to get mad. Not simply because he was convinced of the rightness of his cause, but because Halderling, damn him, was correct in every particular.

"Jesus Christ, General, that fat fucker was a Goddamn traitor! Not only that, he owned boom-boom houses on the side, casinos, bars, hotels, he was running dope into Laos and back again, engaging in massive profiteering and black market activities, using his links with the spooks to knock off anyone who got in his way—Jesus, what more d'you want?"

"Not the point," repeated Halderling. "You should've let the army deal with him. What you don't do in this business is crap in your own backyard. Or," he took his pipe from his mouth again and wagged it at Hardin as he talked, "if you do crap in your own backyard—and you ought to have figured this out after working for me for ten Goddamn years—you don't rub it up everybody's nose."

"*Shit!*" exploded Hardin. "He put out a CIA contract on my fucking cousin!"

Halderling glared down at the asphalt then up at the deep blue of the sky. He sniffed air into his lungs, long and hard.

"Yeah, the CIA are not being at all co-operative with regard to that one, John. Throwing blocks up every which-way. Jesus, they're even talking about a need-to-know situation! They are neither admitting nor denying that any of their operatives had a private deal with Dempsey—and of course, with the drugs thing we're on swampy ground. They're not gonna put themselves on the line and say outright that Air America is running junk all over South East Asia, and even if you do get the bastards into a corner they'll only point out that *if* such a project was in motion it'd be part of a morale-busting operation. No argument against that one, John." He shrugged. "This war's getting more damn complicated by the hour. It's getting so that too many guys simply don't know what too many other guys are doing. Hell, we've always had areas of conflict that have been well under wraps, in every war, but these days even taking a crap's getting to be a sensitive operation."

Hardin reflected that part of the problem had always been that separate government intelligence agencies, of whatever cloth, hated like hell to live cheek-by-jowl with one another. Halderling's own group—SSG—was one of the most secret and little-known in the game. SSG stood for Strategic Studies Group, a bland enough title which looked good on public budget sheets but meant almost nothing at all. Halderling's men did not study strategy, they put it into effect.

It was a wide-flung operation with many men and much materiél at its disposal. Its HQ was located at Bien Hoa, the Saigon air-base, but there was a naval element at Da Nang which ran a fleet of PT boats, and a wing-size air detachment up at Nha Trang. A base near Hue was used for cross-border insertions into North Vietman, and there were a half-dozen camps (of which Da Thong Linh was the most muscular) situated down the western half of the country from Kontum to Loc Ninh, which covered covert expeditions into Laos and Cambodia.

SSG's primary task was, in Halderling's own words of many years before, to "discomfort, discommode and discombobulate" the enemy, but any means whatever, preferably the most unorthodox. Not that Halderling shunned the orthodox approach. It had been suggested that the series of PT boat raids on EnVee secret coastal installations by U.S.-trained South Vietnamese crews and masterminded by him had in fact triggered off the Tonkin Gulf incidents back in 1964. Whether in the long run these raids had been a smart move was arguable, but they sure as hell had been successful.

"And on the subject of taking a crap," said Halderling, "I have to repeat, you are still, believe it, in the shithouse. I've tried my damnedest to cover for you, John, and if I'd been here at the time maybe things might have worked out differently. But the fact is, Command are shitting in their pants. You uncovered a barrel of worms in the EssVee government, and they don't like that. You uncovered a pile of reeking shit in the high echelons of Special Forces, and they don't like that. And you blew away a two-star general, and they really hate that. Whatever the hell your motives, and however much provocation you were under—makes no damn difference. Command are sweating a monsoon and they've run out of Kleenex."

Halderling suddenly laughed throatily. "Oh, yeah. And one other thing. You brought back a bunch of Goddamn murderers and misfits and brig-trash, and Command are beating their brains apart trying to figure out what in hell to do with them. It's driving them over the Goddamn cliff, John! By rights, they should pin ribbons on 'em, even if it's only Green Weenies, but not only should these fuckers not have been doing what they did in the first place, they're all straight outta the stockade! I mean, you had a guy called Garrett on that operation. Turns out now he was a hit-man for the Mob back in the World. You had a medic called Pepper. Jesus, he was popping pills like gum-balls and peddling junk to all and sundry from central supplies. You had a black called O'Mara—he strangled one of his jailers in the brig. Need I pursue this line any further? Right damn down on it, Colonel, you are one big fucking problem."

"The future looks kind of bleak, General," said Hardin.

"No shit," agreed Halderling. "Which is exactly why I pulled you in on this caper, against everybody else's better judgement. George doesn't like the idea and he's in command here. But then I'm in command of George, so that cuts him out." Halderling sighed. "George is getting kind of pompous in his old age."

"Who's the strong silent type? Apart from being CIA, I mean."

Halderling scowled at his pipe.

"Reisberson. Yeah. Couldn't get him off my back, even with the clout I have. Would've been too much of a cat-and-dog fight in Saigon if I'd stuck to my guns and thrown him out on his can. He only has a watching brief."

"CIA watching briefs worry me, sir."

Halderling pondered this for a second or two. Hardin noticed that for the first time faint lines of real worry were etched into the skin at his brow.

Above, a Huey clattered by, disappearing over the treeline to their right. Another chopper appeared, following it. Then another. The day was dying; shadows of tall trees reached out like fingers across the neatly-trimmed grass towards them. A breeze had sprung up.

"To tell you the truth, son, they bother me likewise. They've been getting more and more close-mouthed over the past couple of months. Tighter than an asshole. I get the strong feeling they may have some kind of high-level insertion in the area we're interested in."

Hardin's mouth twitched in silent laughter.

"Oh yeah. The area we're interested in," he said sardonically. "And just where in hell would that area be, General? Like, how about letting me in on this operation I'm supposed to be ram-rodding. Or are you gonna be throwing me to the hungry tigers with only a jock-strap on?"

There was a bench placed beside the path a little way along. Halderling sat down on it carefully, thrusting his long legs straight out. Hardin lit a cigarette and watched him stuff coarse black leaf into the bowl of his pipe.

Halderling said sourly, "Might very well be that way, son. Might very well be exactly like that. You might have to jump in there cold—although it could turn out to be the hottest mission you've ever undertaken."

"So where in hell is 'there'?"

Halderling shrugged.

"That's the 64,000-dollar question. We're still looking. We guess somewhere in southern Laos or the north-western tip of Cambodia. It has to be there, but we've yet to finger the exact location."

"And what is it that's 'there'?"

"Some kind of camp, manned by a strong force of Special Forces renegades."

Hardin's eyebrows clicked up a couple of notches. He didn't really believe any of this. Initially, he'd accepted the proposition that maybe some Special Forces operatives had gone rogue, either for the EnVees, or on their own account. But now it seemed to him to be a bad dream, a Monday morning vision, too fantastic to be true. In any case, the theory had not been gone into in any detail. Shortly after the spook had reluctantly ground out the only words he'd vouchsafed during the entire session, Hardin had been hustled out by Halderling for this "stroll" — "to mull things over." Swales had not bothered to hide his relief.

"Now," Haldering said, "It has to be that, John. It's the only solution that fits."

"Just because some yoyo sergeant gets his ass minced by a couple of madmen one of whom is maybe identificble as a Green Beret?"

Halderling shook his head irritably.

"One, Dettweiler is no yoyo sergeant. He's a very strong man in the field. Two, if you were Goddamn listening, his was the fifth patrol to get iced in around eight weeks. Over 40 highly trained and highly skilled and highly deadly men — wiped out. Officially MIA, but you can draw your own conclusions. We've seen neither hide nor hair of them since they hit the bush. It's getting so that we're loosening our bowels just thinking of putting men out in the field. And like I said, caches are going AWOL like someone's starting a Christmas collection for the Salvation fucking Army. We've lost a hell of a lot of good materiél—guns, ammo, rocket-launchers, MGs, not to mention all the C-rats, dried food, medical supplies and Goddamn clothing we've been sending out. We're doing a low-key count-up on all of our hides right now—and I mean low key. I don't want to lose any more men, for Christ's sake." He paused. "Any case, that ain't the worst."

"Okay. Tell me."

Halderling winced. He looked, to Hardin, to be almost embarrassed. Hardin wondered what the hell was coming now.

"The bastards—whoever they are—really creamed us, not four days ago."

"How?"

Halderling winced again. This time he was definitely spooked.

"They took us for nine Hueys and a lotta men."

"Hueys?" said Hardin incredulously. *"Nine Hyueys?"*

"Yeah."

"You mean, like they blew 'em outta the sky? The Hueys got shot down?"

"Uh-uh. They stole the fuckers."

"Stole?" Hardin's voice pitched upwards. This was not merely a bad dream but an outright fucking nightmare.

"Yeah, stole."

"Jesus Christ, General—that's a hell of a thing! You mean, from one of our bases?"

Halderling's face looked more as though it were made of paper now, not leather at all. It looked to Hardin as though if he were to put his hand out and clutch at it, it would crumple up into a ball.

"Ambush. We had what we thought was very solid intelligence from a CAS about EnVee sanctuary in a ville in Cambodia. It sounded like a good deal. There was a passel of supportive evidence which seemed to clinch it. Ernie Tollmarsh volunteered for the job—you know him?"

Hardin nodded.

"Yeah, redneck son of a bitch."

"Affirm on that," agreed Halderling, "but he notches up kills, no doubt about that." His mouth twisted sourly. "Screwed up on this one, though. He went in and blew the shit outta the ville, then went down and got jumped. It was a trap. Seemed they were hiding in bunkers—deep bunkers. Only one guy had the presence of mind to jump back out again." Halderling glanced up, the glimmer of a smile breaking the dourness of his expression. "Guy you know, I believe. Black called Marco."

"Frank Marco? Sure. Looks like his luck's turned. On the Dempsey fiasco he *lost* two choppers—now he's the only guy to save one."

"Yeah. Ironical."

Halderling had gone back to looking broody again.

"Marco's a smart cookie," said Hardin, frowning. "I can't believe he didn't finger the ville as unsafe."

"So happens he did."

"So why didn't he warn Tollmarsh?"

"So happens he did that too. According to his story. And that's corroborated by his co-pilot, who also made it back. Tollmarsh wouldn't listen. Told him he was out of his mind."

"So much for Tollmarsh."

"Yeah."

"Who was your CAS?"

Halderling laughed, a harsh, barking sound. There was no humour there.

"Does it matter? There were two of them. We haven't heard from either of them since they gave us the dope, and you can bet your ass, John, we ain't gonna be hearing from the bastards ever again."

"They could've been fed."

"Nah, they were turned." Halderling jabbed a thumb at his chest in disgust. "They fed *us!*"

That, thought Hardin, was the problem with CAS agents: you could never be entirely sure of them. CAS stood for "Controlled American Source," and the term was used for live-in agents in bandit territory, native to the countryside. In places like North Vietnam it was often the only way to gather intelligence, where a six-foot, big-boned Caucasian male (however well disguised) stood out like a flashing beacon on a dark night. Mostly, they gave out solid information, and they were well paid for what they gathered. But there had been soom goofs in the past, and CIA foul-ups of one sort or another, and it was as well not to rely solely on their reports, unconfirmed as they usually were by solid supportive evidence. The fact of the matter was, they were by not means as "controlled" as their title suggested.

"So what it is," he said. "we have some kind of hard-nosed force running wild in the jungle knocking off our caches and deep-sixing our men. And they could be Special Forces dropouts."

"Right. 99 per cent sure of that. Captain Marco was certain. He had a run-in with a couple before he made it out, and he has no doubts at all."

"And they could be recruiting other guys?"

"Affirm."

"Or it could be that the guys who've gone MIA aren't dead at all. Maybe they simply decided to cut out, and it's them doing the damage?"

Halderling sucked at his pipe.

"Possibility. But the caches started going astray before these patrols disappeared. Any case, the AWOL statistics have jumped over the past six months. This guy Andrews, for instance. Around the time he split, nine other guys repeated the procedure from the same base-camp."

"You questioned these guys' friends?"

"Jesus, John, we put 'em through the fucking wringer. But they were as surprised as we were. They had absolutely no prior knowledge—not even anything that could be construed as the merest hint—that their compadres were going to take it on the lam."

Night was almost upon them now. Down the slope, lights were flickering on in Quonset huts, and from somewhere beyond the trees came the hum of a generator. Hardin ground out his cigarette in the asphalt with the heel of his boot. He looked up at Halderling who was gazing at where great banks of orange, purple, magenta and cerise bougainvillea spread themselves against the darkening sky.

"Could it be that they've gone over to the EnVees? That son of a bitch Reisberson didn't seem to think so, but what does he know. Be a hell of a propaganda coup if that's the case. U.S. Special Forces' heroes fighting for the Reds!"

"On the whole, I figure not. We'd have heard about it by now. Hanoi Hannah'd be yakking about it fit to bust our ears. They could really humiliate the shit out of us."

"So who in hell *is* in charge of this deal?"

"If we knew that, I wouldn't be sitting here flapping my gums. Whoever it is, he's one smart sackashit. Think about it. Who knows Special Forces routines, camps, bandit territory bases? No one. Except Special Forces. It's the old game warden turned poacher routine, and whoever this fucker is he could crucify us all. We've been trying to figure out a way of nosing round our men without letting too much out, but it's damn impossible."

"Yeah, I can see that. You start asking too many questions—like, Anyone been canvassing you to desert recently?—and morale could drop as low as the bottom of the Marianas Trench. I figure you must have been kind of circumspect when you were putting Andrews's buddies through the mangle."

"You figure right. More damn circumspect than George with you, believe me. But then George is angry. He really doesn't want to believe any of this is happening."

Hardin frowned. "But you must have some idea where these shitheads are operating from?"

"They're in deep. We can rough-guess an area—southern Laos and north-west Cambodia, like I said—but that's about it. Tollmarsh's troop was jumped in Cambodia, Dettweiller's patrol in Laos. We've been concentrating on an area midway between the two. I've had SR-71s and low-altitude RPVs flown over, and I've had the photo interpreters working round the Goddamn clock on the results, but even the infra-red stuff hasn't given us any leads. Apart from anything else, it's a big area. Even with the SR-71s, we could be missing the target by feet."

That was a pisser, thought Hardin, especially the news about the SR-71s. Recon photos could be gathered two ways, from high-altitude SR-71s, operating out of Kadena Air Force Base on Okinawa, whose long focal length technical objective cameras—which covered a swath ten nautical miles wide on the ground—produced unbelievably sharp and detailed pictures, and also from the Buffalo Hunter RPVs (Remote Piloted Vehicles), which were unmanned low-flying drones. The two surveillance methods were technically complementary. The SR-71s shot the general area, while the RPVs gave small-scale, treetop-level coverage for even greater detail. None of which was of any use if you didn't know where to look in the first place. As Halderling had said, it was a big area.

"Sensors?" he said cautiously.

Halderling exploded.

"Jesus Christ, John! We could seed that area with seismic devices until every second fucking bush sprouted an antenna. But you figured out just how long that operation's gonna take?" He calmed down, glancing up at Hardin from beneath his white, tufted eyebrows. "No," he said, "we're just gonna have to throw you in there cold, John."

"You're just gonna have to throw me in there cold," said Hardin thoughtfully, as though he wasn't referring to himself at all. He gazed down at the path.

"You *and* that bunch of brig-trash."

Hardin's head jerked up.

"What the hell is that supposed to mean?" he said tightly.

"Exactly what it sounded like."

"You're putting me on."

"Negative."

"In that case, you old fucker, you're setting me up." Hardin's fascial muscles were taut with anger.

"Negative again." Halderling chuckled, an easy, friendly sound. "Lucky I've known you a long time, John. Lucky you've worked some tough assignments for me. *Very* lucky I know your current state of mind, the way things are with you. Otherwise I'd've run over your balls with a power-mower by now, you calling me an old fucker."

"You really mean this?"

Halderling nodded.

"Sure I mean it. Gets everybody off the hook. Like I said, these guys are an embarrassment. No one knows what the hell to do with them. Likely as not, if you pull this off—find these fuckers, blow their shit away fast—those guys back in the brig are gonna be in clover. And you're not gonna be doing too badly for yourself either."

"So I just step out and find them?"

"Sure. On the ground'll be easier than from the air. *Someone's* gotta know where these jokers are holed up."

"And I just stroll in and say 'Hi, guys, I wanna sign up for the duration'."

"Right. You're my Fifth Column."

"Damn it, General, that's not exactly a muscular force I'd have there."

"You got that big guy Olsen. Real Papa Sierra. The fact that he fragged his commanding officer in a fit of pique sure doesn't make him a pantywaist. Any case, he had a good record, prior to that."

"Well, sure . . ."

"And Garrett, the Mob hit-man—a very hard fellow, as I understand it."

"Yeah, but . . ."

"You'd need a medic in a squad like this, and you've got one—Pepper. Knows his job, from what I've seen on his records. Just keep him away from his own pills, is all you have to do."

"Well, right. But . . ."

"O'Mara and Vogt—well, you may have something there. But it's a challenge, John. Right? You gotta whip 'em into shape."

"Even so . . ."

"You gotta turn 'em into a solid fire-force and roast this crazy guy. As of yesterday I transferred Captain Marco and his current co-pilot to your command. They'll chopper you from here up to Pen Kho."

"Chuck Welland's base."

"Right. You know him. That's your HQ. The brig-trash is there all ready for you. Don't keep 'em waiting."

"Thanks, General." Hardin's tone was not friendly.

"You think all this is kind of unfair . . . unjust—what the Brits'd call . . ." Halderling snapped thumb and forefinger together a couple of times, as though this might help him recall the word he wanted, although this didn't fool Hardin for a moment '. . . unsportsmanlike?"

"Suicidal is more the word I'd use, General."

Halderling's eyes became bleak, stony.

"It's the price the U.S. Army wants you to pay, John, for icing a U.S. Army General—however much of a no-good, corrupt, badass shitstick the guy was. I couldn't pull you off the hook all the Goddamn way . . ."

Chapter Five

"But what about communications?" said the tall man with the thin moustache. "We hit these mothers, all hell'll break loose in seconds flat."

"Relax."

"Jesus, Nulty, how the fuck can I relax when we're in imminent danger of getting our balls blown away by long-range artillery with much experience of bracketing a target then wiping it off the face of the fucking earth?"

"Is that a question?"

"It's a statement of fact."

Nulty—short and squat with a bullet head and a two-month beard on his chin—spat into the darkness. His stubby fingers expertly rolled the makings of a cigarette and then, after putting it up to his lips and flicking along the gummed edge of the paper with his tongue, firmed out the tube, tapping each end against a bitten-down thumbnail.

"You got no faith, Mackinley. The man don't love guys with no faith."

"Aw, shit, Nulty. Listen, cut out the crap. All I'm doing is putting a point of view. It's a fair question. However fast we are, we're gonna hit trouble."

Nulty reached into a pocket for a match and shook

105

his head, then, realizing that his companion probably hadn't seen this in the gloom of the jungle night, said again, "Relax."

Mackinley shifted his position on the dead log then stood up, staring gloomily down at where his feet would be if he could see them. Then he blinked as Nulty's match flared. He saw Nulty's fattish face, lips pursed as he sucked greedily, drawing the flame into the depths of the cigarette. The flickering light threw his face into weird, almost ugly relief. Mackinley didn't like Nulty; there was something secretive about him, something sly. When he spoke to you, you always had the uneasy feeling that there was a distinct probability that Nulty knew something about you that no one else knew, and that you didn't care for anyone else to know, either. He was always chuckling quietly to himself, too. In the past couple of months it had occurred to Mackinley on more than one occasion that Nulty was off his fucking head.

Although not more so, surely, than a hell of a lot of the guys back at the Sanctuary. There were some hard men there, right enough. Mackinley had been in Special Forces for four years and was pretty damned hard himself; you had to be, to qualify. But some of the guys in on this deal were like old granite; it'd take a deal of pasting before they'd crack apart. And the harder they were, the more covertly crazy they seemed to be.

Not for the first time Mackinley wondered if he'd made the right decision.

Sure, the basic idea—as it had originally been put to him—was a solid one. There was no doubt at all that Command was backing down from the Reds, letting the little fuckers trample all over it. The whole direction of the war effort seemed to have veered way off centre. All that hearts-and-minds crap had infiltrated too deep; the war had gone as soft as a wet sponge.

Not only the war, either, but the men who were fighting it, the grunts in the front line. All you saw these days were kids high on drugs, stuffing Goddamn flowers down their rifle barrels.

As this image moved across Mackinley's mind's eye his original resolve stiffened, the momentary weakness (as he now suddenly thought of it) thrust down into the underlayer of his consciousness. Gun barrels filled with fucking flowers—*Jesus!*

His thoughts shifted to the politicos who were pulling the strings, and a sour taste filled his throat. That bastard Nixon, for instance. The guy who'd been so hot for dealing with the Reds like they ought to be dealt with had chickened out, had turned out to be as yellow-skinned as the enemy they were supposed to be fighting. Had betrayed the entire enterprise.

That was how the man had put it: betrayed the entire enterprise.

Damn right. For over 20 years the creep had been hounding the Commies back in the World, against all the odds, against all that pinko Liberal shit that had tried to stop him. He'd told the truth; told it like it was.

But finally, when the chips were down, when the confrontation had come—when it was good versus bad, white versus black, right versus wrong, played out on this south east Asian battleground with freedom as the highest stake—the sonuvabitch had jumped back from the brink, turned tail and run.

Whenever Mackinley thought about this act of gross treachery real rage surged up inside of him. It was monstrous, was what it was. You did your darnedest to defend the American way of life, the values and ideals that had been fought for 200 years before and handed down for generations, and the guys in Washington crapped on you. They didn't deserve to be saved. They sure as hell didn't deserve the kind of guy who was ramrodding this whole scheme to combat the rottenness that was eating its way through the military administration, all levels, here in Vietnam. And—yes—back in the World, too.

As these thoughts slid through Mackinley's mind, he knew this was the only way. Break out, like the man said; cut loose. Fight our own war; destroy the menace in our own way. The brass'd come round in the end; they had to. They'd see it the way the man saw it, that it was the only sensible move to make, even if it meant killing guys on your own side.

To construct anything, you had to destroy first. Rip out the rotten elements so you could start over clean and fresh. And for sure, you had to have hard men to do all that. And okay, so some of them might be a little whacky, a little close to the edge, but that was what war did to you. It was a known fact.

Mackinley shrugged. He'd thought it through. Things seemed somehow better than they'd been a quarter hour before. Even Nulty seemed somehow a little more human, something less than a monster.

But the coming attack still nagged at him, slightly. Hell, the place was small, but it was well defended.

He knew that; he'd been there, had taken off on a couple of missions from there. It still didn't seem to him to be a very smart move to jump straight in, even with the fire-power he knew they had, and risk being wiped out when the defenders called in the heavy help.

He tried again.

"Jeeze, Nulty . . ."

"Now what?"

"Well, hell, isn't that I mind going in there blasting, but if they're gonna whip our ass in double time, what in hell is the point?"

"They won't whip our ass. We're gonna whip *their* ass; whip it good. We're gonna take their choppers and their supplies and all the materiél we can lay our fucking hands on, is what we're gonna do, Mackinley. Now why don't you just shut your fucking mouth."

"Yeah, but . . . they're gonna radio out, and . . ."

Nulty turned on him, reached up and grabbed him by the collar, shaking him violently. His voice lashed out in an irritated snarl.

"Listen, shithead, you ask too many Goddamn questions. You don't keep your fucking mouth closed from now on, I'm gonna close it for you. Right?" He released Mackinley's collar with a final throttling jerk. *"Permanently! Right?"*

Mackinley staggered slightly, clutching at his throat.

"Okay, okay," he muttered, "for Chrissake."

Nulty turned away with an ugly expression on his face. The guy was a dummy. It had been a mistake to pull him on this, and the only way to rectify the error was to get rid of him.

He stiffened suddenly, reached for his M-16, as he heard men moving towards them through the undergrowth. Then relaxed as vague shadowy shapes solidified in the gloom, becoming just recognisable. Bowker, Orlandini, Perez.

"We took out the sensors."

That was Orlandini. Nulty smiled toothily.

"All the way round?"

"All the way round. Was shit-easy. A perfect mission. We set up the mortars and the rocket-men. We're ready to go."

"You took their eyes out totally?"

"They're stone-blind. Stone-deaf. They're wide open."

Nulty nodded.

"Okay. What we do now is move in and take out the LPs. That way we jump right in on the bastards when the go-button's pressed. They won't even have time to crap themselves when we hit 'em." A sudden thought occurred to him. "You got *all* the sensors?"

Orlandini, a barrel-chested Italian with high cheekbones which hinted at a liaison with a reservation squaw a couple of generations back, laughed.

"Sure, sure. They were all there, exactly like we were told. Each in its place. We looked around for more but no more could we see."

"Okay, you know your targets." Nulty chuckled. "Let's get this show on the road."

Arthur Comeraro sucked at his Lucky, took it out of his mouth, stared at it with revulsion, stubbed it out viciously. He was extremely pissed off.

"Jesus. Where'd you get this junk, Top?"

Across the room Sergeant Fuller didn't look up from the cards he was holding. Fuller knew, with a deep-grained instinct that was seldom if ever wrong, that Parrish, opposite him, had something that was more than a merely good hand in his fist, and he was trying to figure out what could be done about it. The problem was that all he, himself, needed was a Queen of Hearts and he could wipe the floor with these assholes, however more than merely good Parrish's hand was. However, more than merely good *anybody's* hand was. All he needed was the lousy Queen.

He nodded to Jessel, who flipped the top card at him. He picked it up, his stomach suddenly constricting painfully, his expression as sour as though he'd just sunk his teeth into a fresh lime. It was a Queen. *The* Queen.

QUEEN OF HEARTS.

"C-RAT CIGS, SIR," HE SAID, IN AS NEUTRAL A TONE AS HE COULD MUSTER.

COMERARO NODDED IRRITABLY.

"FIGURES. TASTES LIKE I'M SMOKING SHAVINGS FROM THE GODDAMN BARNYARD. WOULDN'T SURPRISE ME IF THE DAMN THINGS WERE LEFTOVERS FROM KOREA. DON'T WE HAVE *anything* else?"

"Waiting for supplies, sir," said Fuller, his face as bleak as an Arctic winter, his heart as joyous as a Massachusetts spring.

"I got some Kool, Lieutenant," said O'Brien.

"I don't like menthol," snapped Comeraro.

At that instant, the slate of Parrish's memory was wiped clean, as though a damp rag had been rubbed across it. He'd been playing with Fuller for two or three weeks now, and was beginning to recognise cer-

111

tain signs about the man's attitude to play, certain potents, certain unconscious signals. But now a finger of panic was insinuating itself into his bowels. For the life of him, try as he might, he could not remember what Fuller's stony expression signified.

Did it mean he was furious because he had a shitty hand, or was it a bluff? On the face of it, it seemed like a bluff. With an expression as sour as that it seemed likely Fuller had a winner at his fingertips.

This was ridiculous. He had three Aces, two Kings. It was the best hand he'd been dealt in weeks, and there was a lotta loot on the table. He could really hit these mothers.

If only he could remember what Fuller's expression meant.

"Crisp as an iceberg lettuce, sir," said O'Brien, "cool as a mountain stream."

"I thought that was some other cigarette."

"It's the same principle, sir."

"Whatever," muttered Comeraro, "I still don't like menthol."

He didn't like O'Brien either. O'Brien was a wiseass with a razor-sharp tongue, and had what Comeraro considered to be a strong line in dumb insolence.

He went back to his comicbooks.

Comeraro was a comicbook freak. He was a collector. Back home in the World—in his father's second garage, specially fitted out so that his collection neither disintegrated with the heat, nor went spotty with the damp—he had 8,000-plus comicbooks, many of them (the ones from the late-1930s and the early-1940s) in individual plastic bags. It was by no means a famous collection, nor was it, in collecting terms, a vast collection (Comeraro knew a number of fellow-fans who had upwards of 20,000 and growing). But it was a choice collection.

Although he had selections from all periods and publishers, Comeraro concentrated on Marvel Comics, from the days when they were called Timely, through the 1950s when they were Atlas, right up to the present day. He bought just about every new Marvel (apart from the Western titles and *Millie the Model*) fresh off the newstands. Titles he really dug (*Fantastic Four, Captain America, Thor, Doc Strange*, and so on) he bought two copies of each: one to read, one for storing away. And new titles, he had a standing order with a local distributor to put aside a dozen of each Number One ("first pulse-pounding senses-shattering ish") as a shoring-up against his old age. The local distributor thought he was nuts ("Listen, you're 21, and still reading this crud?"), but what the hell.

Whenever things were grim (in a heavy firefight situation, or when a patrol he was leading was ambushed by the VC, or they were being hotly pursued by EnVee Rangers deep inside hardcore bandit territory, no help within a league) Cameraro thought about his comicbook collection, and visions of *Red Raven* No. 1 (a mint copy, the first Timely comic drawn by the legendary Jack Kirby), or *Marvel Comics* No. 1 (poor condition and with a xerox cover, but shit-rare) or his sets of *Daring Mystery* and *Mystic* (mostly Near Mint) or his beautiful run of *Captain America* (lacking numbers 24, 57, 63 and, oddly, the final ish from the 1940s' series, 74 . . . but that was OK because although it was called *Captain America's*

Weird Tales—title-change on No. 73—it didn't actually feature Cap, and he only wanted it for completeness' sake) acted as a spur to his sense of self-preservation. He felt he had to survive, had to make it back in one piece, if only to experience again the unsurpassable, almost physical thrill of flipping through the multi-hued, ludicrously vibrant pages of a random selection of titles from *Marvel Mystery* through *The Yellow Claw* right up to *Amazing Adult Fantasy* (with all that gorgeous Ditko artwork).

And now, at the age of 24, Comeraro had it all figured out, the direction his life was going to take. He had six months more in Nam and then he had the option of signing up for another three years. He was not going to take that option. He was taking off back to the World, spending a month catching up on two years worth of Marvel back issues, and then he was going into business.

Buying and selling old comicbooks.

It sounded absurd, especially after six years in the military. But two of those years had been spent struggling to stay sane in this hell on earth, and Comeraro had had enough. The idea of a sedentary existence behind a desk or selling insurance out and about did not appeal in the slightest, but the idea of careering round the country looking for old comicbooks, winkling out the rarities, getting a mailing list together, sending out illustrated catalogues—that was really something else. This was 1970; it was exactly the right time, he felt, for the entrepreneurial spirit to be injected into this kind of pastime. Comeraro had visions of pushing comicbooks way up in the rarified sale-room atmosphere breathed by dealers in stamps,

Art Nouveau posters, Persian wall-hangings.

But all that was in the future. Right now, after deliberately not reading a comicbook in eighteen months—after not even glancing at them racked up in all their ridiculous glory in the PX, or stacked and fresh-smelling in Saigon or Da Nang newstands, and then discovering this small cache of tattered and torn and muchread copies—all kinds, all genres, from superhero books to Sergeant Rock winning World War Two for the two hundredth time—now, after all that, he'd spotted Doc Doom (his ultra-favourite villain) on the front cover of a *Fantastic Four* ish ("The Name Is . . . Doom!") and had fallen, had picked it up, had flipped through it, had savoured the pulsating pandemonic power of King Kirby's artwork, the outrageous exaggeration of Stan Lee's dialogue, the crazy intricacies of the plot—and discovered, to his horror, that all he had here were the first three issues to a four-part story.

It was like, Goddamnit, reading a detective novel with the final page torn out; like watching the last part of a serial on TV and the power fails half way through. It was like knocking off the guy next door's wife and then he comes barging in five seconds before climax.

It was truly a pisser of colossal proportions.

Comeraro suddenly winced as a high-pitched keening wail filled the room. The card-players in the corner glared in outrage at the open door leading to the communications room, from which the sound emanated.

"Cut it out, Lantry!" yelled Sergeant Fuller, about to raise 'em yet again.

Cameraro jumped to his feet, strode across to the doorway.

Inside the radio-room Corporal Lantry turned away from the console white-faced, shrugging at Comeraro with an open-handed gesture.

"What the hell is *that?*"

"Jeeze, I dunno, sir. It just came on."

"I know that, for Christ's sake. But what is it? Where's it coming from?"

"All over, sir. All round. Right across the web."

"Well, turn it the fuck down."

Lantry gestured helplessly.

"I . . . I can't, sir."

It was not that the tone was loud, but its pitch was like a needle, driving inexorably into the brain.

"Close down," snapped Comeraro.

Lantry looked aghast.

"Christ, sir, I can't do that. It's against . . ."

"Shut it off!"

The howl died abruptly—but you could still hear it in your head, still feel its unnerving presence as an almost physical sensation. Comeraro shook his head, wincing, rubbing a hand across his face.

"Whatever that is, it sucks," he said.

"Could be it's some kind of freak atmospheric disturbance, sir?"

That was O'Brien. He'd thrown down his cards and was on his feet, holding his M-16 and starting to move towards the door.

"The hell it is. That's Charlie jamming the fuck out of us."

And even as he said this, Comeraro was thinking, And where in the hell did Charlie get equipment

116

that's powerful enough to blanket the entire Goddamn web? That was one sophisticated mother of a jammer somewhere out there, and if Victor Charles had stuff like that at his disposal he was in a bigger league than anybody had previously figured.

He turned to Fuller.

"Get over to Colonel Welland. Wake him and tell him what's up."

Sergeant Fuller, he noticed, seemed to have been turned to stone. He looked, sitting at the table, like some granite statue carved by a genius or a madman. His eyes were wide, his nostrils flared, the muscles on his arms looked as thick as underground telephone cables. Only his hands moved; they were quivering, as though the man himself had been stricken by some appalling ague.

"C'mon, Fuller, move it. You still hearing the wail or something?"

Fuller shook his head, carefully, as though he thought it might imminently topple from his shoulders.

"Nossir," he articulated slowly. "It's just that I hadda fucking Royal Flush in Hearts, sir."

Comeraro had the decency not to laugh, although the urge to break out into a hyena-like bark was almost uncontrollable.

"Shit, I dunno what to say, Top—but maybe you can take it out on the Yellow Peril, because I figure they're almost on top of us." He turned to Jessel. "We'd better get out to the forward LPs . . . start pulling the fuckers right back."

Grinning, Jessel reached for the Armalite.

Chapter Six

All of them saw it—the darkness ripped violently apart ahead of the chopper by four successive eruptions of white light, red-cored, and seconds later, when the light died it did not die completely.

And all of them had expected it.

Only minutes before, their faces lit eerily by the winking lights of the control-board, both Marco and his co-pilot Hanks had simultaneously jerked their heads round to stare, appalled, at each other and torn their headpieces off.

Above the racket of the rotors, Marco screamed, "*Shit!*"

Hardin, in the rear, hunched up against an ammunition box, clambered to his feet and moved fast, sure-footed in the darkness, across the cabin. He saw Hanks leaning across, twisting dials, making hurried adjustments, an expression of baffled outrage just glimpsed on his long face. From Marco's discarded earpiece, hanging loosely from the back of his seat, came a fierce high-pitched howl that cut through the roar of the chopper's engine with shocking ease.

He leaned over Marco, shaking his shoulder. The black turned his head, the console throwing his features into stark relief.

"What is it? What's going on?"

Marco yelled, "Jammin'! We bein' jammed to hell and back!"

He shook his head, wincing, and reached out, flipping switches upwards. The howl, which had been steadily rising in pitch and volume, was cut off abruptly.

Hardin shouted, "It's *that* powerful?"

Hanks glanced round, shrugging his shoulders and gesturing with his hands.

"Right across the net! It's all dead!"

"Might as well be on Mars!" yelled Marco. "We got trouble!"

Hardin glanced at his watch. ETA was in less than five minutes, which meant that Marco was right. The jammer was very close, and that meant in turn that they'd be dropping in on Pen Kho just in time to face some kind of EnVee attack.

He turned and stared at the rushing blackness outside the open port doorway. It was unusual—not unknown, but extremely unusual—for Charlie to mount a night attack. Pin-prick nuisance-manoeuvres, sure. The odd mortar round in the darkness, a few shells here and there, a sniper sitting in a tree suddenly opening up for two or three minutes. You could almost rely on that.

There'd been, at one of the base-camps Hardin had used, a guy they called the "Rack-Out Raider," who regularly, at 0500, sent a broken stream of automatic fire lashing across the perimeters in bursts of five seconds each, which lasted until he ran out of ammo. Then he stopped. And that was that. No fresh mag, no new gun. *Finis*. Until the next day.

And they'd never caught him, because every day he changed his position. Sometimes from the north, then the south, then NNW, then east; all points of the compass in a totally arbitrary fashion. But always 0500. On the Goddamn dot.

And you couldn't send out snipers to catch the little fucker either, because chances were that was exactly what he wanted and his comrades would be ringing the camp waiting for just such a move. So you simply sat back and got used to the fact that you were going to be woken up early by the harsh chatter of automatic fire — and that was smart of Charlie too because after a very short time it got to be extremely demoralising. Subconsciously, in your sleep, you were waiting for the Rack-Out Raider to start up, and a lot of guys began to wake even earlier than five — couldn't help themselves — and would tense, ears straining, fists clenched, minds a deadly vacuum, in anticipation of that first barking stutter of automatic fire. A couple of men went right over the edge because of the Rack-Out Raider.

And then, after twenty days or so of this — nothing. He'd gone someplace else, maybe to plague some other camp. Or maybe he'd fallen out of his tree and broken his neck. Or died in a firefight during the day. Or maybe he'd just gotten pissed off with the whole business.

That was one of the main irritations — a really vicious mind-tic — about this war (and probably, thought Hardin, all wars): there were just too many minor problems you were never able fully to work out, however hard you cudgelled your brains. The big problems — the shifting of supplies cross-country, computation of enemy strengths, movement of troops, order of attack—were, by comparison—Hell, kids' stuff.

But, his mind reverted to the present, a full-scale attack at—he glanced at his watch again, checking the luminous dial—0415? That was so damned unusual as to be unique. Early, sure. But not this early.

And a full-scale and extremely muscular attack it had to be, for certain. Charlie didn't bring up highly sophisticated radio wipe-out equipment simply to give aid and comfort to a lone sniper or pinprick mortar team.

And, yes—*Jesus!*—that had to be *ultra*-sophisticated apparatus to knock out the entire network for miles around. Who the fuck had they borrowed it from? The Russians? Chinese?

He was suddenly aware of Colenso, the door-gunner, a tall, stringy, slow-speaking farmer's boy from Iowa, beside him.

"What gives, sir?"

"Looks like we're about to drop in on an EnVee attack on Pen Kho," Hardin yelled. "Better see to your guns. We could be of use."

It was lucky, he thought, that they were expected at this Godforsaken hour, and at least it was no problem that radio contact with Pen Kho was now totally out of the question.

He moved back towards the pilot's area. Marco turned as he sensed his close proximity.

"Any minute now," he yelled. "Should see the runway lights."

But they didn't see the runway lights. Not at all.

121

What they saw was a chilling firework display that began with four massive explosions and simply got better and more colourful as the seconds ticked by.

"Jesus!" Marco half-turned in his seat to stare up at Hardin. "The way those mothers were placed—they were *inside* the camp! And they ain't no Goddamn mortar blasts either!"

Hardin had already worked this out for himself and his mind was racing on past, delving into the fuller implications of what he'd just seen and what he was seeing now. Incredible as it might seem those explosions had to be the result not of artillery or mortar fire but of charges placed inside the camp and set off either electrically or on a time-fuse. Which meant the enemy had already over-run the camp, and were blowing it to hell before fading back into the surrounding forest.

But that was impossible.

To over-run a camp—even a small air-base like Pen Kho—could take days. This was a Special Forces camp. There were guys down there who would take a lot of killing, and who, in their death-throes, would be twice as dangerous as when they were still alive.

Nor could they have been taken by surprise. There were hidden sensors outside of the perimeters, integrated Listening Posts, all the paraphernalia of up-to-the-minute surveillance and warning systems. There was heavy back-up all round, long-range artillery that could be called in at a minute's notice to home in on the enemy, front and rear.

That was why the fuckers had brought in the jammers, of course. But the jamming had only just started, and that had to mean the attack had only just started too.

Jesus Christ, it *had* to mean that!

So how come the gooks were already inside the wire and planting demolition charges?

Unless.

Hardin's mind did a backwards flip in cold horror. *Unless*.

Jesus, unless it wasn't gooks at all, but the guys they were after—the renegades—and they had men planted in the camp who'd been primed to set off charges—create maximum mayhem—in time with the start of the onslaught from outside.

The chopper hurtled onwards through a darkness that was streaked and seared with flashing eruptions of red and yellow.

Hardin swiftly followed through from this horrifying assumption. The renegades. Right. They'd be after equipment, weapons, ammunition. They'd be after more choppers, it was a cinch. It was going to be a fast raid; speed had to be of the essence. They'd be in, and out. It was more than likely that they'd trekked through the jungle to reach here, but they'd be using—unless they were very stupid, which, it was clear, they weren't—Chuck Welland's choppers for the getaway. Then they'd vanish once more, go to ground in their sanctuary, prepare for the next raid. They could keep on and on repeating this tactic.

Unless they were stopped.

He had, he knew, two options.

One, he could drop down on the base's chopper apron and help secure it. He had the element of surprise on his side and the odds were heavy that he could completely screw them. A rogue chopper lanc-

123

ing down out of the night, cannon blazing and rockets blasting, just when they were about to lift off and were, psychologically, feeling safe and secure, would really fuck up their heads. Christ, it'd *destroy* them!

Two, he could hold back, let the slaughter continue, not give aid to Welland and his men, wait for the bandits to lift off and head back over the border—and follow them. Maybe even join their pack—one more chopper in the confusion would not be noticed. Then tag their hideout and call up the big guns. Blow the fuckers away completely. Total them. As easy and as simple as that.

There were flaws in both arguments. That had to be admitted.

He could get blown away if he dropped down—there'd be a lot of stray stuff flying around, that was for sure. And that would be the end of that.

On the other hand, if he hung around up here waiting for the bandits to escape, a lot of good men down there would die—who need not die at all if he went in and secured the apron, blocked the getaway. In any case, there'd be some survivors from the pirate pack. It would not, surely, take too long for the CID interrogators to pull the sanctuary's position out of one of them, Would it?

Or would it.

"What do we do?" yelled Marco. "I need to know, man. I need to know damn fast."

The words squeezed out from between clenched teeth, Comeraro said, "Just what the hell d'you think you're doing, Jessel?"

Jessel, his M-16 gripped in both hands and held out

124

in front of him, grinned and said, "Pointing this gun at you, Lieutenant."

Comeraro's throat felt constricted.

"And just what the hell is that actually supposed to mean?"

"Well, it actually means I'm actually gonna blow your fucking head off, actually, Lieutenant."

Another explosion went off outside the room, much nearer than the previous ones. The wall facing the main compound shuddered with the blast; the windows rattled.

That, thought Comeraro, was about the ninth or tenth in the past few seconds. He was beginning to lose count. All he could think of was that there was some kind of raid hitting them and he was stuck here in the communications hut menaced by a guy who'd flipped his lid completely.

And not only one guy either. O'Brien appeared to have wigged out too. He'd joined Jessel; likewise pulled a gun on the room. Well, he'd never liked O'Brien. The fact that O'Brien had clearly gone bananas did not at all surprise him.

O'Brien, with an unpleasant smirk pasted across his thin face, was by the door; Jessel was left of the card table, where Sergeant Fuller, still seemingly in a state of shock—though now mesmerised perhaps by the sight of mutiny in the ranks rather than grief-stricken at the loss of the only Royal Flush he'd had in about fifteen years—was sitting gazing morosely at the cards in his hand. Opposite Fuller sat Parrish, frankly incredulous, clearly not believing any of this was happening either. Lantry was standing beside him, hands half-raised in the air.

"C'mon, guys," he said. "Knock it off. A joke's a joke."

"Shut it," said O'Brien.

"Look," said Lantry, as though trying to explain the philosophy of sweet reason to an ill-tempered child, "we gotta get outta here. There's gooks out there blowing the Goddamn base apart."

"*Shut it!*"

The mingled chatter of many automatic weapons could now be heard from outside; the crump of mortar shells; the bark of grenades exploding. Against this heavier tapestry of sound a more delicate interweaving of human cries—shouts and screams; orders being yelled—could also be distinguished.

Comeraro didn't know what to do. There were two M-16s trained on him, either of which—should he be unwise enough to make an untoward movement—could damage him more than somewhat; both of which could cut him in half. Jessel meant what he said, too. He saw that now. At first he had been inclined to think this was some kind of outrageously tasteless joke, but no longer. Jessel was going to kill him and there was nothing he could do about it.

For a second the absurd image flashed through his mind of him jumping across at the table where he'd placed his official issue .45 automatic next to the pile of comicbooks, snatching up the gun and, still in mid-flight, twisting round and firing it, nailing the both of the bastards with two shots. But that was too close to unreality—too near to what Captain America would have done (well, no—Cap'd just sling his shield and it'd smash into Jessel then coldcock O'Brien on the rebound)—to be amusing.

"Look, O'Brien—what the hell is this? Are you crazy, or something?"

"Never saner, Lieutenant. You think that's dinks outside? You think it's Charlie on the rampage? No way, my friend. It's guys who've really got their shit pulled together showing you effete fuckers how this war's gonna be won."

Comeraro shook his head blankly.

"I really don't know what the fuck you're talking about," he said. "I got a feeling, O'Brien, neither do you."

"He knows exactly what he's talking about. He's talking Goddamn sense."

Comeraro, momentarily forgetting the guns pointing at him, turned, startled. Sergeant Fuller had come back to life again, and was now shuffling through the soiled pack of cards as he gazed around the room.

Jessel stared at him.

"Jesus, Sarge. Didn't know you were in on this."

"He's not," snapped O'Brien. "The old coot's crapping us. Watch him."

Fuller's leathery features creased up in disgust.

"Now you *ain't* talking sense, O'Brien. I been in on this from the beginning." He paused to reach into his shirt pocket, took out a short black-leaf cigar. He lit it one-handed, puffed smoke into the air, went back to shuffling the cards. "You better ice these guys fast, O'Brien. We can't piss around here for ever."

O'Brien took a step towards him and was about to take another when the cards left Fuller's hand in a long flickering stream that looked, to Comeraro, like bunting fluttering in a breeze. The cards sailed past

O'Brien's face still in perfect formation, and O'Brien's eyes took in the sight for perhaps less than one whole second. But it was all that Fuller needed. He threw the table at O'Brien.

His arms went under the table-top and he jumped to his feet, heaving the table across the room. It struck the barrel of O'Brien's M-16, knocking it out of his hands, before crashing to the wooden floor. Fuller followed fast in a headlong dive through the air, his hands and arms wrapping themselves around O'Brien's knees on contact. Fuller was screaming incoherently.

Even as Fuller was flying Comeraro briskly stepped across the intervening space between him and his gun, picked it up and, turning slightly, shot Jessel in the stomach. Jessel dropped the Armalite and clutched at himself, staggering backwards before making contact with the wall and collapsing down it in a raggedy-doll slide. He stared up at Comeraro, white-faced, his eyes wide, pleading. Then his eyes squeezed tight shut and he threw up down his shirtfront. Blood was beginning to gather in a pool around him.

Comeraro gathered up the M-16 and turned back to Fuller. The sergeant seemed to have gone mad. He was sitting astride O'Brien's chest, his left hand clutched around O'Brien's throat so that the back of the man's head was fixed firmly to the floor. Fuller was using his right fist as though it was a hammer, pounding at O'Brien's face with bludgeoning force, his arm going up and down, up and down, as though he was trying either to flatten the skull out completely or knock it through the floorboards. O'Brien's face was a mask of blood; his features were already beginning to change shape.

While all this was going on, Fuller still had the cigar clenched between his teeth and was screaming obscenities round the butt.

Comeraro grabbed him by the shoulder.

"Okay, Top. Okay. He's had it. You'll kill him."

"What I wanna do! Kill the cocksucker! Train a fucking gun on me, the shitstick! I'll ram it down his fucking throat!"

Fuller's eyes were wide and his fist rose and fell like a steam-hammer.

"Yeah, all right, all right. Cool it, Top. Jesus—*cool it*, will you."

Comeraro grabbed Fuller's right hand, but it was like trying to stop a hydraulic arm. He swung round on the others.

"Help me pull him off, for Christ's sake. The sonuvabitch's gone berserk!"

Lantry and Parrish piled in and they dragged the still-yelling Sergeant Fuller off O'Brien's prone body. Fuller's fist was bright scarlet; his brown, tanned-teak flesh could not be seen for blood.

"God above." Parrish's voice was awestruck as he stared down at O'Brien's face. "Ain't never seen anything like it, Lieutenant. He's destroyed him!"

"Sure as hell didn't act like he loved him," muttered Lantry.

Comeraro waved these comments aside. All of this was irrelevant.

"I don't know what the hell is going on—why these two scumbags were hot for icing us—but one thing's for sure," he jerked a thumb at the windows, "whoever *is* out there, they're whipping up a real shit-storm.

And I'll be honest with you guys, I don't.know what the fuck to do."

Corporal Lantry stared at Comeraro in bewilderment.

"Christ, sir, hadn't we just better get out there and kill the bad guys?"

Comeraro looked at him in disbelief, as though he'd just offered to do a belly-dance balancing the section piss-bucket on his head.

"I don't think you've been paying attention, Corporal. How the fuck do we kill the bad guys when the bad guys look like you or me?"

Parrish had moved to the right-hand window, and had cautiously lifted one of the blind-slats. He turned back to Comeraro, his eyes wide and scared.

"Jesus, sir—looks like the whole Goddamn camp's on fire!"

There were five men in the cell.

There was Sergeant Walter Olsen, big, solidly-built, with a friendly, crumpled countenance and blond hair; there was little Leroy Vogt, with a baby face and a surprised expression that stayed put no matter what; there was O'Mara, a skinny black kid with large, liquid, almost luminous eyes; there was Doc Pepper, tall and gangling, easy-going, a drifter and a freak; and there was Garrett, who had the build of a boxer and looked like he chewed masonry nails for laughs.

Apart from the fact that all of them had been busted at various Courts Martial (Olsen for fragging his lieutenant; Vogt for killing a sergeant; O'Mara for strangling his jailer in the brig; Pepper for peddling dope; Garrett for icing a big wheel Vietnamese civilian), none of them had all that much in common.

Except for right now, when they were, every mother's son of them, quite literally shaking in their boots—in a state of total terminal flap.

It was Garrett who summed up the situation, when he managed to rasp, in a voice hoarse with panic, the words, "Were gonna fry in here . . . *gonna roast like fucking turkeys!*"

It was actually more of a holding tank they were in than a cell. It was wide and airy, had benches fixed to the wall, a wooden floor, strip lighting that didn't glare in your eyes and reasonable toilet facilities (that is to say, a bucket that could be slopped out rather than a reeking, fly-clogged hole in the floor). The outside wall was concrete, with two small windows set into it; the rest of the walls were made up of steel bars. There were five such tanks in the room, separated one from another by bars from ceiling to floor, with a corridor running down the longest side leading to the guardroom. Olsen and his group were in the tank furthest from the exit, which made their particular predicament at that particular point in time all the more horrifying.

Because where the guard-room had been situated was now only a mass of flames, and the flames were creeping through the complex of barred-off holding tanks towards them. It would take some minutes before the fire reached them—maybe as long as a quarter-hour—and due to some freak of the air-cirulation the smoke so far was slight, most of it being sucked out of the glass-less windows. But that respite only served to make their ordeal more agonising, piled hard time on hard time, crap on crap. The only thing

131

they could do was sit back and watch the fire's slow but inexorable progress across the room.

And slow-roast from the heat.

"I jus' don't get it," whispered O'Mara. "I don't understand what's goin' on . . . why those guys jus' left us . . ."

"Ask me a question on nuclear fucking physics," snarled Garrett, "and I'll be more likely to give you a fucking answer."

Only minutes before—no more than fifteen at the outside—the explosions had started. And the shots, the thud of mortars, the yells, the crackle of automatic rifles. Chilling sounds to be heard on a seemingly secure base-camp at dead of night; sounds that had slapped each of them out of sleep as though cold water had been tossed over them. And almost at express-train rate the noise of battle had hurtled nearer and nearer until it was all around them, an appalling and shocking cacophony.

Then, suddenly, the door to the guard-room had banged open and Corporal Shelley had appeared in the doorway, framed against the light, his shouts lost in a particularly vicious, and loud, detonation. He'd started to run forward towards them—and then the run had turned into a weird kind of staggering leap and blood started pouring from his chest in three or four separate jets before he'd finally collapsed in a head-over-heels heap on the floor.

Two men with blackened faces had appeared, close behind him, laughing, one carrying an M-16, the other a Kalashnikov. Neither was Vietnamese.

In the half-darkness (for a startling couple of seconds Leroy Vogt had been transported back to the movie-house beside the corner drug store in Hannibal, Missouri) there had been only two lines of dialogue.

"Brig-birds! Do we spring 'em?"

"Nah. Let 'em burn."

They'd retreated, still laughing, closing the door behind them, cutting off the light.

But not for long.

A couple of minutes later there'd been a thundering, ear-cracking explosion. The entire building had shivered—as though a giant had kicked it—the guardroom door had been blown off its hinges, and a huge tongue of flame had flared along the corridor outside the tanks then shot back again. Beyond the doorway was a raging inferno—and it hadn't taken long for the flames to invade the tank-area.

Doc Pepper said, "It's gotta be some kind of attack. But who's attacking? Those guys were *ours!*"

Garrett turned on him, grabbing him by the throat and shaking him like a rat.

"Fucking lamebrain!" he howled. "Who cares who's attacking? I don't give a good jack-shit who's attacking! The motherfuckers left us to burn!"

He flung Doc Pepper from him and turned to the nearest window, gripping the bars and screaming out into the flame-racked darkness.

"Get us outta here! For Chrissake—*get us outta here!*"

Outside, it was like—if Garrett had been able to view the scene coolly and dispassionately at that particular moment and had had, moreover, the intellectual capacity to make the allusion—an apocalyptic vision of the Last Judgement—the Great Day of His Wrath—lovingly rendered by John Martin.

Figures, some in groups, some alone, dashed this way and that, black silhouettes against the flames that seemed to be devouring the entire camp. Over to the right an observation tower, its supports and holding-struts awash with flame, suddenly sagged to one side then crumpled, the hutment at the top lurching over and disintegrating. Tiny, doll-like figures were hurled from its interior as it hit the ground, as though ejected mechanically. A truck suddenly split apart as flames reached its gas-tank, and a human fireball sprang from the wreckage and galloped round and round in circles, shrieking as it burned. A man sprinted past the window, only feet away, whirling his right arm above his head as though urging a cavalry troop into a final, desperate charge; the arm was swathed in flames. A group of men with M-16s suddenly appeared round the corner of a hut across the square. They were clearly retreating, running jerkily, turning every few seconds, crouching, firing back at unseen pursuers. They made it to the centre of the square and then, all at once, an MG opened up from somewhere and tracer scythed into them, cut them down cleanly like ripe corn. Every so often—maybe once in every five or six seconds—illumination rounds exploded high above the camp—green, red, white—adding to the hellish aspect of the scene.

Garrett saw all of this but took nothing of it in. The sole thought pounding at his brain was the stone-cold fact that within minutes he would be a charred and blackened piece of meat.

Suddenly rounds began hammering at the outside wall to his left and stone shards sprayed across the window-space. Garrett jumped back, cursing, then

134

leapt forward again as he saw a figure he recognised—Di Gamo, one of the brig guards.

Garrett screamed, "Di Gamo! We're trapped! Get us the fuck out or we're gonna fry!"

Di Gamo had been racing across the square, but now he swerved, veered towards the building, ducking and weaving as he ran. About ten yards away he stopped.

"You're gonna fry?"

"Damn right! Fucking jail's on fire!"

Di Gamo laughed, raised his rifle.

"So fry!" he shouted wildly.

Garrett had never actually looked down the barrel of a gun before. At least, not cold, like this. In a longish career of mayhem and murder he'd been on the receiving end in various gangland firefights, had dodged sub-machinegun fire, had dived for cover down mean streets chased by bullets, had once outdrawn a man who'd been paid money to kill him, and who already had a gun in his hand. And here in Nam, of course, on rice paddies, in swamps, on landing-grounds, trailing through the jungle, a lot of lead had been aimed his way at one time or another. It was a natural hazard.

But not cold. Not from a man who was only yards away, who was supposedly on the same side, who was laughing (albeit crazily), and who had simply raised his piece and squeezed the Goddamn trigger.

Garrett, his heart lurching, actually felt the wind of the rounds as he ducked frantically below the window-line—the vicious cracking through the air above his head which was in a way more terrifying than the appalling clamour of the M-16 itself.

The stream of bullets hammered the opposite wall and howled like hornets of death in a vicious ricocheting spray around the room. O'Mara was already a curled ball in one corner and Vogt had dived under one of the benches, Doc Pepper crouching beside him, hands clutched over his head. Only Olsen was still standing, flattened into the other corner against the bars of the adjoining tank.

From outside came another yell of laughter, pitched high. Di Gamo's face appeared on the other side of the window-grille.

"Know what I'm gonna do? Gonna make you guys dance! Dance-a death, jarheads!"

He started laughing again, his face weirdly highlighted by the leaping flames that were devouring the wooden boards of the floor and advancing with remorseless vigour towards the fifth tank. His expression was almost demoniacal in this red, flickering light, the sound of his voice strangely hollow as it bounced around the room.

Olsen stepped quickly to the window, nudging the shaking bundle of old clothes that was Garrett to one side.

"Look," he gasped, "you gotta get us outta here, son. We don't know what the hell is going on, but less you spring us, the way things are we're frankly gonna be dinner for the crows."

Di Gamo crammed himself even nearer to the bars — which was in fact just what Olsen had wanted. The burly sergeant's panic was now over. He felt very calm. He could view his impending death with a detachment he had not felt in months. But it was not right that he should go out without making some kind of gesture, however futile that gesture might turn out to be in the long run.

In one sense Olsen was a very moral man. Sure, he'd iced his commanding officer — tossed a grenade at him and watched the mother redistribute himself across the landscape — and, sure, that had been, when you got right down to it, a morally indefensible action, despite the fact that the guy had been a real sackashit who'd hated his men, and, what was worse in Olsen's book, led from the rear. Still, no way was that the point. A commanding officer was a commanding officer. Some of them were real nummies (Olsen recalled wryly — the thought hurtling across his mind even at that moment — Warning 3 in *Every Good Sergeant's Rule-Book:* "the most dangerous thing in the world is a second lieutenant with a map and compass" — and that was truly no lie), but a good Papa Sierra could mould a greenhorn, shape him up, sieve the crap out and throw him on the wheel. Turn him into solid performer. Olsen felt he should have maybe persevered with the son of a bitch, not blown him all over the hootch-area. No way, frankly, was that the way to behave — and it could be that death by fire was proper and fitting punishment for such a heinous offence.

Could be.

But it still did not mean he had to walk meekly into the Goddamn flames.

Olsen's right hand shot out, straight through the windowbars like a striking snake, his fingers closing around Di Gamo's collar in a clasp of steel. He yanked hard, heaving the spluttering man towards him by main force, until his head was almost inside the room.

Di Gamo was making gargling noises, his face even redder now as blood pounded through his veins.

Olsen bared his teeth in a terrible smile.

"You *shithead*," he whispered.

His left fist went back then forward, like a piston. The knuckles struck Di Gamo's nose with the dull soggy sound of a cleaver sinking into fresh meat and Di Gamo's nasal bone snapped with a sharp, splintering crack. It was, to Olsen, an intensely satisfying sound; it gave him deep pleasure. Once again his fist smashed into flesh — but this time with such appalling force that he knocked Di Gamo out of his grasp.

Di Gamo fell back with a shriek, disappearing out of sight below the window. Olsen shrugged. With any luck the guy'd get so mad now he'd just up and spray the entire contents of his mag through the window, kill 'em all. Which would be a quicker and probably pleasanter way of going out than all crammed up in one corner with your clothes on fire.

Di Gamo sprang back into sight again. His nose was out of kilter with the rest of his face and there was a lot of blood over his lips and chin. His eyes were glazed; it was clear he'd wigged out utterly. He was clutching a grenade.

He was screaming obscenities but Olsen had flipped the off-switch up in his mind, and was now contemplating his own imminent destruction with something like serenity.

Which made what happened next all the more shocking.

Di Gamo wrenched out the grenade's pin and released the spoon. He was shivering violently, shuddering with unsuppressed rage and humiliation. It was almost as though someone had clasped him by the ankles and was shaking him about. But as his hand came up to toss the grenade in between the window-bars, his head exploded—disappeared in an eruption of blood and bone that sprayed Olsen's face.

On the surface Olsen looked like a phlegmatic man, stolid, slow-thinking—a good man to have with you as back-up in a tight corner, sure, but not the kind of a guy who could make a snap decision and act on it immediately thereafter. Which was tough shit on people who tagged him a dullard and tried to take advantage of him. Olsen was in fact a rapid thinker who could sum up a situation in a split second and do something about it even as the mental pictures were clicking through the relays of his brain.

As Di Gamo's head burst apart two thoughts flashed across Olsen's mind: one, maybe (wild as this might seem) help was at hand; and, two, Di Gamo's grenade was now live.

A third thought careered after the first two: maybe he *didn't* want to die just yet awhile.

He flung himself away from the windows just as Di Gamo's grenade exploded with a cracking detonation. Olsen, squeezing his eyes tight shut and curling himself into a ball, felt the floor shudder. The floor-boards were very hot, and it was with a sudden jolt that he realised that over the past few minutes he'd actually forgotten the fire, now only yards away.

He struggled to his feet, wincing at the scorching heat of the flames on his face. The smoke was now much denser, and he began to cough. He turned, looked at the window.

The outside wall had of course absorbed most of the

blast, but the bars had taken a pasting. They were mangled, twisted. He wondered how long ago this place had been erected, then dismissed the query as an idle one. For the grenade to have done any real and substantial damage, the concrete would have had to have been either very old or very new, but—just their crapping luck—this complex had neither been built a hundred years ago nor last week, and no way would that grenade-blast have weakened this concrete to the extent that it might be heaved down. Still, with the bars in the state they were now in it might be possible for O'Mara, say, or Doc Pepper—skinny fuckers that they were—to squeeze through, and that could mean . . .

A face appeared in the window. Olsen's mouth dropped open. It was a face he knew.

"Colonel . . ." he managed to get out ". . . *Hardin?*"

"Olsen? Sergeant Olsen?"

Olsen reached the window in two strides. He could make out other figures beyond the colonel, most of whom he'd never seen before, but in the hellish light he recognised Captain Marco, the pilot, and that meant there had to be something real heavy going on—something that could well be connected with the hullabaloo here tonight, or maybe something that had no link at all. Whatever, it confirmed his original notion that something was in the wind when he and the rest of his squad (as he now thought of them) had been transferred up here from Saigon only two days before.

Hardin was taking in what he could see through the wrecked window. He said, "The rest of the men here, Olsen?"

"Yessir." Olsen felt himself square away. "It's a little kind of sweaty in here right now, Colonel, but we frankly can't do a damn thing about it."

Even as he said this he began to cough again as thick smoke curled around him, cutting off for the moment his view of the window. He glanced to his left, saw that the bars of the holding-tank nearest the guard-room were now red-hot, actually glowing through the flames, and what had originally been the height of a newly-kindled brush fire—merely eating away at the boards at floor-level—was now ceiling-high. He was suddenly aware of a sickly-sweet smell wafting across his nostrils, and wondered who in hell could be cooking pork at such a time. Then he remembered Corporal Shelly.

"How long can you hold out?"

Olsen grinned crookedly.

"I gotta say, Colonel, not too damn long."

He watched as Hardin turned to Marco and another guy. He couldn't hear what was being said, but the other guy suddenly nodded and swung away at the trot. Captain Marco came up to the bars.

"Stay cool, Sarge."

"Kind of difficult, Captain."

Leroy Vogt, huddled like the rest in the corner furthest from the advancing holocaust, suddenly discovered he had his fingers crossed. Although the heat was now intense—searing to the exposed flesh of his face—he was shivering, his stomach a huge twisted-up knot of tension. It seemed inconceivable to him that they could be saved, even now.

A freak draught of air drove thick smoke at them, blinding them, causing them to gasp and cough.

Olsen reeled against the wall, choking, his eyes streaming. He bellowed with pain as flames curled long tongues at him, singeing his fatigues and searing the hair off his left arm.

The fire now seemed to be all around them; it was creeping along inside the tank from the exterior passageway, one side of the flow hugging the concrete wall, the other making quick greedy darts across the floor-boards towards those crouching in the corner.

Olsen grasped what remained of the bars and yelled, "We got no time at all, for Chrissakes!"

Hardin's face appeared again.

"Get back! Away from the window! Right back!"

Olsen half-turned his head, glanced at what seemed like a solid wall of roaring flames only six feet away from him at this side of the tank. The heat was blistering; the sound of the inferno almost deafening.

"Can't do it! We'll be in the fucking fire!"

"You've got to!" bawled Hardin. "Back as far as you can! On the floor! Heads down!"

Olsen hesitated for a split-second, torn between obeying Hardin or keeping as far from the flames as possible. Then he lunged for the others. He jerked O'Mara to his feet, shoved him towards the fire.

"Move, move! Away from the wall!"

Garrett stared up at him as though he'd gone stark mad. Garrett's face was smoke-blackened and the whites of his eyes seemed to bulge outwards.

"You're crazy!" he screamed. "We'll burn all the fucking quicker!"

Olsen tugged him up by his shirt and hit him, a crisp and solid uppercut to the point of the jaw. Garrett's head snapped back, then lolled to one side;

his eyes were glassy. Olsen stooped, heaved him over one shoulder and staggered towards the rest of the men, now crouching with their backs to the flames, heads down, their hands inter-locking over their necks. As Olsen dropped his human load the outside wall under the window bulged inwards with a thunderous roar, cracking apart and erupting towards him in a brilliant flare of light. A piece of concrete the size of a small boulder caught him on the shoulder and a shaft of pain seared across his neck and breast-bone. He lost his balance as smaller pieces of jagged stonework lashed his face and body, and the shock-wave threw him backwards on to the humped bodies of his men.

Dizzily he clambered to his feet. There was some kind of damn buzzer ringing in his ears, his head hurt, and he wasn't seeing too well, but one corner of his mind was advising him not to panic because his reactions would pull him out, had already automatically jumped into over-drive.

He bawled, "*Out, out, out, out, out . . .!*"—and kept on bawling the word as he kicked and heaved and wrenched at the dazed figures on the floor, herding them towards where a jagged hole had appeared in the wall. Smoke clogged his throat, and brick-dust—a choking combination. Still he worked like an automaton. Last was Garrett. Garrett's clothes were on fire. He reached down, turned him around, rolled him towards the hole, pounding at the flames with his bare hands. Then he shoved the man over the rubble and out of the tank, crawling after him. Hands clutched at his head and shoulders, tearing at his hair, wrenching him through.

Vaguely he was aware of a remembered thought that had crossed his mind hours ago: that it was a hot night.

Maybe it was still.

Out of the tank, however, it felt blissfully like he was in the middle of Alaska.

Chapter Seven

The man moved through the shadows like a crab, sideways, with a limping, shuffling gait. Every so often he would reach a spot where arc-lights glared down, piercing the blackness, and he would pause, wait—even though staying quite still was agony, more horrifyingly painful than keeping on the move. Then, after taking a deep, racking breath and clutching at his left side with a red right hand, he would scuttle across towards the next stretch of friendly darkness, his shoulder-blades almost quivering with tension, prime target for the hail of bullets all etched with his name.

He should be dead now anyway. He still couldn't understand how he'd escaped that one round fired at point-blank range. It was a miracle. But his luck couldn't last.

Could it?

The pain in his side was such that it was as though a huge, invisible animal had its teeth sunk deep into him, and he was dragging this beast along, and the teeth were sinking deeper and deeper into his vital organs with each staggering step he took. That was how it was now, and in a blurred kind of way he realised it would get no better.

Sounds penetrated his consciousness: shouts and cries. The firing had stopped—although there was still the isolated crack of a rifle or very short burst of automatic fire, probably triggered off by spooked sentries flung out on the perimeters to fill the wide gaps torn in the defences.

The *very* wide gaps.

But he was still trapped. He might be able to sneak out—there was a distinct probability; the sentries would be watching for guys coming in, not guys crawling out—but he wouldn't, he knew, last a day in the forest. Not one Goddamn day. Not with this chunk ripped out of his side. So he had to get out some other way.

And if his luck *did* manage to lurch on until he reached the repair-sheds—and maybe just a little way beyond—he had a better than even chance of making it.

If.

Colonel Chuck Welland said, "The fuckers took twenty minutes, no more, no less. But by God they used every second."

Hardin lit a cigarette.

"How many choppers?"

"We're still counting, but far as I can make out everything on the apron—everything that wasn't being worked on. *Every Goddamn Huey we have!*"

His tone was bitter. Whatever the reasons behind this, none of it was going to look too hot on his record. The near wipe-out of a Special Forces base, however small, had never happened before in six years of bloody conflict. Sure, Charlie had invaded bases, scores—hundreds—of times, but always—however much damage he'd inflicted—he'd had to jump back into the safety of the jungle with a very bloody nose and not much else. And it didn't make it any better that this present destruction hadn't been caused by Charlie at all.

Christ, from what Hardin had said, and from what he himself had seen with his own eyes, the "enemy" who'd wreaked such savage mayhem had been a Special Forces muster!

Not only that, it had been guys from *inside* the camp as well as outside.

It was just mind-numbing.

Welland winced as the medic knotted the bandage round his shoulder, where a stray round had punched through flesh, just missing the bone.

"I'll take another look at it later today, sir."

"Yeah, yeah," Welland muttered grouchily. The medic helped him on with his shirt—with a few grunts and minor curses from Welland—then left, picking his way carefully over the debris-strewn floor of the office and out through the hole in the wall where the door had once stood.

"Don't feel too bad about it," said Hardin.

"Don't feel too . . ." Welland's voice was an angry squawk that came oddly from the neat, trim-bodied man he was (though he looked anything but trim or neat right now, with his bruised and smoke-blackened face, torn shirt, dust- and mud-streaked fatigues). "Shit, John, they're gonna tear the balls off me for this. Toss me out on my can quicker'n you can spit. They'll say I'm not running a very tight ship here, and believe me I got a feeling they could be right."

"Look," said Hardin reasonably, "if it had been an EnVee attack, sure. But the fuckers who hit you, outside and in, were ours. Those inside set off mines and started throwing lead around, those outside took out all your perimeter defences. And that's the point." He jabbed the cigarette at Welland. "Charlie wouldn't have done that—Hell, Charlie *couldn't* have done that. But these guys knew where to go to ice the Listening Posts, knock off the sensors. They knew *exactly* where to go. Jesus, most of them—the raiders—probably used this base a hundred times before they lit out for the jungle and deserted. It's a whole different ballgame."

Welland shook his head dourly.

"And what *about* those guys who set off mines and threw the lead about? Before jumping in the choppers and heading Christ knows where. Hell, John, I'm commanding officer here. Why didn't I spot the undercurrents . . . feel the fucking pulse-rate rising?" He scraped a blood-smeared hand across his chin. "You know how many took off?"

"Tell me."

"We don't know exactly, yet, but the way it looks maybe as many as fifty men. That's nearly a quarter of my current complement, Goddamnit, not including mechanics, fitters, linesmen, and such." His voice rose to an outraged bellow. "That's a *fuck* of a lot of men, John!"

He rose stiffly to his feet, gazed sombrely down at his dust-coated desk.

"Any case," he went on, "whatever the reason, Command won't give a shit. They'll go by the rule-book, and there ain't no reasons for fuck-ups in there.

You know the way it is."

Hardin stubbed out his cigarette, glanced up at his dishevelled colleague.

"And did you?"

"Did I what?"

"Spot any undercurrents."

Welland sniffed long and hard.

"Nary a Goddamn one. Been racking my brain for the past half-hour, but I can't even put my finger on the tiniest fucking hint of a hint that everything wasn't entirely tight." A bleak smile licked at his lips. "I'll probably find out everyone else knew about it. It's the way of things. I got already word that one of my sergeants—guy called Fuller—sniffed something in the wind but dismissed the whole idea of guys deserting in droves because he thought it was too fucking ludicrous for words. Thought it was some kind of joke, until it all started happening."

"Joe Fuller?"

"Yeah."

"Solid guy."

"Sure. Just wish he hadn't been so damn solid between the ears and a mite more forthcoming. Still, he and the guys down in the comm-hut did manage to salvage something from the wreck—the only two live ones, although one of those got beat up pretty bad."

Hardin shook his head irritably.

"Shit, only *two* prisoners?"

"Yeah, and the one who's still conscious says he had no idea where they were gonna be heading for, once they were in the air. I got a couple of medics working on him."

"He could be lying. On the other hand, he could be

telling the truth. Whatever, I don't have any time to wait around until he cracks."

"It was a pro job," said Welland ruefully.

"That's the whole point. Special Forces are pros. That's what makes these guys so fucking dangerous."

"Not even the stiffs did they leave behind. What they must've done was pick up the dead and wounded as they went along—took 'em with 'em in the choppers." Welland laughed bleakly. "A very sanitary bunch."

"And they left no one behind? At all?"

"Uh-uh." Welland rummaged in one of his drawers, pulled out a cigar. He lit it one-handed. "Was the first move I made just before you bounced in—search for survivors, guys who missed the boat. I got another, heavier sweep going now, just in case, but it sure seems like all the raiders and the deserters, and the bodies, made it to the choppers in time."

Corporal Koentiz heard the metallic crash behind him in the deep shadows of the shed and sprang round, jabbing his Armalite in the direction of the sound and yelling *"Halt! Don' move!"*

He could see nothing but darkness. His eyes were adjusting, but slowly. He'd only just entered the building from the landing-area, now washed with bright lights, and as yet he could not even distinguish the darker shapes of solid objects against the general blackness.

He shouted *"Move towards the main door, cocksucker, or I'm gonna spray the whole fuckin' shed!"*

Still there was nothing. No sound, no movement. Koenitz felt a frizz of alarm running up his spine and wondered whether he ought to fire and the hell with it. Trouble was, there was no knowing what he might hit if he simply opened up. Drums of gasoline, crates of ammo, anything. He could blow his nuts away, add to the scores of fires raging outside over the rest of the base, just by giving the M-16's trigger a slight squeeze.

Whoever was in here could not see him, because he'd made sure, on entering, that he was not silhouetted against the door or any of the tiny windows. On the other hand, whoever was in here had maybe been here for a while . . had had time to adjust.

Jesus! Maybe whoever was in here *could* see him!

He began to sweat. The silence extended. Vague shapes began to shift into focus, but nothing that looked human. And nothing that moved.

This was a crazy business altogether. He didn't know the in and outs of it, but from what he could make out the incredible raid that had just hit them had been mounted by *Americans*. And it wasn't some kind of heavy Special Forces battle-test either; the burning huts, the destroyed vehicles, and, more to the point; the bodies that now littered the camp testified to that. In any case, he thought, he had had firsthand experience of the total shambles that, for a half hour or so, had gripped the camp. Hadn't he come running out of his hut at the first explosions and been shot at by Kowalski—*Kowalski*, damn it: a guy he'd partnered on at least two raids into Laos—who'd suddenly appeared from the direction of one of the howitzer emplacements?

He'd managed to dive for cover—feeling almost whoozy with shock—but after that things had just gone from bad to worse to right out demented. No one knew what the hell was going on, and after about five minutes no one even knew who was who. It had been, and this no one could deny, an all-time high in shit-storms.

Koenitz's sight had now fully adjusted, but as his eyes flicked from left to right and back again, he could still see nothing that remotely resembled a human figure amongst the boxes and crates and drums that were stacked up at the far end of the shed.

Could be it had just been something that had been dislodged naturally, for one reason or another. A small box, maybe, teetering on the edge of one of those crowded workbenches and crashing to the ground when he'd entered?

He couldn't believe it.

And he was just about to take a step forward when the gun-barrel pressed coldly into the nape of his neck.

He froze.

"Drop the gun or I'll blow your head off."

The voice was hoarse, rasping. Koenitz, even in his state of shock, thought he recognised pain there.

"Drop it!"

Koenitz opened his fingers, not moving any other part of his body, and dropped the M-16 on the ground. It fell clumsily, clattered away from him across the concrete.

"Put your hands round the back of your neck. Clasp 'em."

Koenitz did as he was told. He still did not attempt to move, did not even try to shift his feet. He was thinking of what one single round could do, fired through the back of his neck.

"Gimme some answers. All the Hueys here gone, right?"

"Yeah," croaked Koenitz.

"Yer a liar!"

Koenitz's head jerked forward as the gun-barrel nudged hard into his flesh.

"They've all gone, Goddamnit!" he got out. "The guys . . . the raiders . . . whoever, they took 'em."

"The one up near the hutments?"

"Christ, something else. I dunno. That one came down as all the rest were going up. Got holed in the gas-tank, what I heard."

"Okay." Another nudge. "Just don't forget things, right? Just tell me everything. Don't crap me around."

"Sure, sure."

"They only took Hueys, yeah?"

"That's it. The Loaches were parked in the hangars."

"What about the Loach that's out back?"

Koenitz swallowed.

"Outta commission."

This time it was not a nudge but a savage blow. Koenitz squealed as the gun-barrel thudded into his occipital bone.

"You are one Goddamn fuckstick of a *liar!*" hissed the voice. "I been over it. She's sweet."

"For Chrissake! How the fuck do I know how it is?" Koenitz's bowels were churning. "You say it's sweet, it's sweet."

"Right." The voice chuckled throatily. "Sweet as a nut, shithead. And you know what you're gonna do?"

"No, I dunno. I dunno."

"You're gonna crank me outta this shit-hole, is what you're gonna do."

"I feel as though a lot of this is maybe my fault," said Hardin.

He stared bleakly at the destruction that lay all round him, the chaos that still reigned across the base.

Ahead, just beyond where a sheet of pierced-steel planking, pitted and burn-blasted black on one side, stuck up out of the ground at an angle, medics were dragging dead men from out of the bunker of a howitzer emplacement. The medics looked dispirited.

A fire-truck raced by, heading for the chopper apron, where black smoke rose into the dawn sky in a thick, ugly column. More fire-fighters were laying down a blanket of foam over blocks of rubble, or what could have been a giant's set of toy-bricks, kicked over in a temper-tantrum, but was in fact all that remained of the cookhouse and stores. Weary men, smoke-smeared and bandaged, trudged off to the rear, some carrying buckets of sand; walking wounded making themselves useful in a useless situation.

"Should've stayed in the air, caught 'em as they came up. Could've crucified the bastards."

Welland shrugged, then grunted angrily as pain flared down his left arm and up again from the wound in his shoulder.

"Bullshit, John, and you know it," he muttered. "Not your fault a stray holed you. Lucky it didn't blow you out totally."

Hardin coughed at the smoke-soured air that rasped at the back of his throat.

"How long will it take to get fixed?"

Welland made to shrug again, but remembered not to just in time.

"Not too long. I got men working on it now." He laughed bitterly. "It's the only operational heavy chopper on the Base, as of a couple of hours ago. We got some baby Loaches and two CH-54 lifters, but no way are they going to be of use to you. Damn lucky," he said thoughtfully, "you managed to get your men out of the brig."

"We had some *plastique*. It was the only way. I need those guys. They're the only outfit I have."

Welland caught the unspoken thought which ran through Hardin's mind, and was quite clearly outlined on his face: Small and ineffectual as it may be.

"Why in God's name didn't they give you a bigger force, a force with more clout, for Christ's sake? Those guys are the guys you brought out of the jungle. Jail-birds."

Hardin grinned sourly.

"You could say it's Command's revenge for past misdemeanors," he said.

"Jesus."

"It's a cruel world, Chuck."

"No lie."

Welland pondered the problem as they picked their way over spaghetti trails of canvas hosepipe, taut with water, across grass that was scorched black and poked with craters, past still-glowing steel skeletons of trucks and jeeps.

"Listen," he said suddenly, "I can maybe shove some men your way. We can forget about the paperwork; got too many other things to worry about right now."

Hardin said, slightly warily, "I'd appreciate that."

"Yeah." Welland had a self-absorbed expression on his face. "Sarge Fuller, now. Solid guy, like you said. A real roisterer in a firefight. You could maybe do with a radioman, too. Corporal Lantry is one I have in mind. Sure knows his networks. And then," he took a thoughtful pull at his cigar, "seeing as how you might be a little top-heavy on Sergeants, I could ease Lieutenant Comeraro into the squad. Chain of command. You'd need that." The cigar-tip burned redly as he took another slow drag at it. "Yeah. One other guy, let's say. Specialist 5th Class Parrish. Been on a few patrols; knows how to handle his shit." He glanced across at Hardin. "How's that sound, John?"

"Sounds fine to me," said Hardin.

This mood of sudden altruism on Chuck Welland's part didn't fool him for a moment. Although he didn't know the other three guys, he recognised that Welland was, in giving him Fuller, getting rid of—if only on a short-term basis—a source of potential embarrassment. Welland had said something to the effect that Fuller had somehow picked up on disgruntled undercurrents amongst the men, and the fact that he hadn't informed Welland was beside the point. If a sergeant could spot the rot, why not Welland? In the enquiry which was doubtless being organised even now at Command HQ (news of the disaster having already been radioed out on a secure line, once the activities of the jammer had ceased), this question would be high on the list. Welland could clearly well do without the presence of Sergeant Fuller just at the moment.

It was even possible that Welland hoped Sarge

Fuller would get his fool head shot off, tagging along behind Hardin on this crazy mission.

Hurrying footsteps from behind made both men turn. The newcomer was Welland's number two, Major Bill Stroklund. Stroklund had a field dressing over one eye, streaks of dried blood down his face. He looked puzzled.

"They found what could be the jammer, a half mile into the forest."

"Could be?" queried Welland.

"Almost certainly, and seems like it was highly Goddamn sophisticated."

"Have to be," said Hardin, "to blank out the entire web for miles."

"Was?" Welland was becoming irritated. "*Was* sophisticated?"

"Yeah, heavy-duty truck equipment in the back. But they blew it."

"Jesus," grunted Welland, "wish to hell we had their quartermaster, if the mothers can afford to drop materiél like that."

"Also found some more men from the forward Listening Posts, sir."

Welland glanced up, catching something extra in the man's tone.

"So give me the bad news."

"We haven't found their heads yet."

"*Christ!*" Welland exploded. "What are these fuckers—animals?"

A tide of anger was welling up inside of Hardin, too.

"Just going about their lawful business, Chuck," he said tightly. "You teach 'em it's cool to lop Charlie's head off, why not our guys' heads? What's the difference? They've gone rogue—you expect them to act any other way?"

Welland glared at him, his mouth working but only incomprehensible noises coming out.

"Still," Hardin plunged on, "it does kind of prove the point that these guys have to be nailed right fast. They *are* insane. They're mad dogs." He gestured round at the devastation. "Indiscriminate slaughter. Some of these stiffs might well have joined the renegades, who knows? But they weren't even given the option. They weren't even . . ."

He didn't finish. A series of thudding blasts erupted from the direction of the chopper sheds, cutting him off. Oily smoke boiled up into the murky air.

"Aw, *shit!*" snarled Welland. "Now what?"

They began running across the apron, and as they passed Hardin's Huey, they each became aware of the high-pitched whining clatter of an engine bursting into roaring life. Ahead, a tiny Loach scout suddenly soared up into the air through the smoke-cloud, then raced away across the far end of the Base, disappearing over the trees.

Hardin skidded to a halt, wheeled round, sprinted back to the Huey. He wasn't interested in what had happened. That was instant past-history; let Welland sort out the details. He looked for, spotted, then grabbed the sergeant in charge of the repair-squad.

"How long on this?"

The man shrugged dubiously.

"Jeeze, Colonel, I dunno. You took more hits than you maybe thought. To do a good job . . ."

"I don't want a good job," snapped Hardin, "I want a fast job. I want this crate patched in four minutes." He jabbed a finger at the man's chest. *"Dead!"*

Chapter Eight

The chopper shadow raced ahead of them pursued by the rearing sun. To the left was an unbroken canopy of green; to the right wooded ridges became heights that became hills that in their turn soared to ragged-peaked sierras. Where the sun touched tree-tops on the uplands steam rose from the jungle like a fine fog; the valleys huddled in deep shadow still.

"Bastard could be anywhere," said Marco over the intercom.

"Keep heading west," said Hardin.

"Could be over the hills an' far away."

"Whatever."

He half-turned in the bucket-seat immediately behind Marco and glanced at his squad, now somewhat beefed up.

Lieutenant Comeraro, Parrish and the radio-man Corporal Lantry were there on recommendation; he knew nothing of their form. But although he figured that Chuck Welland might, for one reason or another, have wanted to get rid of them, he knew it wouldn't have been because they were useless. Sergeant Fuller was known to him: a man with 20 years' experience of killing, a man the jungle could not break. Pepper the medic, Sergeant Olsen, Vogt, O'Mara, and the brutish Garrett. Well, Olsen and Garrett were good and solid in a desperate situation, and Olsen would ride herd on the rest well enough, push them up to scratch if things got really hairy. And that left Marco and his crew—Hanks and Colenso, the gunner—who, in any case, were not a part of the mission, save in that they were acting as ferryman.

Hardin hoped that somewhere out front they would catch a sighting of the Loach, watch it drop down on the hidden sanctuary.

Not that that would solve too many problems. Only the most immediate.

The biggest problem after that was what to do when they got there, positively identified and actually reached the target. Radioing its position back and letting a bunch of B-52s turn it into a wasteland was not the answer. Halderling didn't want that. Not immediately. Nor did he want to send a battalion or two over in a massive assault. That might turn out to be too messy: too many men could get killed; too many men might escape. He wanted the kingpin of the operation lifted and brought back for secret trial, and he wanted his materiél returned. *Then* the bombers could make the hit.

Hell of a task for ten men Hardin thought.

Not grabbing the mastermind, whoever he was; that could turn out to be a sweet in-and-out job. It was the materiél that bothered him—the guns, ammo, stores, choppers. How in God's name was he going to pull that stuff out with only ten men?

"Hey I got him!"

Marco's voice was excited. Hardin clutched the back of the black's seat as the Huey canted over to the

161

left and dropped in a sliding sweep. He got to his feet and eased himself between the two front seats.

Marco jabbed a finger downwards, and Hardin saw, far below, the tiny Loach buried nose-deep in the trees, its tail boom sticking up like a stumpy radio beacon.

"Look like another good idea up the spout," said Marco cheerfully. "Less all this," he gestured expansively at the sea of greenery that stretched away to the south, "their sanctuary."

To the north Hardin saw narrow-necked valleys cutting into the densely wooded foothills; beyond were high sawtooth ridges marching away into the distance.

"If it is," he said, "that's a novel way of parking his chopper. Can we go down?"

Hanks gestured with his thumb.

"We just flew over a clearing. Could be he was making for that and overshot."

"Why would he overshoot?"

Hanks shrugged.

Marco pulled up on the collective to give the blades more bite and eased off on the throttle. The Huey rose high. He turned then swooped down over the trees, banking slightly as a small clearing slid into view. He circled it twice—his eyes taking in knee-high elephant grass, bushes, a clump of banana trees to one side, but nothing that seemed at all out of place—then began spiralling until the altimeter showed 50 metres and he could feel the ground effect, as though he was sinking into a quagmire. Seconds later the chopper sat down bumpily amidst the flattened grass.

While Colenso glared out at the encircling jungle and swung his M-60 round in lazy arcs at the port door, Comeraro jumped out the other side, followed by Fuller, Lantry and Parrish. Covered by Olsen and Garrett, each with M-16s, they sprinted across the clearing, ducking low, and dived into the tangled green wall. The *wap-wap* of the Huey's rotors died; ceased altogether. Hardin listened to the sound of the jungle: the howls of terrified monkeys, the screech of parrots. He heard the gruff cough of a tiger, but it was some way away, the sound carrying maybe a mile or more on the morning air. Slowly, the dwellers of the forest returned to their normal preoccupations — hunting, fighting, killing; whatever else they'd been doing minutes before — satisfied that this giant bird meant them no immediate harm.

Hardin reached for the AK-47 he'd picked up on a previous mission, tapped Marco on the shoulder, said "Look after the shop," then nodded to Olsen and Garrett.

Their progress through the 300 yards or so of dense jungle was not fast. All three used machets honed to a razor-edge on the undergrowth, mostly bamboo and elephant grass ten feet high. They worked in shifts, one man hacking at the tangled, matted wall, the other two heaving it down bodily while the first man rested. Then one of the others took over. In all it took nearly forty sweaty, lung-racking minutes to reach the crashed Loach.

The tiny scout was wedged securely in the trees, its plexiglas canopy shattered by the smack-down impact, its blades twisted and bent. Even from where they were they could see the cockpit was empty.

Hardin gazed around in the high-light.

"So where is he? Did he climb out, or is he dead?"

"If he's dead," said Garrett, "the stiff's gotta be around somewhere. Decomposition hits you fast in this crappy climate, but not that fast."

Olsen had ventured further into the clinging tangle of vines and bamboo. He suddenly turned.

"Colonel!"

Hardin stepped quickly across and stared down at the twisted body. The top of the cervical vertebrae bulged outwards like a tent-pole against the taut flesh at the man's neck; his head lolled sideways, resting on a tree-root. His face was a bloody mask. Hardin reached down for the dangling ID tags.

"Koenitz." He shrugged. "Whoever he was. Came straight out the windscreen on impact, you bet. Like Captain Marco said, another good idea up the spout. This guy is going to be leading us nowhere."

"Hey, Colonel!"

Garrett was a couple of yards away, bending over some bushes. He pulled branches aside and Hardin saw scarlet splashes on the wide, serrated-edged leaves. He leaned down, touched them. The tips of his fingers came away wet.

"More over here, sir," grunted Olsen, squatting under the trees.

"Shit!" Garrett stared down at what was in fact a small pool of blood. "This fucker's pushing a gusher!"

"How far can he go?" pondered Hardin.

Olsen pushed onwards a little way through a less dense clump of bamboo, following the trail of specks and splashes of red, easily spotted against the lighter green of the vegetation.

"I gotta say, Colonel, not too damn far. Like Garret says, this boy is spouting. With all respect, sir, the fucker could be feet away."

But as Hardin made to follow him, the first ragged chorus of automatic shots crackled off behind them.

The man watched them go, trying not to laugh. There was a bloody foam on his lips; trails of deeper, richer crimson ran down his chin, trickling sluggishly but steadily through the tangled scrub of his beard.

He was lying on his right side with his right arm jammed underneath him, the hand clamped into his left side, just below the ribs. The hand was like a surgeon's glove, slick and wet and red.

He was trying not to laugh because although everything seemed so funny, every time he did laugh it hurt. It hurt so unbelievably badly that the shock—the jolt of agony after each quiver of his stomach—nearly caused him to faint. The beast wasn't merely attached to him now, it was actually eating him, its teeth like knives.

He was beginning to hallucinate, too. Sound was only getting through to him in fits and starts, and the men crashing away from him through the bamboo and creepers seemed to be taking the hell of a time going. In fact they seemed to be running on the spot, their legs pumping up and down but their bodies not moving. Then they seemed to be moving towards him again, backwards. Then they receded into the dark tunnel that had suddenly and magically appeared around them. Then returned, faster this time, then shot away again. Then . . .

The man mumbled a curse which echoed around inside his head as though he was hearing it in a vast, vaulted cavern. He closed his eyes, nuzzled his cheek against the ground.

Suddenly, it wasn't funny any more.

Nothing was funny any more. There was only a soulsucking weariness, creeping through his system like a black tide. And as he relaxed and began to drift he felt the pain begin to flow slowly away from him, ooze out of his limbs and bones, seep through the pores of his skin and out into the soggy moss of the forest floor.

He was dimly aware that he was lying on something—a log, maybe, a dead branch—that was making his position slightly uncomfortable. Only slightly, but enough to cause him to consider trying to shift whatever the hell it was so that he could at last drift off in comfort.

He seemed to have lost his right arm, so his left hand would have to do. It took a long time to drag it round, humped at the elbow, but at last he could feel what seemed like some kind of lump sticking into his side. He grasped it; made to shove it aside . . .

. . . And instantly a shaft of pure agony shot across every nerve-end on his body, as though he was being roasted with a flame-thrower. He tried to scream—but all that came out was a thick, wheezing, bubbling sound, as the intense and excruciating pain wrenched him out of his stupor. Confused images fled through his mind, a dark kaleidoscopic turmoil of figures falling and spinning away from him against a back-cloth of roaring fire and vivid explosions. And one man's face superimposed, eerily highlighted by the flickering flames: a mask of sneering scorn.

Hatred boiled through him like molten magma about to spew upwards out of the nethermost pits of the earth. He grunted, bared his teeth at the pain, opened his eyes. All trace of the deadly lassitude which had threatened to wash over him completely had vanished. His mind and his vision were clear. All he could think of now was to get up, plough on through the jungle, reach his destination.

He scrabbled at dead leaves and dug his fingers into the wet earth, heaving himself over on to his back.

And found himself staring up into two grinning yellow faces.

The only other thing he registered was the barrel of an assault rifle pointing down at him, before he launched himself upwards with a throaty howl of animal-like fury.

Hardin came to a dead halt at the crouch. He froze as though he'd been turned to stone. He let his breath out slowly, although his brain was racing with the velocity of a high-speed train.

From the direction of the clearing the sounds of battle were now more intense. Someone was using a machine-gun—probably Colenso—in a highly professional manner, throwing off short but deadly bursts. Threading through this heavy hammering noise Hardin recognised the high-pitched, clean chatter of Kalashnikov assault rifles, and the deeper, blunter stammer of Armalites.

But from where he was Hardin could see nothing of the clearing at all—mainly because five yards away his view was blocked by bushes and two NVA infantryman, one of whom was hefting an RPG-7 rocket-launcher up to his shoulder.

Hardin began to sweat, appalled. He had no doubt

that the NVA's target was the chopper, but this was like cracking a nut with a mighty sledge. Although the PG-7 grenade was percussion-fired it had a secondary-boost rocket motor which automatically fired after the grenade had sped about ten yards through the air. The range after that was anything up to around 300 yards, but since the chopper could only be, at most, 15 yards beyond the bushes the explosions would be devastating. The chopper and all inside it would be, literally, quite blown away.

He was suddenly aware that the nose of an M-16 was edging forward beside him. His hand went out fast, clamped itself round the barrel.

Garrett hissed in his ear, "We can take 'em. Easy."

Hardin shook his head.

"No noise."

His hand unclasped, slid behind him, and he flicked up the tabs of his knife-sheath. He eased the weapon out, balancing its length on his palm. His arm went back then snapped forward like a piston. The eight-inch blade thudded into the rocket-man's back up to the hilt and the impact sent him sprawling forwards on his face, the launcher tumbling from his grasp.

The second man didn't have time to turn; he didn't even have time to yell. Almost as the knife left Hardin's grasp, Garrett had sprung forward, wielding his rifle like a club. The butt smacked into the side of the man's neck and he crashed down into the grass.

Hardin jumped forward and dived for the ground; peered out from beside the bush. Ahead was the chopper. Colenso had dragged his MG to the other side of the cabin and was shooting into the jungle; this side he could see Vogt, crouching beside the skids, M-16 thrust out in front of him. Vogt was staring straight at him, or at least in his direction. To Vogt's right, Hardin could just make out O'Mara in the long grass, firing off bursts at the trees, where flickers of flame stabbed back. He couldn't see Marco.

Marco was helpless, of course; was having to sweat it out. However fast he could lift off, the EnVees would nail him, take his rotors out with a long burst of MG-fire and bring him crashing back to earth. It was an uncool situation.

"How many you think there are, Colonel?"

That was Olsen, dropping down beside him. Hardin shrugged briefly.

"Who knows? Could be a Goddamn regiment hidden out there, but I doubt it. They'd've rushed the chopper by now. Most of them are the other side of the clearing."

"Yeah," said Garrett, "right where that Lieutenant Comeraro and his squad are. Bye-bye Lieutenant Comeraro."

"But they don't know we're here," said Hardin.

"Does it actually make any fucking difference?" grunted Garrett.

"Actually, it does," Hardin gestured sideways with his head. "Eleven o'clock left. EnVee group massing. And Vogt's looking the other Goddamn way."

Hidden by thick frontal foliage, shapes were materialising under the trees.

"But don't they know that any minute now it's gonna be fireball-time for the chopper?"

"Maybe that rocket-man was sighting up, just in case, when I hit him. Maybe he wasn't aiming to fire at all. Whatever, those punks are going to be flooding out any damn second." He tapped Olsen's shoulder. "Round the back about ten yards, fast as you like." Olsen squirmed off through the underbrush. Hardin turned to Garrett. "When they come out, hit 'em hard. I'm gonna be running for the bird."

A wolfish expression spread itself across Garrett's craggy features.

"Texbook stuff, huh, Colonel? A sweet enfilade."

Hardin crouched up on one knee, the toe of his boot dug hard into the earth. He was trying to count numbers, but it was difficult; the men he could see kept shifting around in the gloom. Then he muttered "This is it!" as fire from the trees lashed the chopper's nose. It went on for five seconds, and then the bushes sprouted human beings. Hardin sprang out of cover like a sprinter off the block, hearing Garrett's Armalite rattling off its staccato death-song, joined an instant later by a searing blast of rounds from Olsen's direction.

As he ran Hardin pumped bullets in a tight arc to his left and saw EnVee grunts go down like pins in an alley. Those behind were running and yelling, but the yells turned to screams when two grenades sailed out the trees and exploded in front of them, hurling them back with a roaring detonation and a red-cored eruption of fire. Hardin folded his gun into his stomach and dived forward the rest of the way in a head-over-heels roll that slammed him into Leroy Vogt. Both of them bumped over the Huey's skids as MG tracer arced over the spot where they'd been.

Hardin disentangled himself from the younger man and barked "Get the MG!" as, twisting round, he slid under the body of the chopper. Both he and Vogt poured fire at where the tracer was coming from, their rounds raking across the thick green canopy of the jungle-edge, flaying leaves, ripping branches to shreds of wood-pulp. The MG stopped.

But the rest of the weaponry homed-in on the sitting-duck helicopter didn't. If anything the decibel-level was hitched up several notches as lead from all directions pounded at the machine, smashing the plexiglas canopy, hammering along the fuselage, ricocheting off struts and panels with an appalling clamour.

Then, above the storm of sound, a voice boomed tinnily across the clearing.

"Dung lai!"

The noise-level dropped to zero. Only birds screeched in outrage in the vacuum of silence.

Crouching under the chopper, Hardin heard Frank Marco's voice above him.

"When the man say stop, they stop? How you doin', Hardin? Some dude got a bullhorn out there, an' I got a feeling that bad news for us."

Hardin grinned wryly. The same thought was crossing his own mind. He wondered what would happen if he tried to swing himself up into the chopper interior. He wondered what had happened to O'Mara. Not to mention Garrett and Olsen. Then he ceased to wonder about anything as the bullhorn-distorted voice crackled out again.

"Colonel Hardin. I have four of your men. Let us talk."

Above him in the chopper, he heard Marco say, "Hot *damn!* What the fuck *is* this? Is we set up?"

171

Hardin didn't know. He couldn't even begin to figure the situation out. The voice was totally unrecognisable through the loud-hailer—no help there—but in any case he still couldn't for the life of him think who of the enemy would know his name. And one thing was for sure, Comeraro and his men wouldn't have let it out.

It would be simple to destroy you. I have many more men. Many more. Let us talk. Our objectives may be similar."

"You gonna talk?" came Marco's voice.

"Either that, or lie here and get creamed."

"No contest," agreed Marco.

Hardin wriggled out from under the belly of the chopper, got to his feet. He slung his AK-47 and half-turned to call in the direction of Olsen and Garret.

"Don't fire."

He padded across the clearing towards the far side, and as he did so a small group of EnVees emerged from the trees. Heading them was a dapper little man in his late 40s, maybe early 50s, wearing an immaculately pressed uniform but no topee. He smiled a wide, jolly smile at Hardin and held out both hands. Hardin's stomach flipped over backwards, then righted itself.

He did know the man. Sure, he knew him. He knew him so well that the last time they'd met, the guy had split a bottle of 1962 Marguax with him. Then had proceeded to dump buckets of water down his throat.

He was an EnVee top brass—a *thieu tuong*, equivalent of a U.S. major-general.

His name was Hoang Van Tho.

Despite the jolly smile, he was a very tough and

vicious cookie indeed.

Hoang Van Tho said, a shade regretfully, "No wine today, I am afraid, Colonel. Unlike the last occasion we met."

Hardin shrugged.

"The wine was good. I didn't care for the chaser."

Tho laughed, a rich, deep-bellied chuckle of genuine amusement.

"That was the impression I received. You left in something of a hurry."

You are not kidding, Hardin thought.

Hoang Van Tho had been a part of the Dempsey business. He had been pulled out of the abortive Paris Peace Talks by his superiors and sent back to South East Asia, to take delivery of the information Dempsey had been selling to the enemy. Hardin, with the package of highly sensitive documents on him, had fought a near-last ditch battle with Tho's men in a Laotian ville before Chuck Welland's choppers had dropped in and napalmed the place. All in all, it had been a close thing.*

Hardin had not expected to see Tho ever again. The fact that he was now facing him across a shaky table in a tent open on three sides with scores of EnVees hanging around outside and his own men bunched up and guarded out of the now fully-risen sun some way away merely provided strong back-up to a theory he'd long held and often mooted that life went in circles. But that was beside the point.

Tho said, "Well, Colonel, despite our past differ-

*See *GUNSHIPS: The Killing Zone* by Jack Hamilton Teed.

ences, it is good to see you again."

"I'm not sure the feeling's mutual."

The Vietnamese waved a hand airily.

"You can surely afford to be magnanimous? After all, last time you were the winner."

"Now it looks like I'm the loser."

"These things are relative."

As he said this a group of men broke through the circle and advanced toward Tho. One was staggering, helped along by the rest. He looked as though he'd taken two or three trips through a harvester. His face was bloody, his tunic in rags. One of his eyes were closed completely.

Tho stared at the sight and Hardin saw his expression tighten. He guessed that whatever this was, the Vietnamese knew nothing about it, and was, moreover, extremely angry.

The man started to jabber in Vietnamese, but Tho cut him off abruptly. Without even glancing at Hardin he pushed the man backwards, out of earshot.

Hardin lit a cigarette, sipped at the water the *thieu tuong* had provided for him. The water was pure and cool, tasted like some kind of mineral water, maybe French or Italian. That figured. Tho had expensive tastes, and, seemingly, the clout to indulge them.

He thought about what the man had gabbled out before he'd been hustled away. Hardin could speak Vietnamese like — and probably better than — a native, but the guy had been almost delirious, certainly in a state of considerable shock. He'd caught the words "madman" and "crazy animal" and had gotten the gist of some kind of wild attack. Beyond that was only speculation. He sipped more water and didn't bother

174

speculating; Tho would either tell him about it or would not tell him about it. In any case, on the face of it whatever had happened had nothing to do with him.

After about ten minutes Tho returned. He sat down heavily in his chair, stared at Hardin. The smile had gone from his face and there was only disinterest there, a cold detachment, as though Hardin was the prize specimen in an over-enthusiastic colleague's collection of fauna, for which Tho himself had no enthusiasm whatsoever.

"Your men fight like wild beasts," he said in a neutral voice.

"Your guys don't exactly use kid-glove tactics," countered Hardin in a voice that was just as colourless.

"You are not worried about him?"

"Worried about who?"

"From what I gather, he had lost much blood."

"Much blood?" Hardin was about to glance across at where his men were corraled, when he remembered. "Oh. Yeah. Much blood."

Tho half-turned, snapped his fingers once. An orderly trotted across with a large aluminum bucket stuffed with ice. Embedded in the ice was a bottle of Evian water. Tho nodded and the orderly unsnapped the cap and poured out more; Hardin first, Tho second. Hardin didn't bother commenting on the utter strangeness of the situation.

Tho took a sip at his glass, then a long pull. He said, "And then here is the scout helicopter in the jungle, and the dead man beside it."

"Yeah."

"I ask myself why you are here, Colonel."

"I sometimes ask myself the same question, Major-General."

Tho laughed. Suddenly, he seemed relaxed again.

"I do not believe the man who attacked my men was of your party."

"Oh?"

"Despite the fact that he appeared to be in very bad condition, he killed one of my men with a single blow to the neck and, as you will have noticed, seriously wounded the other."

"To put it mildly."

"My man said the American had the strength of ten."

"Probably because his heart was pure."

"I suspect you were following him."

"I suspect you may have something there."

"It is my opinion, Colonel, that this man was fleeing to a certain valley very close to where we are now, where are gathered others of like mind and disposition."

"That's an interesting way of putting it," said Hardin.

He took a final drag at his cigarette then dropped it to the ground and heeled it. Through the divine revelation of hard experience—both of men and of all kinds of situations—he suddenly realised that if the renegades were causing Special Forces problems, it followed they were causing the enemy problems, too. After all, that was what they were there for; that was why they'd gone rogue. And if they were causing the EnVees even half the hassles they were causing U.S. High Command, the EnVees would have to be extremely pissed about it.

So why hadn't the EnVees creamed them?

"Let me show you something, Colonel," said Hoang Van Tho.

Chapter Nine

The heads hung from the trees like cocoanuts from the stall of a poverty-stricken travelling carnie. On each, the thick black glossy hair had been pulled back into a topknot, tied with thin cord, attached to a branch. They revolved slowly one way, then back again as the cords payed out. They were placed so close together that every time a random breeze caught the end pair they bumped, one against the other, setting off a bobbing, thudding chain reaction along the line. On all the heads the ears had been neatly sliced off, and the noses; small pieces of wood had been wedged into each mouth so that it gaped open, revealing the fact that the teeth had been extracted — though not neatly at all — and the tongues had been torn out, or cut off, too. There were nine heads in all, glazed-eyed and crusted with recently dried blood. Fat flies gorged on them.

"We have not found the bodies yet," said Hoang Van Tho, then shrugged. "But then we have not looked very closely."

Hardin glanced at Tho's entourage — four officers and a dozen guards. All had impassive faces. He offered Tho a cigarette, but the Vietnamese shook his head. Hardin put the crumpled pack away without taking one himself, his fingers touching the tiny linen bag as they thrust downwards into his breast pocket. That sparked off a weirdly out of context picture of Eileen Satkis's lightly-tanned limbs, and the juxtaposition of that and what he was now gazing at was gruesome indeed. Yet he almost had to physically shake himself to shift the memory away.

"With all due respect, as a sergeant of mine has a habit of saying," he said carefully, "this is a kind of commonplace sight."

Tho's face flushed with anger.

"It is uncivilised," he hissed, thrusting his face close to Hardin's. *"Barbaric!"*

Hardin made no attempt to placate him. All this was outward show on Tho's part; he knew it, Tho knew it. And Tho knew he knew it. Atrocities of this nature were almost a part of the natural order of things in Vietnam. Both sides indulged in them, often with an enthusiasm that would have been better expended on other areas of the war altogether. The fact was, Tho had only shown him these grisly objects in order to be able to bawl him out in front of his men. Having gotten that out of the way, could be they'd get down to the serious stuff.

"This is what their honchos teach them!" Tho suddenly screamed at his men, gesturing energetically at the swinging bobbing heads. "This is the freedom the treacherous United States confers on our peace-loving land! They torture and rape our women! They mutilate our young men, so fierce and so proud to fight for their birthrights! But the imperialists shall never subjugate us! Their violence, their brutality, their despicable banditry and rapine only serve to make us stronger! Only serve to put steel into our hearts and minds! Only serve to ensure that *we* shall destroy *them!*" He went on like this for some minutes.

Hardin watched Tho's men out of the corner of his eye and noted that their wooden, almost doltish expressions were now quite transformed. Real enthusiasm almost sparked from their eyes. They were drinking in Tho's tirade as though the *thieu-tuong* was speaking words that had never been spoken before in the history of mankind. It was quite extraordinary. Hardin tried to recall when he'd last seen a group of grunts so truly metamorphosised by a peroration that—intellectually, at any rate—was nothing more than a farrago of simplistic, rabble-rousing junk. Of course, he couldn't. And nor was it because these were peasants and the U.S. grunts were, generally speaking, not. In fact, the mentality of many of these men was exactly similar to that of the average grunt. What they were all after was a wife, a home, kids, basic provisions, security from attack. Hardin wondered if U.S. grunts would go underground, fight for their territory, if America were invaded. The thought crossed his mind that the vast majority might not; that the vast majority would accept whatever was ladled out to them by whoever ladled it out. But these guys here had a vision, and they believed in that vision however speciously—as now—it was presented to them. That was almost frightening.

Charlie Cong had been battling for over two decades now, and he wasn't even half-way tired. Not for the first time, it occurred to Hardin that this war was an utterly hopeless venture, and had been so for years.

"This way," snapped Tho loudly, shoving him in the back in the direction of the trail again. Hardin smiled wryly. There seemed to him no pressing reason why Tho should not have his fun.

"Good speech," he said. "Lotsa pep."

They were now about 25 yards in front of the rest of the men.

The *thieu tuong* said, "You liked it?"

"Mmh. Especially that bit about putting steel into their hearts and minds. A neat twist."

"Ah, yes." Tho smiled broadly. "I use that phrase often. It came to me one night in an inspired moment. It was like the Greek philosopher . . ." he snapped his fingers ". . . the bath . . . water displacement . . ."

"Archimedes, his principle."

"Yes."

"He jumped out of the tub and hollered 'Eureka!'"

"Precisely."

"But you knew that anyhow."

Tho shot him an amused glance.

"Perhaps, Colonel. Yes, perhaps I did."

"Just checking out my general knowledge, maybe?"

"Maybe."

Hardin said, "Let's cut out the crap, shall we?"

Tho turned to his men, gestured at them. They halted. Tho looked round, selected a log that did not seem to be covered with ants, and sat down gingerly, hitching up his pants to preserve the crease. Hardin put one boot on the log, rested an elbow on his knee, and relaxed. He set fire to a cigarette and drew smoke into his lungs, deep. It actually tasted not too offensive.

Tho said, "These men are inflicting much damage on our forces. Out of all proportion to their strength. They are, to put it no stronger, more than a nuisance."

"Looks like they're doing a fine job, in that case. We should be awarding 'em A for Effort."

"Come come, Colonel. I am not a fool. Our intelligence is by no means as amateurish as your people appear to believe. Up there," he gestured vaguely to the north, "are men who can be compared to rogue tigers. They are bandits. They owe allegiance to no one, least of all the American Military Assistance Command in Vietnam. They are destroyers. They are destroying our men, and they are destroying their own men—that is, *your* men. It is a situation that cannot be allowed to continue."

"You mean, they're not playing fair?"

Tho glared at him.

"This is no laughing matter, Colonel, believe me."

Hardin shook his head.

"Believe me, it's fucking hilarious. Right damn down on it, we should be cheering them on."

"But that," said Tho, in a reasonable voice, "is precisely what you are not doing. These outrageous bandits are hurting your own side as much as they are hurting ours. We know that. In fact, the damage inflicted on you is greater by far than that inflicted on us."

"That's arguable."

Tho irritably slapped a hand against the log.

"Not at all, Colonel. So far, over the past few months—before, during and after the disgraceful American incursion into Cambodia, I might say—you have sustained a variety of grave losses: equipment, armaments, men. A helicopter patrol has been led into a trap: no survivors. Now, these rebels have actually raided one of your own bases, causing much destruction. As far as our side is concerned, we have been subjected to mere pin-prick attacks, no more. Small patrols tortured and murdered. Some weapons captured. That is all. The losses are quite different."

Hardin knew that Tho was not coming out with the entire truth. Too, his information—excellent as it seemed to be on the surface—was flawed. He knew about the chopper-steal, but he didn't know there'd been a survivor. On the other hand, he also clearly knew about the disaster at Pen Kho, only a couple of hours after the event. That at least showed that EnVee agents in the field were earning their piastres.

But still, Tho was dissembling. The North Vietnamese High Command simply did not send men of the calibre of Hoang Van Tho out to deal with mere pin-prick attacks.

"So where does that get us?" he asked.

Tho shrugged.

"It is to be hoped, into a position where we may pool our resources, Colonel."

That, thought Hardin, was unusually blunt for a Vietnamese, of whatever persuasion. These guys had to be worrying the shit out of the EnVees, truly giving them a hard time. But that still didn't explain why they didn't simply jump in and blow 'em away.

"Look, Major-General, all this is so much horseshit. I have nine men, plus a three-man chopper crew. How many guys do you have at your disposal? Goddamn thousands. How come you need me?" He paused.

"Any case, how come you're so sure *we're* not trekking out to join these guys?"

Tho smiled and looked Hardin straight in the eyes.

"What you Americans would call a gut feeling, Colonel Hardin. As soon as I recognised you this morning, I was one hundred per cent certain that you were here to annihilate them, despite the comparative weakness of your force. That was why I offered a truce."

"Okay." Hardin took a deep breath. "Now here's the biggie, Major-General. Why for Christ's sake haven't you just wiped these guys from the face of the fucking earth?"

"Their sanctuary," the Vietnamese said slowly, "Could not have been better created if a committee had sat down at a table and planned it. But a committee would have taken a long time, Colonel. Nature did the job millions of years ago, and, I should say, in seconds. It is, in a word, impregnable."

He stood up, stared down at the ground, then began to trace the outline of a bottle in the mud with the heel of his boot.

"The valley is shaped like a bottle," a brief smile flickered across his face, "a claret bottle, Colonel, rather than a Burgundy bottle—the neck is long and narrow. You are only able to reach the valley or exit from it in single file. A few marksmen hidden in the cliffs above the bottle-neck could, quite literally, decimate an army. Thus, one may only enter the valley in force from the air—and that would be a simple action: part of the valley floor is a natural helicopter apron. Except that invaders have to run the gauntlet of tremendous firepower from caves overlooking the run-in. Invasion is, in one word, impossible."

Hardin tossed his cigarette away into the bushes, following its downward curve with his eyes.

"So why not just blow their shit away? Bomb the fuckers to hell?"

"Again, the valley is so placed that attack from the air could not be entirely certain of total success."

And that, mused Hardin, nicely fudged round the issue. Not that he was going to force the point. He wanted Tho to believe his explanation had been accepted.

"Sounds a hell of a place."

"It is a more than adequate hiding-place for these dogs of renegades," said Tho after a brief pause. "I am able to understand why your people should be so concerned about them that they should send a man such as yourself, Colonel, to root them out."

Flowery, thought Hardin, and easing the conversation away from a possible danger-area.

"I think maybe you're right, Major-General," he said. "I think maybe we ought to think about working something out."

"It would be to our mutual benefit," said Tho brightly, "believe me."

"So let's talk."

"Man," said Frank Marco, "that got to be the farest-out deal I ever heard. Fuckin' grand-slam, babe, on a mighty scale."

Hardin spooned C-rat spiced beef into his mouth and said, "You figure so?"

"Damn right! A deal with Charlie, to blow our own

guys away?"

"No guys of ours, Marco. Not any more."

"Yeah, but—shit, man! It's like—*wow!*"

"It's a marriage of convenience. Simply that. Nothing more."

"Sure wasn't made in heaven." Marco suddenly frowned at the can he'd just opened. "Fuckin' date-pudding. Jesus, the pits." He offered the can to Hardin. "What you have?"

Hardin shook his head.

"Beef, Marco. No trade."

"Lootenant Com-uh-rah-ro?"

Comeraro grinned.

"Uh . . . no thanks, sir. Don't like dates."

"You me both. How 'bout you, Sarge?"

Olsen shot him a worried look.

"With all respect, Captain, I gotta say that stuff has a bad effect on me. Internally. Frankly, sir, I'd rather eat my beans."

Marco said, "*Beans?*"

Hardin finished his beef and used the spoon to dig a small hole in the earth. He shoved the empty can in and pushed dirt over it, tamping it down. That was habit. That was so old Charlie Cong didn't come along and spot you'd been there. Under the circumstances, it was also kind of redundant.

He looked around. The rest of the men were further down the slope and into the trees, eating and smoking and chattering. Above, over the top of the wooded ridge they were on, a clear view of the entrance to the renegades' valley could be seen. Or so Tho had said.

He wondered if Tho truly believed that his bluff about the bombers had been successful. It was

186

possible he did. All things were possible. On the other hand, Tho had insisted they leave the chopper, and Marco and his crew go with the main group. That might be a hint that Tho didn't fully trust him. And the business about Corporal Lantry's radio was an even more positive indication.

The radio had been taken off Lantry when he'd been captured, and then, when Hardin had asked for it back, it couldn't be found. Tho had been angry—or at least had seemed to have been angry—and had explained that, quite inadvertently, the radio had been taken back to his own main base-camp with other equipment.

On the whole, Hardin didn't mind Marco and his men along. He positively welcomed Frank Marco himself, who was utterly reliable, worth two or three other guys in a hairy clinch. It also meant he now had a dependable MG-gunner—Colenso—which was no bad thing. Garrett, who'd previously been hefting the MG, had other uses, other special talents—the swift and silent kill when you wanted it that way. Hardin patted his fatigues pants pockets, and made a mental note about Garrett.

There was one other reason, too, he was grateful for the extra men—a prime reason. He'd have to start working on that right soon.

He got to his feet and nodded to Marco, who followed him up the rising ground still clutching his date pudding.

At the top of the ridge the ground fell away in a bumpy, bush-studded slope, back down to the forest. Mountains ranged around them on all sides, but higher to the north. The sun was easing downwards towards the western horizon.

Hardin lay on his stomach on the springy grass; pointed to a narrow cleft in the cliffs maybe a mile away. The jungle ended almost in front of it.

"That's the one."

He opened out his binoculars then squirmed across to a thick bush, pushing himself head-first under the foliage where the sun's rays would not catch the metalwork or the glass. He peered through the eye-pieces, and ran his gaze over the rockface.

Tho was right. The cleft looked to be only two or three feet wide. No way could you storm through with men, armaments, equipment. Tho had said the path itself ran through the rocks for about a quarter mile, then opened out into the valley itself. That would make assault even more out of the question. Hardin ranged upwards to the top and around.

"You see anything?"

"No, but then they'd only need a handful of guys spelling each other up there. They probably have some comfortable nooks back of the path itself."

"Man," sighed Marco, "what I could do with a comfortable nook, dig?"

"Uh-huh."

"Hey, listen. This deal way outta line, Hardin."

"Way out."

"Way I see it, the slope honcho gonna do us, babe. Do us all. The big DC."

"DC?"

"Double-cross, man."

"Oh sure. I wouldn't trust the little fucker further than I could flick him with my pinky."

Marco nodded. "Yeah. No altruist he." He looked

at Hardin. "Way I figure it, we jus' walk in an' say we wanna join the fun. No reason why not, way things are. Disaffected, right? Then we knock out the guards on the entrance, let Charlie in. Yeah?"

"Yeah. We're the only way the EnVees can get inside. That's why Tho wanted a deal."

"So the bad guys are minced, and Charlie duck out, havin' done his piece. Big fade-off. Hands across the jungle, an' now we can get back to killin' each other like regular guys. No more complications, right?"

"Right."

"But we only got this dude Tho's word that that's it, that the finish."

Still staring through the glasses, Hardin said, "Captain Marco, I believe you have placed your coal-black finger on the nub of the matter . . . the quintessential crux, as we college boys might say."

"Fuckin'-A, as we slum-scum have it."

"Come on, Marco, you have a fucking degree in social anthropology, and I know it." He put the glasses down. "Tho has the hots for that valley. He handed me a lot of crap about how bombers couldn't bomb it, but the truth is, the reason the EnVees haven't ripped the place apart is because they want to jump in there themselves. It's an ideal base. Work on it a while and it could be the perfect COSVH HQ. And a *real* HQ, not a fucking fantasy."

As he was talking, Hardin's mind spun back to the time, only a few months back, when U.S. troops had rolled into Cambodia looking for VC sanctuaries. That was the main reason for the incursion, the destruction of the vast network of hide-outs and bunkers that was supposed to have been erected in the

189

dense, almost impenetrable jungle. COSVN HQ—or the Headquarters of the Central Office for South Vietnam—even had a vague description tied to it: a reinforced bunker buried 30 feet underground, housing maybe 5000 technicians, tacticians and high officials.

Only trouble was, most of this—and especially COSVN HQ itself—existed only in the fertile imaginations of hotshot CIA assets, and the nightmares of army chiefs of staff who simply could not believe that the VC did not have some kind of central organisational controlpoint. Hell, that was the reason Charlie was still around, still fully operational, the sanctuaries. Had to be. Eliminate them, and the tide would turn.

That was the theory.

But COSVN HQ and its satellite sanctuaries were a myth, no more.

Sure, there were central points where VC and EnVee officials gathered to plan out the direction of the war. But these were moveable, sliding from area to area, shifting to wherever the action was; Charlie would give his right hand for a reinforced, utterly safe, and, above all, stable HQ. They'd probably been looking for a site for years. Decades, even.

And here one was, ironically snapped up by a bunch of U.S. Special Forces renegades: a remote, impregnable, unassailable valley, with deep caves in the surrounding rock walls and, for good measure, a natural chopper apron.

Certainly, it was not entirely secure from high altitude air-attack. But once the EnVees had captured the valley it would take them no time at all to transform it. They could seed the entire area with missile silos, dig the caves deeper still, and sit back in the sure and certain knowledge that they had the tightest stronghold in South East Asia.

Even more ironical, Hardin thought, was the fact that none of this could be achieved by the EnVees without his help. He and his men were the key to the door; without them the North Vietnamese were helpless.

Marco said, "You don't think we could maybe take out these scoundrels ourselves?"

"No way. Too many of 'em. Look, this whole thing's been fluid from the start. First we had to find this place, in a hurry. One plan was to walk in, get to a radio, let Halderling have the coordinates. Another was simply to locate the place, and likewise. But the old man wants his materiél back. That's a problem. He also doesn't want to waste men in a chopper drop that could go wrong. Sounds to me these guys have the air approaches sewn up, so that's a problem, too."

"Sound to *me*, babe, we don't have a chance with this mother."

Hardin shook his head.

"We go in, buddy-buddy for a couple of days, then take out the entrance guards and let Tho in. There'll be all hell let loose then, and that's when we hit their communications and tell Halderling to send a posse, pronto. We then take out the air defences and sit back. When our guys drop in, it'll be like the Goddamn Day of Judgement. Total shock. We can wipe out the renegades and cream some élite EnVees at the same time."

"Yeah, man," said Marco through a mouthful of

date pudding, "but what if—an' this only conjecture, dig?—we don't get to be able to call Halderling? Lines could be bad, you know? Maybe these dudes get fidgetty 'bout strangers usin' the phone. Me, I prefer back-up when my head on the block."

Hardin fished a map from one of his pockets, opened it out.

"Sure. And Tho gave me back-up when he forced you fly-boys down my throat." He traced across the map with his thumb. "Let's see—the chopper would be about three miles back down in the jungle. I think we could spare your co-pilot Hanks, and Corporal Lantry from Pen Kho. My wild cards, Marco . . ."

Hardin decided to hit the valley the next day. He wanted to give his two wild cards time to get clear and dig in for the night. As far as trying to grab back the chopper went, an early-morning raid had a better chance of success than an attempted snatch when the sun was high and Charlie was fully alert. The reverse was the case for entering the valley. He wanted to march up in the full light of day, make no secret of his presence. Any incursion earlier than mid-day was likely to be misinterpreted by itchy-fingered guards, and would almost certainly end in disaster.

They emerged from the forest a couple of hundred yards from the opening in the cliffs, and that was, Hardin thought, an optimum distance. Walking towards the entrance, they would be in full view of anyone high up on the cliff-face.

The sun was hot but, up here in the mountains, not sweltering. Fresh breezes played on and around them, cooling them. It was a fine day with an ultramarine sky flecked with a few wisps of cumuli meandering northwards high above.

"Be ironical," said Marco, "if some of our guys turned. You know, man: went over the other side, blew our cover."

"The only one who could be on the hinge is Garrett."

"What I was thinkin'."

"But he won't."

"You figure?"

"He's very pissed with these guys. They left him to burn, kind of. Garrett doesn't forgive and forget that easy."

"He lack that spirit of turnin' the other cheek."

Hardin turned and beckoned down the line. The big man ambled up towards them, his craggy face alive with sharp insolence.

"Wanted me, Colonel?"

"Got something for you, Garrett."

"For me, Colonel? Now what the fuck—beggin' your pardon—could you be wanting to give ole brig-trash like me? Sir."

Hardin reached into a pocket and tossed him something that flickered as the sun caught it. Garrett laughed and snatched it out of the air one-handed. There were two wooden toggle-grips which he pulled apart expertly, revealing that what the sun had caught were strands of thin, shiny wire twisted tightly together and fixed to the toggles.

"Well now, Colonel, that's right civilised of you. Sure appreciate it. Been feelin' naked without a sweet cheeseslicer like this."

"That's what I thought, Garrett."

"Right. Sir."

"Could be you'll be slicing cheese damn soon."

"Could be I'll be lookin' forward to that, Colonel."

They filed into the opening, Hardin on point. Here it was dark and chilly, the sun unable to penetrate the narrow defile for overhangs of rock that, in places, blocked off the sky completely. The walls of the cleft rose sheer above them for hundreds of feet; the floor was uneven, boulder-strewn. At its widest the passage through the cliffs could not have been more than four feet.

Hardin's stomach tightened as he moved onwards through the cold twilight; he felt naked, exposed. Tho had been right. One marksman on each side of the cliff above, firing from a ledge or a cave, could truly wipe out any large body of men who tried to penetrate this stronghold. It would be the simplest thing in the world. There was nowhere to hide — even cowering under an overhang would not save you from an MG-gunner who knew his business — and your pace was governed by the narrowness of the path, its unevenness, the way it twisted and turned. Under fire, you could not move faster than a panic-stricken stagger.

They trudged on until, quite suddenly, turning a tight bend in the rocks, Hardin stepped out into brilliant sunlight. He winced, shielding his eyes with a hand, coming to a halt so sharply that Marco, behind, stumbled into him.

"Shee-*it!*"

Marco gaped at the scene.

"Fuckin' para-*deezo!*"

The description fitted, Hardin decided. It was as

though they had been warped out of the hell-hole that was Vietnam—South East Asia, mud, blood, bullets; all that that implied—and into another place altogether; another country. Possibly another planet. He was reminded of a story he'd once read—a famous book, the name of which escaped him for the moment—about travellers discovering the fabled valley of Shangri-La, where life was eternal and peace infinite.

The valley was lush and luxuriant. It stretched a mile due north away from them, and was maybe a half-mile wide. Cliffs rose high all around, and to the west these lifted even higher, rearing majestically into the mountain chain. At the end a ribbon of water plunged down the sheer rock-face, disappearing beyond a grove of tall pines into what was probably a large pool. For the most part the valley floor was densely forested, but Hardin could see small glade-like clearings patched in amongst the darker mass of the trees. North-east, he glimpsed the caves Tho had spoken of, raggedy-edged black roundels in the grey and blue of the cliff-face, a network that clearly began below the treeline. Hibiscus blazed colourfully; orchidlike flowers hanging in clusters from high bushes grew in profusion beside the trail that led into the woods; the forest floor was green with ferns.

Shadows suddenly flickered raggedly in front of them across the long slope of scree and broken rocks that fell downwards to the valley floor, and Hardin tensed, his right hand gripping the strap of the AK across his chest, his eyes darting upwards.

Two eagles wheeled and swooped and peeled away from each other high in the sky.

"Yeah," said Marco, "I thought we about to be iced too."

"Jesus," said Hardin, almost in awe, "this is some place. Really some damn place."

"It reminds me," said Marco, "of that place—you know . . ."

"Shangri-La."

"Naw, the Big Rock Candy Mountain."

"I don't think the cops have wooden legs here."

"Could be right."

Comeraro said, "No one seems to want to stop us, Colonel."

"Yeah, so let's move on down."

It took them nearly an hour to reach the valley, and Hardin thought again how incredibly defensible the approaches were. Even were you to get your men through the entrance and along the gorge, you could still be cut to hell on the downward slope by two or three machine-guns placed strategically in the trees, and arcing across in long, deadly sweeps. Not forgetting those snipers hidden atop the cliffs and firing down at your rear. Every so often quick chills went rippling up his spine as he thought of them, the snipers. He knew for sure that they—or someone—was watching their progress even now, undoubtedly reporting it to the caves.

They filed up at the bottom of the slope preparatory to entering the trees. Here the ground was a carpet of lush green moss interweaved with short springy grass. It was like, Hardin thought, stepping on the comfortable pile of a millionaire's rumpus-room; it was so thick you could sleep on it. There was a smell about the air, too, that was sharp and clean and fresh, as unlike the rank stench of rotting vegetation that filled your nostrils through most of the day out in the jungle as it was possible to imagine.

They'd gone maybe a couple hundred yards when Olsen stepped up beside him.

"This is pretty good, sir," he said briskly.

Hardin stared at him, not at all sure how to take this unusual, for Olsen, approach.

"Certainly is, Olsen."

"Gotta say, Colonel," Olsen's voice plummetted to the pit of his stomach, "we got company, rear and flanks."

"Ah. Got you Sarge."

Not that it mattered. Ahead, three men suddenly stepped out from bushes on the right of the pathway, M-16s raised and levelled.

"Far as it goes."

Hardin lounged to a halt.

None of the men wore rank-tabs. They could have been Specialists, NCOs, any rank up. The man who'd spoken—tall, and with a thin moustache—gestured with his rifle.

"Put your pieces across your shoulders, grip 'em with both hands."

Hardin shrugged. He turned to the file of men behind him. Other figures could be seen in amongst the trees on each side of the path.

"Do it," he said.

They were in.

Seated in a canvas-backed chair at the edge of the clearing, his right leg resting negligently on his left knee, Hoang Van Tho regarded the burning wreck of

197

the Huey with some amusement. It had reached a height of perhaps 100 feet before he had nodded, briefly and dispassionately, and the PG-7 rocket had blown it out of the sky.

Tho felt it was right he should feel a certain amount of satisfaction. He had gauged the time of the escape attempt to within six minutes, and although in many ways the Yankees were very predictable, still six minutes seemed to him to be a degree of accuracy that could not really be faulted.

He could imagine the elation, the surge of triumph welling up inside the pilot as the helicopter lifted into the air—a surge that would have been abruptly cut off as his world exploded around him. That was very amusing. Tho hoped there had been a split second of horrifying awareness before nothingness had been achieved.

He took a thin, coarse-leafed cheroot out of a packet and placed it in his mouth. His aide—an unusually tall Vietnamese with an oddly wizened face—leaned forward from behind and snapped an American lighter into flame. Tho drew on the cheroot and contemplated the future.

It looked promising.

Chapter Ten

Hardin said, feeding self-righteous anger into the words, "How long the fuck as I going to be kept here?"

The man called Nulty shrugged his shoulders.

"Hell, Colonel, hard to say. I just don't know."

"So far it's been nearly a week, and I've seen nobody."

"Right on the line, you have a kind of a strange rep. Wouldn't do us no good if you turned out to be some kind of . . ." Nulty tapped spatulate fingers on the table-top, "well, you know, Colonel, double-crosser, anything like that."

"A Trojan horse," said Hardin.

Nulty frowned.

"Guess so, Colonel. Something like that."

He tossed a pack of Winston down on the table, shrugged again, grinned—slightly comtemptuously—turned and went out. Hardin watched the door close with relief. He remembered Nulty from a year or so back, a man of not much education, with a hatred of the Vietnamese that hinged on the pathological, and a shaky temper. Precisely the type who would sign on for an operation such as this.

He yawned, stretched his legs out, rose to his feet. It took two short paces to reach the only window in the hut, which otherwise contained a small table, a bamboo chair, and a makeshift bunk. It was by no means luxurious.

Out of the window he could see other huts amongst the trees, men chopping wood, the helicopter apron under camouflage netting that could be part-rolled back for access, a sand-bagged emplacement (probably for a mortar), and a glimpse, far over to the right, of the lower caves, where the choppers were hidden.

He wondered where the rest of his men were. He'd gotten the impression from what Nulty—the only individual of any seeming prominence with whom he'd thus far had any intercourse—had let drop that they were not under any strong restrictions. He hoped Marco was making proper use of his time, and that Olsen was keeping a tight rein on Garrett.

Otherwise, frankly, this entire operation was starting to slide right down the chute. He'd wanted, once the target had been identified, a rapid tying-up of the business; which could easily have been achieved. But all he'd had—once he'd been identified and separated from the rest—was the view from this window for nearly a week. He still didn't even know who was in charge here.

Whoever it was, it seemed like he was running a tight ship. The men he saw outside were well-fed, confident. The approaches to the actual camp itself well-guarded and probably even better booby-trapped (he'd spotted evidence of at least three trip-wires in the brush that would have been invisible to anyone who had not been rigorously trained by Special Forces to notice the tiny but unnatural detail that even the most experienced saboteur often did not allow for—but that did not mean invaders would notice such things; it simply meant that he himself was just slightly more skilled than the guys who'd laid the traps).

He'd noted that the majority of the renegades were white, although there was a sprinkling of blacks and other ethnic groups. He wondered if that fact was of any consequence, but then realised that speculation of any kind was idle until he could get out of here and mix with the men.

He took three paces to the right and lay down on the bunk, smoking. The afternoon died into evening. A chopper clattered in. Darkness fell. Lights flickered on.

Not only a tight ship, thought Hardin, as he listened to the muted hum of a nearby generator, but a very well-stocked ship. He remembered the jammer the rebels had used, and had then discarded without, he assumed, a thought. It had occurred to him more than once, lying there and sorting the problem through in his mind, that there really had to be more to this than a bunch of guys getting pissed off with the status quo.

Without warning the door slammed open and Nulty entered the room, M-16 at the trail. He was smiling. Behind him were three or four men.

Hardin tensed, wondering if something had fouled up and these guys were here to take him out.

Nulty said, "You got your heart's desire, Colonel."

Someone snickered in the darkness back of him.

"Yeah?"

"Yeah. The man, he wants to see you."

They took him through the pines towards the caves. Low-wattage naked bulbs hanging from cables drooped from trees like fairy lights. There was a smell of cooking in the air. As his boots crunched through dead needles, Hardin thought all this reminded him of summer camp back in Vermont a million or so years ago.

Next to the caves a separate complex of hutments had been built, some connected, some having stoops, a number on a rock outcropping that led to the chopper apron. Slatted duckboard walkways covered the ground all round. Followed by Nulty, Hardin climbed the three steps up to the main door of the largest hut. Inside was a passage with doors leading off it.

"Sophisticated set-up," said Hardin.

"No expense spared."

"The only thing I don't hear are typewriters."

"Crap like that we can do without," said Nulty, pushing open a door.

Hardin walked in. The room was empty. There were closed blinds over the windows and a shaded lamp on a desk that would not have looked out of place at Nha Trang HQ or Bien Hoa air-base. There was a filing-cabinet, a cushioned settle under one of the windows, a waist-high cabinet with one louvred door open, revealing bottles of Jim Beam and Johnny Walker Black Label. On the desk, beside the lamp, was a mounted photograph of a plump, dumpy middle-aged woman in a print dress, smiling inanely.

Hardin tapped the desk with his knuckle, just to make sure it was really there.

He sat down in a chair in front of the desk and lit a

cigarette. He thought, If I'd used a match I'd've been able to toss it into the U.S. army issue trash-bin beside the door. Or flick it into the U.S. army issue glass ashtray on the desk. Or pop it into the U.S. army issue desk-litter can in between the lamp and the photograph.

He began to feel disoriented.

Footsteps sounded in the passageway outside, brisk and businesslike. The door opened, banged shut. A short, bulky figure crossed the room quickly, almost fussily, and tossed a white Cavalry Stetson and a briefcase on to the top of the filing cabinet. He plumped himself down behind the desk, beaming widely at Hardin.

"Colonel John Hardin," he said, with short gaps between each word.

"Well, well," said Hardin. "Ernie Tollmarsh."

"I see it," said Frank Marco, "but I don't believe it."

Lieutenant Comeraro said, "You read comicbooks, Captain?"

Marco took his eyes off the man with the briefcase under his arm and the white Stetson on his head hurrying towards the cave area, and stared at Comeraro as though Comeraro had just belched in his face.

"Comicbooks? What?"

"Stan Lee of Marvel Comics always uses that phrase, sir, when he wants to get over real shock, real disbelief. Only he writes it in a kind of a stammer. Like, 'I s-see it, b-but I d-don't believe it,' accent on 'believe.' Literary device, sir. Adds to the incredulity."

"Yeah? Well, I incredulous, babe. I real incredulous. I just seen a guy I figured was dead."

"You mean that stumpy little major, Tollmarsh?"

Marco said, "How in hell you know him?"

"Bumped into him a couple times, sir. He had a Cav squad near the border."

"So why ain't your eyes poppin' outta your head to see the little booger here, Lieutenant?"

Comeraro shrugged.

"I guess nothing surprises me any more, sir. Not in this shooting war. Anyway, this outfit had to have some ranking guy as headman. Why not Tollmarsh? What I heard, he's strongly gung-ho."

"Strongly gung-ho, Lootenant Com-uh-rah-ro, a mild description of that little fucker."

Marco leaned against the trunk of a pine, watched the darkness swallow up Ernie Tollmarsh. This, he thought, was one for the books right enough. Tollmarsh, the honcho of the outfit. But it fitted, it all fitted. Sweet Jesus, it truly did fit. The ambush in the deserted ville had been a set-up from the start. Maybe information had been filtered through to Command, but Tollmarsh had been behind it, no lie. That had been his method of getting out. The perfect cover: missing, believed KIA.

But if Tollmarsh was in charge here, that was bad news for Marco. Tollmarsh sure as hell didn't love him; apart from anything else, he'd escaped from the ville and iced a couple of Tollmarsh's men for good measure. Why hadn't Tollmarsh thrown him in the camp brig as a precautionary measure?

Maybe Tollmarsh had been out of circulation, sniffing out some juicy new target outside the valley?

A lone chopper had dropped in an hour before; maybe Tollmarsh had been on that? Certainly no one had threatened him for the five or so days they'd been here. All that had happened was that they'd been relieved of the rifles and pistols and grenades, but not personal weapons like knives. Otherwise, it had been almost like a normal Special Forces non-operational period, even down to the pre-breakfast calisthenics — eight repetitions of the daily dozen (better known as Army Drill One) followed by a two-mile run round the valley perimeters. That latter, thought Marco, had been particularly useful; he now knew the terrain pretty damn well. He'd also, with Olsen and Comeraro, fingered the guardposts up in the entrance ravine. There were only two; it would not be difficult to take them out from behind.

And it looked like it might come to that right soon. Tho had now been kicking his heels outside for nearly a week; could be he might lose patience, try to storm through on his own. Which would fuck up everything. Marco was glad he'd already made certain preparations.

Whatever, Tollmarsh's arrival could be the match to set the powder-train alight, the switch to trigger off the ignition, the goose to make the lady jump, the . . .

Marco decided not to stand there pissing about with metaphors. He poked Comeraro in the chest.

"Go get Garrett. Tell him, cool it. Tell Olsen, get out there."

"We ready to go, Captain?"

Marco O'ed his thumb and forefinger.

"Had to do it, Hardin," said Ernie Tollmarsh. "Too

much corruption in Nam. Goes to the top, too. Goes right up to the very top." He stabbed at the desk surface with a stubby finger, as though ramming each word home into the metalwork. "There's Reds up there, screwing us off. All the Goddamn time, telling us to hold back, hold up, hold fire. *Jesus!* I could get to the pinko trash, I'd hold okay. Hold their Goddamn nuts and squeeze."

He stripped cellophane off a cigar, balled it, tossed it into the desk-litter can. He snipped the end off the cigar, warmed it with a match, began to draw on it. Hardin noted that it was a Havana Partagás, which hinted at all kinds of connections, illegal and otherwise. Tollmarsh might be — almost certainly was — the moving force of this outfit, but Hardin was becoming more and more convinced as each second ticked by that he hadn't set it up at the start.

"Why are we in Nam, anyway?" asked Tollmarsh.

It was clear to Hardin he needn't bother replying.

"To screw the Reds is why," said Tollmarsh. "But have you noticed, Hardin, has it not become crystal fucking clear to you that we are not, repeat not, doing a very terrific job? I started asking myself why we were not doing a very terrific job, and it became crystal fucking clear to *me* that there was only one Goddamn answer." He smacked the palm of his hand down hard on the desk-top and the lamp shivered. "*Corruption!* Corruption in the White House, corruption in the Pentagon, corruption in MACV! It turns your fucking *guts!*" He prodded the air in Hardin's direction. "Tell you, Hardin, it wouldn't surprise me to find there's a Goddamn hotline between Creighton Abrams and Ho Chi Minh."

"Difficult," said Hardin.

"And another thing . . ." Tollmarsh was about to launch off again, when he suddenly frowned. "Huh?"

"I said, difficult. Ho's dead. Last year. You hadn't heard?"

Hardin said this with a perfectly straight face. Tollmarsh stared at him for some seconds then reached up for the briefcase and unzipped it. He slid papers out on to the desk.

"How'd you get here, Hardin?"

"Sniffed around, caught rumours in the breeze."

"*Why* did you come here?"

Hardin shrugged.

"Same as you, I guess. Sick to my gut of the corruption, venality, and sheer stupidity of the U.S. High Command in Vietnam."

The ironical thing was, thought Hardin, that that was exactly right, what he'd just said. But Ernie Tollmarsh would not have appreciated the joke in a thousand years.

"Been away," said Tollmarsh, "checking things out. Have to say, I was surprised when they told me you were here."

"Stranger things could happen."

"Not to say downright fucking suspicious." Tollmarsh's eyes were bleak.

"Look," said Hardin, "I wanted out. It's as simple as that. I had it up to my nostrils with the stink of incompetence. I'm a good fighter; one of the best. But they are treating me like rat-shit."

Tollmarsh nodded abruptly.

"Know what you mean. Way things are, you don't get to see the fucking gooners for paperwork." He jerked a piece of paper from the pile in front of him. "You have a man named Marco with you."

This fact had been running through Hardin's mind ever since Ernie Tollmarsh had entered the room. He did not need even a micro-second's pause to say, "Yeah, and frankly I'm not happy with the guy."

"Oh?" Tollmarsh gave him a pop-eyed look.

"For one thing, he's a nigra."

"Damn right," muttered Tollmarsh.

"I noticed you got a few nigras here."

"A few. Red-haters. They have to be. But I could do without 'em."

"Other thing, he's a wise-ass."

"Jesus," said Tollmarsh in disgust, "him and all his fucking breed."

"Got a chip on his shoulder the size of a redwood."

"I'll tell you," said Tollmarsh seriously, jabbing a finger at Hardin, "what's wrong with the nigra. They weren't reared like us. Not like you and me, Hardin. They'd've read Horatio Alger at the pickaninny stage, be a deal different."

Hardin nodded briefly, to show he agreed wholeheartedly with Tollmarsh's brilliantly unconventional but entirely logical reading of the situation but that time was far too short to pursue this sociological line—interesting though it was—further. In any case, Tollmarsh had risen to his feet, crossed to the cabinet, and begun to pour large fingers of Jim Beam into two chunky glasses. He brought the uncapped bottle back to the desk.

"The hell with the Commies, dinks or otherwise," He threw a liberal measure of the whisky down his throat. "You know what I see? I see a dead land from the Annamites to the sea and right on down to the Mekong Delta. A *dead* land. Nothing that grows, nothing that moves, nothing that lives. *Nothing*. Then I'd bomb the North, and I mean *really* bomb the North. I'd bomb the fuckers back to *beyond* the Stone Age. You think it couldn't be done? You think maybe it's been tried? A pissant effort, Hardin. I'll tell you, Rolling Thunder'd be ant-shit to what I have in mind. Nuke 'em out, is the way I see it. That's how I'd sanitise the situation."

He glared at Hardin, and Hardin nodded cautiously.

"Not the easiest thing in the world to do."

Tollmarsh laughed, and there was a chilling quality about the sound that sent a faint shiver up Hardin's spine.

"Shit-easy, Hardin." Tollmarsh sank some more whisky and poured himself another heavy slug. Fat beads of sweat stood out on his reddish face. He smiled a death's-head smile, all teeth and blank eyes. "I'm going to show those half-assed clowns in Saigon how to fight this war, Hardin. The fuckers won't forget Ernie Tollmarsh in a hurry, no sir."

"I'm beginning to get the picture."

"You like what you see?"

"It's a hell of a view." Hardin leaned forward, injecting a touch of controlled tension into his voice, as though he might have grave difficulty not stabbing a finger at the first hot-button he saw. "Jesus, why stop there? Why stop at the North? China's only one Goddamn footstep across the border."

Tollmarsh laughed again, a fat, relaxed chuckle. He gulped at more whisky and splashed another dose into the glass.

"Right. You *are* getting the picture. And the scenario gets even better after that. Tell you, Hardin, this thing's been brewing a long time. This is no shit I'm giving you, but a very solid deal." He winked suddenly. "And the pay's *very* good. You want in, you're welcome."

"I'm in."

"As long," said Tollmarsh, with a smile that was several degrees cooler than before, "as you realise who's honcho round here."

"Goes without saying," Hardin shrugged.

"And as long," and the temperature dropped even lower, "as you check out."

"Take your time."

As Hardin said this, a door banged outside, boots thudded in the hallway. Nulty came in without knocking and gave a sharp salute.

"Communications, sir."

Tollmarsh pushed the Jim Beam across the desk.

"Fill her up, Colonel. Be my guest."

Grinning, he reached for his Stetson, crammed it on his head. The two men exited.

Hardin sat back in his chair. All this talk of nukes had sent needles of real panic sparking through his brain—not simply because nukes were an appalling ultimate, a final destructive solution from which there was truly no deliverance, but because he had a strong presentiment that Tollmarsh was, as he'd said, giving out no shit. No shit at all. What really unnerved him was that Tollmarsh—although he surely was very close to the edge—didn't act crazy. On the contrary, he seemed totally sure of himself, totally in control, as though bolstered up by far more than a belief in the righteousness of his cause. As though he had backing, and that backing was so Goddamn solid that a block of granite would seem like toothpaste beside it.

It occurred to Hardin that he'd been closer than he'd thought when he'd felt there was more to this than a few guys getting grouchy and taking to the jungle. There was a closely-extrapolated scenario here, a game-plan that had been worked on meticulously, almost fastidiously.

It also occurred to him, with a kind of icy foreboding, that it was the kind of intricate and devious game-plan he and Halderling used to toss around in the old days, when he was a tyro freelance and Halderling—the master of entrapment and subterfuge—was teaching him how to set up a target, human or otherwise.

Hardin got to his feet slowly and went to the door. He opened it, and was immediately aware of movement down the passageway. Two men lounged against the wall with slung rifles.

"You be wanting something," pause, "sir?"

"A match, soldier. Just a match."

One of the men tossed him a book, and Hardin nodded and closed the door again. He had not expected anything else. He briefly wondered what the message was in Communications, and whether it concerned him. Then thrust the thought out of his mind. There were other things to think about, now he was out; plans to be made. He felt that some kind of resolution must be achieved as soon as possible—Christ alone knew what Tho was doing outside the valley. He would be getting truly pissed by now.

Hardin decided that he was going to have to deck Ernie Tollmarsh when he came back, cold-cock the fucker fast and take his piece. He was tired of inaction.

He glanced at the book of matches, then thrust two fingers into his breast pocket for the pack of Winston.

And froze.

"Shit!" said Marco. "They fingered Hardin! We in big trouble, boy!"

He said this to Garrett in the deep shadow behind a hut that sprouted aerials from its timbered roof.

"I didn't hear any of that," said Garrett.

"Couldn't get the full picture myself, but Tollmarsh jus' stormed outta the hut breathin' fire. He was talkin' to some dude across the aether."

"Gotta hand it to you, Captain Marco, sir, the way you do use them fancy words."

"The trouble with you, Garrett, you the realest, uneducatedest poor white trash I ever did come across."

Garrett's lips pulled back in a feral smile.

"We go in and ice these fuckers?"

Marco pondered this. His first plan had been to quietly take out the guys in the Communications hut, get through to Halderling, pick up some weaponry, then find Hardin. Olsen and his squad—Sergeant Fuller, Doc Pepper, Vogt and O'Mara—were already on their way down-valley, towards the entrance pass and the guards high in the rocks, and Marco had no qualms at all about them getting through, and opening the gates for the EnVees. Even so, that would take time, and suddenly time was at a premium.

With him, Marco had Comeraro, Garrett, Colenso and Parrish. He knew Garrett's capabilities, and was satisfied that the other three, all with Special Forces experience behind them, would swiftly meld into a tight fighting force when action was thrust upon them. What he hadn't wanted was for the action to start just yet.

But now the balloon had gone up. From what he'd heard, his ear jammed to the rear of the hut, Tollmarsh had just been informed that Hardin was a plant. And if Hardin, so was his squad. They'd be out looking for them; very soon the entire camp would be in an uproar.

"Yeah," he said, "we go in, take out these dudes. We can use their weaponry and ammo."

"How many in there, you think, Captain?" said Comeraro.

"What I could hear, three. An' that one too many. I don't dig the idea of jumpin' three guys in a large room. We gonna have to extract one."

They slid along the rear of the hut, down the side. There was a stoop out front, overlooking grass that dropped to the pines; a naked bulb hung from a cable-connexion at the far end, lighting the immediate area. Marco could just see, peering through the stoop railings, his eyes just above floor-level, that the main door of the hut was open. There were two windows, one each side of the door; both had their blinds down.

Marco said, "I gonna go round back, take out that bulb. One of them exits, you take *him* out, Garrett."

"Shit, Captain—how?"

"From behind, my man."

"You mean I gotta clump along the stoop, in full fucking view of that open door?"

"Take your boots off."

"Why the fuck don't you gut him with your blade, when he reaches up for the bulb?"

"Because," said Marco patiently, "I reach up through the railings, I jus' may not be able to reach, or only stick two inches in an' he start screamin'."

"I think it's a dumb idea."

"Do it, soldier, or your ass is grass an' I gonna mow it."

"Jesus Christ," muttered Garrett.

He unlaced his boots, and said sourly to Comeraro, "Goddamn fuckin' jigs. S'what happens when they get educated. They get Goddamn dumb ideas."

He waited, crouching below the level of the board-floor. Three minutes ticked past, then Comeraro whispered, "He's there."

Garrett looked up, caught a glimpse of Marco's lean form stretched out beyond the glare of the bulb. Then the light blinked off. Above the fizz and crackle of static from an open radio, they heard voices from within the hut.

"Light's gone, out front."

"Could be the bulb. I'll go take a look."

Garrett swung himself silently up and over the rail and stood in his stockinged feet on the stoop, beside one of the windows. A man came out of the door, turning sharp right, not even glancing in Garrett's direction. Garrett followed him fast, not stopping or even pausing when he reached the doorway but moving straight on past like a confident wraith, his eyes taking in what he could see then flicking back to the dark shape of the man in front. The man had stopped by the railing, was staring up at the bulb-holder in the darkness. Garrett already had his garotte out, and now, in one fluid movement, he looped the wire over the man's head and down, and cross-toggled, feeling the familiar instant of skin-resistance before the strand of tightly-twisted piano-wires sliced through flesh and jugular as though it was cutting into a ripe peach. The man didn't make a sound, just stiffened momentarily then relaxed as a dead weight in Garrett's arms. Slowly, Garrett lowered him to the boards.

"You see?" whispered Marco, sliding over the railing beside him. "Cool."

They padded back towards the door. Already, Comeraro was flattened the other side of it, and, beyond him, Colenso and Parrish could just be seen in the shadows. Marco peered into the lighted room.

One man was sitting at a radio, cans over his ears, his back to the door. The other man was leaning across him, reaching for something, a cigarette dangling from his mouth. Marco nodded to Comeraro, then strolled into the room as though about to enquire what was for lunch. The man with the cigarette did not even glance up as he said, "S'matter with the bulb?"

"Dead," said Marco.

The man's head jerked up and round, the cigarette dropping from his open mouth. Panic careered across his features.

"Like you," said Marco.

His hand shot out, the fingers stiff, like rods. The extended fingertips punched into the side of the man's

215

neck with a meaty thud. The man gagged out something that sounded like *"Ugghhk!"* then collapsed on to the radio bench. As he fell, Comeraro lunged past him, his left hand scything round in a chopping blow that connected with the radio operator's exposed throat with such devasting force that the man was knocked backwards in his chair. Garrett jumped forward and caught the chair before it crashed to the floor. He glanced down at the man casually.

"Lotta power behind that, Lieutenant. Looks like you ruptured something. He won't wake up this side of hell."

Marco was across the room now, humming to himself as he sorted through a small stack of weapons leaning against the wall: M-16s, M-14s, an AK-47 or three. He chose a Kalashnikov, weighing it in his hands then checking the mag, nodding in satisfaction. He slipped a Russian .45 automatic into his belt-holster and stuffed clips of ammunition into the pockets of his fatigues.

He said, "Jus' take your pick, an' don't forget spare clips. Colenso, shut the door. Parrish, check out the radio. I want a line across the border."

Parrish shifted the dead operator off the chair and sat down, picking up the cans. As he did so, a door at the far end of the room opened and a man sauntered out.

He seemed to be in no hurry. He had an oily rag over one arm and an automatic in his hands, and he was in the middle of fitting the magazine up into the grip. He glanced up.

"You guys got the coffee yet?"

Then he saw the bodies.

It flashed through Marco's mind that this was one cool dude, a real professional. The guy took in the whole scene in, it seemed, rather less than a microsecond before he acted, and it was the act itself that fired Marco's admiration and caused him to mentally shake his head in sorrow that such a guy should have to be deep-sixed. He could almost see the logical sequence of images that were racing through the man's mind, and acknowledged that, in a similar position, he would act in exactly the same manner.

The man rammed the clip hard up into the butt, spun the gun and fired one shot at Parrish.

The thinking behind this action run thus: *There were dead men here, this was some kind of invasion, the guy at the radio was summoning help—therefore he was the most important of the group and had to be killed first.*

The bullet took Parrish in the throat, knocking his head back in a cloud of bloody spume and punching him in a wild flailing of arms across the radio.

It was a perfect illustration, Marco had to admit, of the adage that was hammered into you again and again and again in Special Forces training: Mission first, self afterwards.

Now the guy was thinking: *These fuckers don't dare shoot because of the noise, but I can make it back to the door and give the alarm.*

He was actually in the air, in a backspring towards the open door, when Garrett caught him, and even in the large room the raking burst of automatic fire was ear-splitting. Garrett had chosen an M-16 from the pile, and its bullets tore into the man, jerking him to one side and sending him, fountaining blood, into the closed blinds of the window and beyond, with an appalling jangle of shattering glass. The body thumped down, half-in and half-out of the room, slumped across the sill.

"*Cunt,*" said Garrett, with deep feeling. He turned to Marco, "I didn't even check, for Chrissake. Just flipped the safety and let him have it." His voice rose. "I didn't know it was on automatic. The fucker would've got away. He was too far to jump." He said, "I *hadda* do it!"

Marco said, "Better get your boots, boy. You be needin' them."

Chapter Eleven

Hardin knew someone had blown the whistle by the fact that when Ernie Tollmarsh re-entered the office he didn't quite close the door.

Tollmarsh marched round to the rear of the desk, spun his Stetson up on to the filing-cabinet, and reached for his drink. He tossed the contents—nearly two-thirds of the glass—down his throat, and banged the glass down on to the desk.

"Jesus," he said, staring at the desk-top, "it's all harrassment. Tell you, Hardin, some Goddamn times it's like being back in Nam here . . ." He paused—Hardin surreptitiously tightening his grip on the haft of his knife—and then went on in exactly the same tone of voice ". . . you fucker."

He looked up, his face ruby-red in the lamp-light, sweat running down his cheeks in an almost continuous stream.

"You fucker!" he howled.

An arm whipped round Hardin's throat from behind, but Hardin had been prepared for just such a move. His knife—double-edged and with an eight-inch blade, souvenir of a piece of business he'd attended to in Barcelona nine years back—thrust smoothly upwards into the wrist, turned and carved, and suddenly blood was jetting over his face from a severed artery. There was an animal-like scream from behind him, but by that time Hardin had shot off the chair and down, feet-first, and was plunging beneath the desk. He let go the knife, thrust his hands up at the desk's underside, and shoved down at the floor with his feet, heaving himself and the desk upwards into the air. He jerked at the desk, let it go. The light in the room spun crazily as the lamp slid off on to the floor, miraculously landing on its heavy base, and the desk crashed away behind him with an appalling clatter mixed in with human yells and gasps — but Hardin was already stooping, plucking at his knife, and launching himself at an astonished Tollmarsh. He hit Tollmarsh across the face, hard and damagingly, with the haft of the knife, grabbing him by the shirt at the same time, then swinging him round to face the room. Tollmarsh gave a pig-like grunt of pain, and then Hardin was behind him with the blade rising towards his throat.

But just too late.

Even as he was lifting the knife an explosion of sound and agony and fierce white light seemed to erupt around his head. A violent ripping shaft of pain cracked through his brain, and he reeled sideways, dropping the knife. He staggered, fell to the floor on hands and knees, half-blinded, not even sure whether he'd been shot in the head or brained with a rifle-butt. Something fell on him from above, flattening him, and hands gripped his wrists, dragging them back and round, twisting them half up his back.

"Get up, get up, get up!"

Someone was yelling in his ear, and tugging at his arms at the same time. Dazedly, he decided to drift with the tide, roll with the pitch, do anything anyone wanted him to do. For now. He heaved himself up on to his knees, staggered to his feet.

His head was, quite literally, buzzing. It was like a berserk swarm of bees rampaging around in there; he could only just hear extraneous sounds, sounds that occurred more than a foot away from him. Nausea rose in a black tide, then receded, then rose again. He decided he hadn't been shot, just lammed with something heavy. He peered blearily at the scene.

The guy he'd sliced was being hauled out of the room, moaning incoherently, one arm drenched in blood; they were dragging him through the wreckage of the U.S. army issue desk, which now lay in two splintered sections on the floor. Across from the door four guys were pointing rifles at him. They didn't look happy. But probably the most important ingredient of the entire scene was Ernie Tollmarsh, who was coming at him waving the knife.

Tollmarsh screamed, *"I'm gonna cut your fucking heart out!"*

Hardin shook his head, tried to clear it of the buzzing. The buzzing persisted.

"You don't have a hope in hell, Tollmarsh," he croaked.

"You think so? You think your pissant effort's gonna stop me? Your squad's already being wrapped up for body-bags, shithead. By the time my men've finished with 'em they'll be the sorriest-looking bunch of stray-dog fuckers you've ever seen. Not that you'll live that long, you sonuvabitch."

Hardin said, "I sent two men back, before we came in here."

"He's bluffing, sir. The scumbag's fulla shit." That was Nulty, behind him. That meant Nulty had been the guy who'd decked him.

Tollmarsh shook his head violently. It seemed to Hardin that the stocky little man was having trouble concentrating.

"He's an ass-wipe, sure enough. That's right. Damn right."

He stood there, the knife thrust out towards Hardin, but his eyes were elsewhere, darting around the room, up at the ceiling, down at the floor. A crafty smile suddenly tugged at his lips, and this was made more grotesquely foxy by the lamp on the floor, which was now shining directly up at his face. The shadows, Hardin decided, were all wrong; they masked his chin, the bridge of his nose, his forehead.

Tollmarsh said, "I'm gonna personally . . ."—then he stopped, took a deep breath. He said ". . . personally . . . peel ya . . . person . . ." He seemed to be experiencing some difficulty taking air into his lungs; his breathing was short and quick and jerky. He tried again. "Peel ya . . . ya . . . peel . . . ya . . . like . . . like a . . ."

He suddenly stooped, stared fixedly at the exposed lightbulb, his eyes wide and unblinking. He chuckled fatly. All at once he seemed to have lost all interest in the proceedings; seemed to be in a world of his own.

"Sir?" said Nulty, puzzled.

Tollmarsh moved back from the light, still in a crouched position. He began to wave the knife slowly back and forth in front of his face, following its progress through the air with his eyes. He licked his lips, an expression of eager, greedy anticipation on his face.

"Major?" said Nulty, his voice cracking up slightly

on the final syllable.

Tollmarsh didn't appear to have heard him. He seemed to be utterly divorced from his immediate surroundings, oblivious of everything and everyone in the room. With infinite — almost exaggerated — care he turned in a quarter circle, his left arm reaching slowly outwards, the fingers extended. The fingers began to twitch and clutch, as though they were trying to grasp something. He looked like some kind of New Wave ballet dancer rehearsing an intricate piece of mime.

Tollmarsh said, "It's not there." His voice rose. "Not there!"

He thrust his hand out, swept the arm round wildly, his face creased up into a mask of stunned bewilderment, as though he'd just been rammed with a cattle-prod. One of the men holding rifles stepped across to him, grabbing him by the shoulder. Tollmarsh's right hand — the hand still clutching Hardin's knife — brushed him off, and the blade hacked across the man's chest. The man staggered backwards, open-mouthed, as his shirt parted across in a neat, sweet line, and a gush of blood welled up from a long furrow in the flesh.

Nulty said, "Sir, for fuck's sake . . ." — and Ernie Tollmarsh began to shout.

"They're all around . . . all there . . . sweet Jesus . . . coming at me . . . on all sides . . ."

His arms began to windmill and flail around in furious, crazy, spasmodic gestures — up and down, to each side of him, thrusting and heaving and shoving at nothing. His sweat-slick face contorted itself into a death's head rictus of pure grinning terror.

"There . . . *there* . . . THERE!" he shrieked, whirling

around in a wild dervish dance, his arms now flapping at the air as though he was trying to lift off in flight. Grotesquely distorted shadows flared jaggedly across the wall behind him, in nightmarish imitation of reality.

"The light!" he screamed.

His head jerked back and his right hand swept round in a tight circle—light from the lamp catching the blade and transforming it for an instant of time into a coruscation of glittering fire. Then the fire blinked off suddenly and shockingly, drowned out in a pumping surge of dark crimson as the razor-edge of the blade sheared across the taut flesh of his exposed throat, sinking deep, opening up a second mouth across the jugular.

Tollmarsh, spouting blood, toppled backwards and crashed to the floor, his body juddering in spasms that seemed to be timed to each pumping scarlet gout.

"Jesus," breathed someone in awe, "he flipped. The man truly wigged out."

Hardin was shoved to one side roughly as Nulty strode past him towards the twitching figure.

"I don't believe this," he muttered, "I don't fuckin' believe it." He turned sharply, pointing at Hardin. "What the fuck goes on here?"

Hardin shrugged.

"How should I know?"

Nulty's face darkened with rage.

"You know something about this, shitstick—I know it! I can smell it! What happened to the guy?"

"You ask me, he OD-ed."

"OD-ed?" yelled Nulty. "What on—*Jim Beam?*"

"All I can say," said Hardin, "he was acting very weird. Primo case of *folie de grandeur* if ever I saw one." He felt he was beginning to regain shape now.

224

His brain had settled down; though still aching, his head was not buzzing any more. Everything was much less distorted.

"Folly? What?" Nulty stepped towards him, his voice pitching low. "Mister, I'm gonna nail your nuts to the fucking wall."

Ignoring the rifleman, Hardin crouched slightly, grinning, his arms loose at his sides.

"You and Godzilla, Nulty? You couldn't take a bed-bug in a boom-boom house."

Nulty wheeled round, stooped and reached for the knife still clutched in Tollmarsh's hand. He was in this position when the sudden distinctive *crump* of a mortar shell exploding sounded outside, followed by the chilling stammer of automatic fire. Nulty jerked upright.

"What in hell's name was that?"

"Sounded to me like a mortar," said Hardin. He knew it could only mean one thing: the EnVees were in the valley. Either Marco had caused them to be let in, or Tho had gotten tired of waiting and had stormed the entrance. Whatever, resolution of this particular situation was clearly not too far away.

Nulty turned on him.

"You think the fucking cavalry's arrived to save your ass?" he screamed.

"Not exactly. I think the little yellow men are flooding into the valley."

"What the fuck is that supposed to mean?"

"The EnVees. I made a deal with them. I let 'em in; they take you out. Simple."

Nulty's expression was almost comical: a mixture of rage and bafflement and panic, with a touch of real anguish dabbed in. Hardin almost felt sorry for him.

"You made a . . .?"

The thud-thud-thud of mortars was closer now, shaking the ground on which the hut-piles stood.

"Jesus!"

Nulty lunged for the door and disappeared, his boots hammering in the corridor outside. Adrenalin suddenly burned through Hardin's system as he simply reached out at the nearest guard and plucked the rifle out of his hands.

It was a Kalashnikov, already on automatic. The man started to say "Hey!"—but the ejaculation ended in a coughing scream as Hardin opened up. The four men were roughly in a line stretching towards the door and Hardin mowed them down with a burst that lasted possibly four seconds; certainly no longer. Each man screamed and danced and fell in sequence, Hardin's rounds unstitching them across their chests, blowing blood back out of them in long spouting spurts that paint-sprayed the wooden wall behind.

Hardin lowered the weapon, took a deep breath, wiped blood off his face wearily. He reached down and pulled his knife out of Tollmarsh's stiffening fingers. The killing—and it was an almost invariable after-effect of killing for him—had flicked some psychic switch in his brain, and plans and game-runs and moves were tumbling through his mind at breakneck, yet still graspable, speed. The most logical move of all was clearly a fast link-up with Marco, wherever the hell he was. Tollmarsh had said that Marco and his men were being mopped up, so that could be a problem. On the other hand, there seemed no doubt that the EnVees were inside the valley and only Marco or one of his group could have let them in.

There was something else that had to be considered, too. Tollmarsh had seemed willing enough to accept Hardin into the company—as long as Hardin checked out. Clearly Tollmarsh had set up a call to someone as soon as he'd returned to the valley. When that call had come in, Tollmarsh had discovered that no way did Hardin check out. But who had he called? Who'd been his informant? Whoever it was had to be the real honcho of this outfit, the guy who'd dreamed it up and set it into motion, the guy who was pulling the strings.

Some disgruntled top echelon brass in Saigon, maybe, out for escalation at any price? Or maybe Swales, the gung-ho-for-glory Lieutenant General and Special Forces coordinator? The cap would fit him. Swales was power-hungry if anyone was.

Or was it—and again Hardin experienced an icy tingle in his mind—Halderling?

On the face of it, it seemed a crazy notion, way over the edge. But Halderling was deep, there was no damn doubt about that at all. He might be coming up for retirement, but he hadn't lost his grip on events and his mind was as convoluted as a labyrinth. At the briefing back in Nam, the old man had seemed seriously worried. But that, frankly, didn't mean jack-shit. Halderling was a bunco artist supreme, who made Ivan Kreuzer seem like Anne of Green Gables.

Was this whole deal part of some wild scheme he'd dreamed up? More to the point, was Halderling setting him up as a juicy shooting target, object unknown?

Hardin turned as hurrying footsteps sounded in the passageway. A big man suddenly sprang into the doorway, M-16 levelled, covering the room.

"Hold it!" yelled the man. And relaxed, lowering the

rifle, taking in the scene. "Jesus, Colonel, high body-count. I gotta say, it's frankly like a fucking slaughterhouse in here."

The man was Olsen. He stepped through the doorway, followed by Joe Fuller, Doc Pepper, and a winded, sweating Leroy Vogt. Vogt gazed round the room, gaping incredulously at the bodies and the scarlet splash-marks on the walls and the floor, as though plasma had been collected in a bucket and then thrown around by a drunken intern.

"Let's hear it, Olsen," said Hardin.

Olsen said, "Those sneaky little assholes."

"What's the story?"

"A pig-fucker of a one, Colonel, beggin' your pardon. Captain Marco said to bring 'em in. The EnVees, that is. We'd already tagged the sentries, so me and Joe Fuller, O'Mara, Pepper and the kid here, we took off down-valley, took the fuckers out. Real sweet operation, Colonel, I gotta say. Took no time at all. Captain Marco said to beat it fast once we'd flared Charlie. Just in case, you know, sir, they reneged on the deal, tried to nail us. We had to get back down to the valley, down the scree, right?" Olsen paused, a disgusted expression sliding across his face. "The fuckers were waiting for us, Goddamnit. They must've bellied in. You know, sir, like — sneaked through the pass in the fucking dark sometime. They could've been waiting there the past fucking week, living on rats, tabs, like that. They couldn't finger the sentries up above, but they just stuck it out there's what I think, waiting for us to do the fucking job. The little crappers blew the spade kid right out, just as we climbed down the Goddamn rocks. There were three, maybe four, I dunno. I nailed one of the sonsabitches, and I think maybe the kid here got one, but then we frankly fell down that crapping scree like God was shitting on us, you know? *Jesus!*"

Olsen's final imprecation was heart-felt. Hardin could now see that all four men were weary, done in, their fatigues ripped and torn by rocks and sharp stones. And the news was bad. Hardin had known that Tho would double-cross him first chance he got, but it had seemed to him that the Vietnamese would make his play only when the valley was secured. Now he was another man down, and the odds against him were lengthening drastically.

"Okay," he said, "so the EnVees are in."

"And close. I gotta frankly say, sir, tight up our ass. They must've had everything set up just right and ready, because they started throwing mortars at the trees and everything when we were still running. What I think, sir, with all respect, we gotta get our butts mobile. I figure the gooks are gonna maybe pull an encirclement, up both sides of the valley. They could squeeze our balls, Colonel."

Hardin nodded; that had already occurred to him. He gestured at the bodies.

"Pick up spare clips. We'll go find Captain Marco."

Doc Pepper stared down at Tollmarsh. The blood had stopped pumping out of his slit throat, and was now merely oozing blackly. Flies were already beginning to gather for the feast.

"Eyes look kind of weird. He do that himself, sir?"

"He surely did, Pepper."

"Wow. Kind of a dumb thing to do wouldn't you say?"

Hardin smiled wolfishly.

"He partook of strong liquor, Doc. It blew his mind."

Doc Pepper took this in, thought about it for a couple of seconds, scratched his nose.

"Man, this fucking conflict gets heavier and heavier," he said.

Hoang Van Tho gazed at the flame-lit darkness with satisfaction.

All his men and matériel were now safely through the pass. It could not take longer than two hours at the most to secure the entire valley.

Already the Yankees were fighting off an attack on the right flank, and were doing so with a measure of success. This did not matter. The group he'd sent up the right-hand side of the valley, close to the cliff-wall and heading directly for the cave-area, was a token force only—a feint on which the Americans could expend as much energy and fire-power as they liked. Just so long as they remained under the impression that it was the main attacking force.

In fact it wasn't. Tho's largest body of troops was on the left of the valley, to the west, even now heading through the trees towards the waterfall where it would regroup, and then smash its way through to the caves. It was the classic hammer-and-anvil manoeuvre, much favoured by Vo Nguyen Giap and other senior North Vietnamese tacticians.

And why not?, thought Hoang Van Tho, as he began to make his way down the scree towards the valley floor.

The simplest moves were invariably the best moves. And the simpler they were, the more unexpected they were, and thus the most likely to succeed.

Certainly, the success of this particular venture was absolutely assured. Thanks to the Yankee Colonel, Hardin, of course, but he would be, in the long-term assessment of the operation, of minor importance only; merely the key in the lock, so to say. He was a foolish optimist. Soon he would be killed. Tho dismissed Hardin from his mind, and concentrated instead on thinking of the glory that would so very soon be heaped upon his head by the high-cadres in Hanoi.

The trees were burning.

Marco sniffed the air appreciatively as he fired his Kalashnikov, relishing the pine-sap fragrance that wafted through the firefight stink.

"Some damn smell," he said as he caught a bunch of figures, blackly silhouetted against the back-cloth of flames as they sprinted for cover, and sent them skittling over with a three-second burst.

"Hey, Captain, we gotta get outta here," yelled Garrett above the thunder of weaponry. "All it needs is a couple grenades and we're gonna be hamburger."

They were in a shallow culvert that ran under the treeline at the edge of the cantonment. At first Marco had been inclined to hold the comm-hut, but had rejected the idea almost as soon as it had slid into his mind. Too claustrophobic.

Any case, the bad guys could decide the hell with the radio equipment (like they'd done with the jammer back at Pen Kho), and simply blow the hut away.

They'd exited fast, sprinting across the clearing as men started to boil out from surrounding huts, alerted by Garrett's burst of fire and its immediate consequences. They could have made it to the trees but some quick-thinking dude had magicked a couple of MGs from somewhere, and cut off their retreat with impenetrable lines of tracer.

Huddled in the ditch they'd poured fire back at the huts and had only been saved from full-scale assault by the sudden *woof-woof-woof* of mortars in back of them. That had taken the pressure off considerably; Tollmarsh's men had split up and the mainforce had headed off down-valley (hopefully, thought Marco, through the pines).

Which still left an unhealthy number of guys blasting off in their direction.

Marco fast-crawled up the ditch in the flame-lit darkness, heaving himself along on his elbows, his rifle held out in front of them. Other smells were crowding out the odour of pine now; less agreeable ones: hot oil, the choking tang of cordite, and—what had become ubiquitous in Nam—the sickly-sweet pork-roast stench of burning flesh. Marco had never smelled burning flesh before he'd arrived in Nam; it had certainly never occurred to him that the odour would so soon become an important part of his sensory experience; that he would almost feel deprived without it. He reached Comeraro, wincing as a particularly heavy mortar-blast shook the earth beneath him.

He said, "They walkin' mortars up towards us. We gonna have to move, an' the only way is back where we came from."

"We'll be running straight into MG-fire, Captain."

"So we gonna have to take the fuckin' MGs out." Marco jerked a thumb over his shoulder. "Ditch curves round back there, but flat for maybe ten yards. We get across that ten-stretch, we got us a clear field to the

MGs, blow their shit away."

Tracers, glowing the dark, lanced low, cropping the grass, as they squirmed back along the ditch, taking Garrett with them, Colenso following on behind.

"Grenades," snapped Marco. "Two-second sequence."

He flung an arm back, hurled a grenade, counted "Thousand-one, thousand-two," hurled another, then ran, bent low, his stomach churning. The darkness was torn apart by the grenades, and the crash of a third explosion erupted just as he dived into the ditch-continuation, scrambling along it fast to give the others room.

There was another thudding blast and Garrett, cursing vitriolically, landed in the ditch in a spray of dirt. Marco lifted his AK-47 and cut loose at the two MGs, now exposed to fire. He glanced round and saw Comeraro sprinting and diving, with Colenso tight behind him. Colenso didn't make it.

Two separate lines of fire lashed him and flung him sideways, bundling him like a blazing Catherine-wheel head-over-heels into the brush.

By now Garrett and Comeraro were firing, and the three of them raked the two MGs from side to side, back and forth, up and down. Marco experienced a feeling of savage satisfaction as they turned the nest into an abattoir; not because he'd liked Colenso—Hell, he hadn't even known him—but because these renegade fuckers had just wiped out his own MG-gunner, a useful card in the deck.

Marco slammed Garrett on the shoulder, pointed, and jumped to his feet. All three men sprinted the 50 yards or so to the wrecked MG-emplacement, ducking and swerving as rifles barked and chattered from the direction of the huts. Garrett banged himself down behind the nearest MG and Comeraro belt-fed him as shapes suddenly seemed to erupt from nowhere, charging down the grassy slope towards them through drifting clouds of smoke. Garrett swivelled and started to laugh in genuine glee, but the sound was drowned by the hammering death-song of the MG as he opened up. He dragged the shuddering weapon from right to left and back again, his mouth open, his teeth bared, his eyes mere slits. Rounds kicked earth-clods into the air around them and howled off ammo-boxes, but Garrett scythed through the line of men, cutting them down at ankle-level in one sweep and blowing their heads apart as they collapsed on the second. The line dissolved; all that was left was a bloody shambles of dead and dying men.

Marco tensed to spring up, then said "Oh, *shit!*" in a despairing voice, as, up the slope, the nearest hut disintegrated in a blossom of smoke and fire. Bits of wood, railings and metal spiralled up into the air in the midst of the wash of light, disappearing as darkness fell once more. Then a second hut powered apart in a blaze of orange fire, but this time the after-effect was utterly fearsome. Rounds cracked and fizzed and popped, grenades detonated viciously, shells erupted in fierce, ear-splitting explosions. Light pulsed and bloomed angrily, searing the eyes. It was like a solo from an ensemble of *avant-garde* drummers crazed on acid, lit by a strobe-operator with the DTs.

"Hit a fuckin' ammo-dump," screamed Marco through the enormous blast of sound. Then, "Hey, up to the left!"

Up to the left, shadowless in the geysering light-show, was Hardin, making signals with his hands.

"Far as I can tell," said Hardin "the EnVees are on the perimeters of the pine forest, mortaring up. Olsen figures that more of 'em are sweeping round the outer edges by the waterfall, to take the caves and hit these guys from behind."

"Yeah," nodded Marco. "Nut-cracker."

They were huddled by the rock-face to the rear of the hut cantonment. Olsen and Vogt were on guard at the north end of the long-house wall, Fuller and Garrett to the south. Hardin and Marco and Comeraro squatted in a circle near the centre. Doc Pepper sat back against a boulder, smoking.

"Tho," said Hardin, "could have a couple thousand men out there, maybe more. Tollmarsh never had more'n 400, top score."

"Which mean he gonna get creamed," said Marco.

"Tollmarsh already is. A messy one."

"Oh? You ice him?"

"Not exactly. I slipped some junk I had on me into his whiskey. Mescaline derivative."

"Jesus. He go out a happy man?"

"Not so's you'd notice."

"His name was writ in water," said Marco solemnly.

"What it means is, his men are gonna be running around like a chicken without a head. Tho is gonna beat the living shit out of them." He paused. "And us, if he catches us."

"You think the wild cards got home, Colonel?" said Comeraro.

Hardin shrugged.

"Lap of the gods."

The mortars were exploding every few seconds now, and the thunder-crack of their detonations was almost deafening.

"So what we gonna do?" said Marco.

"Grab a chopper," said Hardin.

The thinking behind this was simple. Once they were in the air, in a weaponed-up gunship, they had some kind of command of the overall situation; also they could radio out. The hell with Halderling and his matériel (especially if it was Halderling who was behind all this); let the EnVees and the renegades fight it out amongst themselves. Whatever happened, the renegades were finished and Tho would soon hold the valley —although his victory would be short-lived; strangled at birth in fact. It would not take long for a formation of B-52s to truly sanitise the situation. Tho would not even have time to rough out sites for the missile silos in his head, let alone build the Goddamn things.

Tollmarsh, the titular head of operation, was dead so no one was going to be standing trial back in Nam—unless they made that guy Nulty (the only other man who seemed to hold some kind of rank here) the scapegoat, but that depended on finding him amongst all this chaos and carnage, and Hardin had no intention of wasting his time going looking for him.

Then, chased by rounds as he dashed across the open space between two huts, Hardin grinned suddenly. Not that he needed to. It was typical of life—in the nature of things so disordered, muddled, fucking sloppy—to suddenly present him with a smooth and harmonious pay-off when he least expected it.

There was Nulty, at the edge of the wide slab of smooth rock that served as the chopper apron, screaming at a bunch of guys to drag the lone Huey (clearly, the one Tollmarsh had flown in on) into the caves.

"Nail 'em," yelled Hardin, "but leave the short guy."

Comeraro cut loose with an Armalite, Hardin wincing as rounds hammered at the chopper fuselage. But men went down screaming and at least Comeraro wasn't hitting fuel tanks.

He saw Nulty head for the nose of the Huey then jump back as Olsen, ahead, opened up, cutting off his retreat with a long burst. Nulty dived for the chopper's skids and barrelled under the belly of the bird; when he came up again, he was firing back, sending a stream of lead spraying across the apron.

To the right, Hardin could see the cave-openings, eerily flame-lit in the furious darkness. He could see the vague shapes of parked choppers, placed well back from the vaulted, wind-sculpted entrances, and knew that from their size—from the fact that they could accommodate so many birds—the caves must stretch back deep into the heart of the mountainside. The perfect position for a last-ditch stand; trying to winkle determined (possibly suicidal) Special Forces vets out of there was going to be difficult, well-nigh impossible.

Hardin concentrated on Nulty, a problem with a simpler solution, and saw that now Olsen and Comeraro had been joined by Joe Fuller, and all three men were holding him down with interlocking lines of fire. The poor fucker couldn't even lift his head for fear of having his eyes ripped out by flying shards of stone kicked up by three vicious streams of rounds.

Hardin sprang to his feet and sprinted across the apron, his boots pounding at the smooth rock. The murderous hail of fire ceased abruptly as the gunners saw him, and Nulty, too, at this sudden let-up, raised his head. In the flickering firelight he looked like some thwarted demon as he recognised Hardin, an expression of pure rage boiling over his features.

He pulled at his rifle, but Hardin was already flying through the air, lying sideways on nothing, his feet kicking out at Nulty's face as he hurtled in. Nulty screamed as Hardin's boots connected, and then Hardin was thudding down on to the rock-pad and, using his Kalashnikov, sweeping Nulty's rifle out of his hands with a tremendous clubbing blow. He scrambled round, clutched at Nulty's throat with his left hand, and landed a jarring roundhouse jolt to the right side of his face. Nulty went limp.

"Move!"

That was Marco, already on his feet and running. Hardin dragged Nulty's dead weight up and over, into the chopper interior. He shoved the recumbent figure to one side, then dived into a crouched position beside the port door, cutting loose with the AK as his men sprinted across the apron towards the bird.

Marco took a flying leap past him, yelling "No time for talkin'! This place is walkin'!"

Garrett thudded in after him, firing from the hip straight through the open starboard door and out into the blazing night at a group of men on the other side of the apron.

"So get your ass in gear and outta here, Captain!" he bawled. "We're a sitting fucking target!"

As Hardin pulled men into the chopper he was aware that Nulty was blearily coming to. The man started babbling, something about "booby-traps." He was beginning to get wild-eyed.

"What the hell is he talking about?"

"Captain Marco's idea," said Olsen. "Him and me

and the Lieutenant, sir, we shifted the trip-wires around in the pinewoods, turned the safe paths into fucking death-traps. I frankly figure that when these sonsabitches ran out to hit the Cong, half of 'em must've blown themselves to hell before they even started."

Despite the situation, Hardin started to laugh. Nulty jerked himself up on to one elbow and screamed "Bastard!"

"That's *Mister* Bastard to you, shithead," snarled Garrett, jabbing him viciously in the ribs with the barrel of his Armalite.

Above them, the rotors began to stir lazily—too lazily, thought Hardin, aware that Garrett had been appallingly, blindingly right. They *were* a sitting target—for anyone who cared to home in on them. Charlie or the renegades, it made no difference—both parties wanted to blow them away.

And as he thought that, the bullhorn blared.

"Colonel Hardin! You and your party are already dead men!"

The sound was clear, the words intelligible, even through the crash and clamour of the firefight; Hardin knew that Tho must be very close. He scrambled forward to the pilot's area.

"Where d'you think?"

Marco nodded towards the plexiglas windscreen.

"He about there somewhere. Where the trees ain't caught yet. Right in front of us."

"You are hoping for a miracle, Colonel. Do not hope. Just pray. Your chopper-man did not get home."

"Right in front of my sweet tubes," said Marco, leaning forward.

As the turbine took hold with an ear-splitting bellow

and the Huey's fat nose dipped slightly as the big bird lifted, six 2.75" rockets exploded from each side-mounted pod and streaked into the trees. There was a blare of sound; a blaze of fierce and blinding irradiation. Then Marco was wrestling with the Huey's controls as the shock-wave billowed outwards, pounding at the chopper like a succession of mighty hammer-blows.

The rotors clawed air as the chopper canted over to one side, loose fittings avalanching out of the port doorway. Then she rose into the blackness of the night sky at any angle and, it seemed to those desperately clinging on inside, with the gut-churning speed of an express elevator. Leroy Vogt, lying flat on the floor, one hand gripping the handle of an ammunition box while his boots dangled in space, screamed in panic, the contents of his stomach slopping around like a ship's bilges.

Hardin gazed down at the scene below. It seemed as though the whole of one end of the valley was awash with fire; in some places the flames looked to be over twenty foot high. You needed no night-scope to penetrate the darkness for there was no darkness, only a lurid, flickering light that transformed the whole valley into some weird and wild outpost of Hell.

Even as he watched more angry, red-cored eruptions bloomed amongst the pines towards the waterfall; a whole succession of explosions, one after another, in almost orderly progression. It was clear to him what was happening. The valley might be judged to be impregnable from assault on the surface, but Tollmarsh had not trusted this judgement; had taken no chances at all. He'd seeded linked lines of booby-traps across the entire area and now they were detonating with a domino effect. The bulk of the EnVee forces would be caught in the centre of the appalling holocaust.

And there wouldn't be much left of the renegades, either.

"Hey, Colonel!"

Comeraro, sitting in the co-pilot's seat, was yelling at him, pointing frontwards. Hardin blinked, screwed up his eyes, finally decided that what looked to be a vast control-board of winking, flashing lights sweeping down towards them through the darkness was no figment of his imagination.

"The radio!"

As Comeraro flicked switches, swept the dial, Hardin grabbed for some headphones. A voice suddenly burst through the hiss and crackling sludge of the net.

". . . chopper? D'you read, lone chopper? Read me damn fast, or we blow you to hell outta the sky!"

It was the voice of General Lewis J. Halderling.

Chapter Twelve

Halderling said, "So you sent two men?"

"Yeah." Hardin Zippoed a cigarette, blew a plume of grey out of his mouth into the reeking, smoke-soured dawn air. "I had to sacrifice Hanks. Knew he wouldn't make it; knew Tho'd be watching the chopper like a hawk. But I figured Tho'd be satisfied if he nailed Hanks, and wouldn't think I'd sent another guy by another route, especially on foot. But all Lantry had to do was get to a Khymer ville only 30 klicks to the east where the honcho's been holding a radio for me for two, three years."

Halderling nodded, fed tobacco into the charred bowl of his pipe.

"He radioed the coordinates out a couple of days ago. I'd've been here a whole lot sooner, John, but I needed the time to pull a really muscular force together. Okay, I said I wouldn't move until it was a secure situation, but then I figured, what the hell — we could get our asses shot off, but on the other hand we could be of use. Frankly, I figured you'd somehow turn the trick." As he lit his pipe, Halderling glanced around. "What I didn't figure was that you'd turn the Goddamn place into a crematorium."

Some of the trees down-valley were still burning;

most were now blackened, defoliated—stark fingers pointing up through the smoke-laden air at a stone-grey sky still heavy with the rain-bearing clouds that had already soaked the holocaust down to a manageable level.

Halderling and his flying armada had—once Hardin had made contact—sheered off to a holding position to let the fire run its furious course. Just before dawn the clouds had opened up, deluging the burning valley and its immediate surrounds. The downpour had lasted an hour, but it had been enough. Halderling had swooped in, rocket-blasting the gun-emplacements in the cliff walls and dropping men from three big Chinook troop-carriers like eggs from hyper-fertile hens.

It had been a smooth operation, a sweet and simple mop-up. Most of the EnVees who had been moving up the west side of the valley had been unable to escape from the effects of the booby-trap detonations and there was a lot of grilled steak in what was left of the undergrowth; those who'd managed to flee in time had regrouped near the entrance, but had then been destroyed in the chopper rocket-strikes Halderling had ordered when the rain had eased. And those who were left were quickly dealt with when the Hueys had landed. Of Hoang Van Tho there was no sign.

The renegades, too, were in a sorry and dispirited state. Many had been blown to shreds amongst the pines, or mown down by EnVee-fire. The survivors had holed up in the caves, while the holocaust raged outside, but had offered only token resistance when Halderling's chopper force landed on the rock-apron; the last-ditch syndrome seemed to have been seared out of them.

"Looks like I'll be getting most of my matériel back in

one piece," said Halderling. "Which is, I guess, something."

"And you got yourself a scapegoat too," said Hardin, watching as a blank-faced Nulty was prodded towards one of the Hueys.

He was still not entirely sure how to approach the general on the wider implications and ramifications of this whole business, mainly because he was still not entirely sure how deep Halderling was implicated, or even if any responsibility could be laid on his desk at all. *Someone* had been behind Tollmarsh (someone, Goddamnit, had contacted Tollmarsh and blown the whistle on *him*) and Halderling — all things considered — seemed like a prime candidate. The fact that he'd turned up like he had made no difference — didn't in fact mean a fucking thing. Halderling was enough of a pragmatist to change his mind about a firm decision if other options, of whatever nature, presented themselves.

"Ernie Tollmarsh," muttered Halderling, rubbing a leathery finger across the bridge of his nose. "Goddamn! A redneck, sure, but I wouldn't've fingered him for the honcho of a wildcat outfit like this. Good at his job, maybe, but he had the planning capabilities of a sick roach."

"Yeah, well," said Hardin, "he didn't plan this, did he?"

It was not a question, and Halderling caught the stripped-sour tinge in Hardin's tone. The General surveyed his bleak-faced subordinate and was about to comment when an aide scurried up from the direction of the gunships.

"You're gonna kick me, sir, but I lost the fucker."

Halderling frowned irritably.

"Lost him? Jesus, Landau, we're not in the Thieves' Market here, for Christ's sake!"

The aide looked unhappy.

"Well go Goddamn find him!"

"Who've you lost?" said Hardin, not really interested.

"The pissant little spook. He tagged along for . . ."

"The spook?" Hardin stared at Halderling as though the general had just gone into an impromptu tango.

"Yeah. Reisberson. The Company man. Just wanted someone to keep an eye on him, see he didn't . . ."

Hardin turned fast and sprinted away as though EnVee rounds were kicking up mud at his heels again. The jigsaw had fallen into place, neatly and without any fuss at all, and as he ran he cursed himself. It was a question of lateral thinking, he thought. The image that had been in the forefront of his mind the whole time had been of one man, shadowy, amorphous, but — whoever it was — a single entity. He should have known better.

No one man could've dealt with the logistics on show here — no one man could've arranged the transport of the hut building materials, the generators, the desks and chairs and tables, the sophisticated electrical equipment (Jesus, no wonder these guys had dumped that jammer; they knew they could re-order at the flick of a transmitter switch). Or the food, cartons of cigarettes, cigars, comforts, good whisky. No one man could have pulled all that together — but a company of men could.

Or — *the* Company.

The Goddamn fucking rat-bastard CIA.

Hardin ran. He knew where Reisberson would be.

He ran through the flame-stripped pines, his boots

thudding into ash and mud and muck, and burst through a knot of Halderling's men escorting prisoners towards the choppers. Most of the cantonment was still intact; the fire had not been able to gain a purchase on the rock-shelf on which most of the huts stood. Hardin sprang up the steps leading to Ernie Tollmarsh's nerve-centre, and pounded along the corridor. One mighty shove with his boot at the closed door sent it crashing inwards. He sprang in, the Kalashnikov thrust outwards.

Reisberson swung round, a sick grin on his face. As though he'd been caught with his hand in the till.

The steel-frame filing cabinet yawned emptily against the wall; its drawers had been wrenched out and placed on the floor. Reisberson had been stuffing thin card files into a briefcase. In his stooped position, he now made a slight movement with his right hand.

"Don't," warned Hardin. "One more twitch and you've had it." He said, "I'm not gonna kill you, shithead. Just blow your kneecaps through the wall. You'll be okay to testify."

"Testify, shit," said Reisbeson. "You're outta your depth, Hardin. This thing's too big for you, buddy. Back off and out, close the door. Just forget it, right."

"*Nukes,*" spat Hardin.

Reisberson's face was expressionless; the grin had gone.

"Jesus," said Hardin, "you'd've let a clown like Ernie Tollmarsh get his paws on a bunch of nukes and fire 'em off at the North, China, Russia, all points of the fucking compass. Christ, I've heard of some moronic schemes before now, Reisberson, but this one gets me to thinking you guys at Langley got as much brain as a whoopee cushion."

"Look . . ." said Reisberson.

"Guy I know told me you guys had a plan for making Fidel Castro's dick fall off. I didn't believe it. Not until now."

"Listen to me, Hardin . . ."

"You're really an inept bunch of assholes, you know that? Nukes. My God."

"For the greater good, Hardin," said Reisberson tightly. "That's the name of the game.

"For the greater lump of horseshit. At back of this there's a power-play, Reisberson. All this pissing around was to jockey Halderling and the SSG out of a desk in Saigon. Of all the Special Forces groups the SSG was the hardest hit by these renegade fuckers, which means—or so the whisper goes, you bet—that Halderling isn't running a very tight ship these days; getting past it. And he doesn't dig the Company, either. Get rid of the old fart and you clowns have yourselves another slice of territory. Smart work."

He stepped further into the room, nearer to Reisberson, but not near enough for the CIA operative to be able to do anything about it. There was a faint sheen of sweat on Reisberson's brow now.

"Then one of your assets discovered this valley—the perfect location for any number of interesting schemes. And some genius in Thong Nhut comes up with the idea of filling it with disaffected Specials with a real Red-hating redneck ramrodding them—and, hey, even better, how about giving 'em a few nukes after a while, so they can destroy the world as well as the SSG? Wow, that's terrific! What I'm beginning to wonder, Reisberson, is, does even that failed used-car salesman currently occupying the Oval Office know anything

247

about this? I have a feeling, not. I have a strong feeling all this is the work of some tight little bunch of crazies out at Langley, VA, playing global checkers."

"Look," said Reisberson in a stifled voice. "Those guys—Tollmarsh—the whole bunch, they were getting pissed with the army, pissed with all the troop pull-outs. Our idea was to . . ."

"My ass," said Hardin. "You're trying to turn these motherfuckers into heroes, but it won't go. What was it Tollmarsh said to me? The loot's very good, he said. Now where would Tollmarsh get all this very good loot from, if not CIA coffers? Probably some of the laundered profits from all that sweet heroin you guys are running across Laos. Sure, there's an element of anti-Red in the mix, but I figure most of these sonsabitches loved money more'n they hated Commies or Luke the Gook."

As he was speaking Hardin was suddenly aware that Reisberson was no longer focussing on him but on something behind his back. The CIA agent's eyes were wide; there was a tinge of shock in his expression.

"Jesus," said Hardin disgustedly, "you make a play like that, and you'll get me to believing you're even more of a Goddamn amateur than I figure you for anyway."

Which was when something barged into him from behind.

Hardin caught a strong sour odour—a whiff of the jungle mixed in with the dark, ugly stench of festering rot. Then, even as he lurched to one side, the AK falling away from him, he saw an automatic appear in Reisberson's right hand, heard the crash of a shot, and felt a tremendous blow in his left shoulder, as though he'd been socked with a baseball bat. By the time pain began to rasp across his nerve-ends, he was a dazed heap in one corner of the room, sprawled behind the open door.

A figure, gaunt and filthy, staggered into view. His fatigues were ripped and torn, half off his back, and crusted with dried mud and blood and slime; bits of creeper, leaves, twigs, grasses adhered to him, not only to the tattered remnants of his clothes but to his scarred and blood-smeared skin. Round his waist was wrapped some kind of scarf or strip of thick-weave cloth which might once have been white or at least cream, but was now, at the side, black with blood. To Hardin, staring through blurred and watering eyes, the tatterdemalion figure seemed to have shambled straight out of the pages of *Tales from the Crypt* or any of the other horror comics he'd devoured as a kid.

The man came to a halt, uncertainly. He was clutching something in his right hand, but his left arm was in the air, fingers extended; the arm moved in a slow and wavering half-circle. The head turned in his direction, and Hardin saw that his right eye was partially closed and where his left eye had been was now only a scarlet hole, black-encrusted round the rim. It was clear he was stone-blind.

Reisberson said, hoarsely, "Jesus Christ . . ."

Instantly—shockingly—the head whipped back round to face in Reisberson's direction. The man whispered, *"Nulty . . ."* and took a step forward.

He said, "Got . . . something for you . . . Nulty" in a rasping croak, and pushed out his right hand.

Reisberson gasped "Fucking grenade!" in a voice that was soaked in terror, took a step back, and shot the man twice in the vicinity of the heart.

Still holding the grenade, the man staggered backwards without a sound, pitched up against the door, and seemed to bounce right back into the centre of the room again. He kept on going until he slammed into Reisberson and curled his left arm, almost affectionately, round the CIA agent's neck. The two men collapsed into an angle of the wall.

Hardin watched all this and felt that none of it could possibly be happening. He'd passed out, was what it was; was seeing visions, nightmares. Or he was dead and this was Hell. But he knew it was as real as anything he'd experienced in the past ten years.

He was aware that he'd fallen very close to the cold, stark, glaring-eyed corpse of Ernie Tollmarsh, and Ernie Tollmarsh had a .45 in his waistband still, and Hardin wanted Reisberson alive and in one piece and not just gobbets of flesh scattered around the room.

As he reached out and tugged at the .45's butt, he heard two muffled thuds and realised that Reisberson was still pulling the trigger of his automatic and the barrel was jammed up against the scarecrow's body somewhere. This seemed to make no difference whatsoever. The man was still tight into Reisberson as though welded to him and even though he'd taken several rounds at point-blank range was now babbling incoherently.

Despite the jolting shafts of agony throbbing down his left arm from the shoulder, Hardin gripped the .45 two-fisted, his back against the wall, and waited several seconds for a side-shot. This came when Reisberson and the man seemed to waltz to one side, lurching towards the doorway. Hardin breathed out, blinked sweat from his eyes, and squeezed a round into the man's head, not unadjacent to the parietal bone.

The back of the cranium burst outwards in a fuzzy shower of red and grey and the scarecrow jumped back from Reisberson, both hands up in the air, as though jolted by a severe electrical charge. The egg dropped.

Reisberson shrieked *"Spoon's off!"* in a voice that sounded like he'd just been castrated, and Hardin had just enough time to throw his good arm across his face and curl over into a tight ball before the room powered apart with a sound like the crack of judgement.

Hardin yawned. The morphine was taking over. The clouds had begun to soften, drift, flake apart at the edges; a watery sun bathed his face.

"Makes sense," said Halderling, "in a weird kind of way. The spooks tend to see things differently from the rest of mankind."

"Way different," said Hardin.

"Yeah."

Hardin shifted slightly under the blankets, stared up at the angled stoop-roof above. The stretcher was placed beside the steps alongside Halderling, who was sitting on the bare boards staring out across at the chopper-apron, pipe clenched between firm white teeth.

"When d'you think they found this place?"

"You said yourself you thought they could have some kind of high-level insertion in the area. My guess is they've been setting it up a long time."

"Figures. And part of it was to discredit me, right? Sounds feasible. I'll have someone's balls for this, John. They're gonna find out there's life in the old dog yet, plenty life."

"You shouldn't have too many problems firming the evidence out. Tollmarsh wasn't entirely stupid. He must've kept papers; a kind of insurance policy. That was what Reisberson was after. The grenade mainly took Reisberson and the other guy out, so there should still be plenty of documentation lying around."

Halderling frowned.

"Who was that guy, anyway?"

"They call him the Lone Ranger." Hardin chuckled tiredly. "Christ knows. Seemed like he had some heavy grudge against Tollmarsh's number two, Nulty. Looked like he'd been out in the jungle for a week, so he could've been the survivor of that chopper crash we ran into. Something was burning up his guts, for sure; he took half of Reisberson's mag and it didn't seem to bother him any. Pity he blew Reisberson out, though."

"No matter."

From where he was, Hardin could just see Halderling's profile. It looked like something carved out of teak.

"I'm gonna march into the Embassy on Thong Nhut with a claw-hammer and a bag of nails. I'm gonna crucify those clowns, hang 'em by their Goddamn nuts." He puffed smoke-rings into the air. "Gonna have me this valley, too." He chuckled dryly. "A sweet little jumping-off point in bandit territory's what I've always hankered after."

Hardin said, "Listen, Lew."

Halderling glanced down at him. He could not recall the last time Hardin had called him Lew.

"I want executive clemency for Olsen, Garrett, the rest of them. I want honourable discharges, ribbons, money. Good ribbons; a lot of money. No quibbles."

"Sure, John. Sure."

"I want your word on that."

Halderling blew a couple more smoke-rings. He thought about it for a while.

"What if I renege?"

Hardin shook his head.

"No. You wouldn't do that, Lew. Not to me."

Halderling nodded slowly, got to his feet with a slight wince as his kneecap cracked.

"No," he agreed. "I wouldn't do that to you."

Hardin yawned again as he watched the general striding off down the slope.

He forgot about the war, Charlie Cong, blood, rounds, booby-traps, chopper gunships; he forgot about rain, mud, the jungle, the indifferent immensity of the natural world; he forgot about his wounds, because he was now no longer aware of them. It occurred to him—a split second's flash—that he could do with a cigarette, but then he forgot about that too.

He thought Steeger might be interested in some of this.

He thought about Eileen Satkis.

He drifted off.

MORE EXCITING READING!

VALOR AT LEYTE (1213, $3.25)
by Lawrence Cortesi

Leyte, The Philippines. The Japanese were entrenched and willing to sacrifice everything to hold the island. And as troop ships carrying reinforcements for the Emperor's line steamed into Ormoc Bay, the valiant American fliers came in on one of the most important missions of the war!

IWO (799, $2.75)
by Richard Wheeler

For five weeks in 1945, Iwo Jima saw some of the most intense combat in history. This is the story of that devastating battle, told from the perspective of both the U.S. Marines who invaded the island and the Japanese soldiers who defended it.

VICTORY AT GUADALCANAL (1198, $3.50)
by Robert Edward Lee

For six months and two days, combined U.S. Army and Marine forces held off the Japanese assault on Guadalcanal. It was the longest single battle in the history of American warfare—and marked the end of Japanese advances in the Pacific!

PACIFIC HELLFIRE (1179, $3.25)
by Lawrence Cortesi

The Japanese were entrenched at Truk. We had to take it before we could move into the Marianas. And before the battle was over, many valiant American sailors and airmen sacrificed their lives. But sixteen Japanese ships went to the bottom—shortening the war by at least a year!

Available wherever paperbacks are sold, or order direct from the Publisher. Send cover price plus 50¢ per copy for mailing and handling to Zebra Books, 475 Park Avenue South, New York, N.Y., 10016. DO NOT SEND CASH.